AFTER
HOURS

NATIONAL BESTSELLING AUTHOR

ROCHELLE ALERS

AFTER HOURS

HARLEQUIN® KIMANI PRESS™

Recycling programs
for this product may
not exist in your area.

AFTER HOURS

ISBN-13: 978-0-373-09145-4

Printed in U.S.A.

™ www.Harlequin

Dear Reader,

I have a confession…

I can't take credit for the story line for *After Hours.* It was during a Thanksgiving holiday weekend that I'd attempted to jot down ideas for my next women's fiction title. Then I did something I'd never done before: I asked someone for an idea for a plot. That someone was my daughter. She came up with not only the plot, but also the character profiles. It then became her task to complete the character dossiers, and two days later she admitted she had a very healthy respect for what I do, because the prep work is very intensive.

The writing of *After Hours* forced me to take off my romance hat and replace it with one for women's fiction blended with a dash of street lit. I found myself mesmerized with the lives Dina, Karla and Sybil— three very different women who share scandalous confidences that could not only destroy them, but also their marriages. You will be given a glimpse into exclusive neighborhoods boasting multimillion-dollar mansions and manicured lawns—a world of desire, seduction, hustling, sex clubs and closely held secrets.

Writing this novel permitted me a sense of freedom because I was able to push the literary envelope. Karla, Sybil and Dina are able to define their destinies living by their own set of rules.

Happy reading…

Rochelle Alers

With gratitude to Noemi Victoria, who saw the vision for *After Hours*. Thank you for Dina, Karla, Sybil and the men who love them.

Truthful lips endure forever, the lying tongue for only a moment.
                    —*Proverbs* 12:19

Chapter 1

Inserting the key card into the slot, Adina waited for the green signal and pushed open the door. The motel room was small, clean and functional. It wasn't a four-star Four Seasons or Ritz-Carlton, but it would serve her well until she found permanent lodging. The modest motel would become her sanctuary and temporary home.

She wasn't certain why she'd gotten off the bus in Irvington, New Jersey, but there was something about Irving that called to her. Perhaps it had something to do with the boy who'd sat next to her in third grade. He was the kindest boy she'd ever met or known. There wasn't anything Irving Gordon wouldn't do for her, and that included sharing his lunch and letting her cheat off his paper during a test.

The neighboring state of New Jersey was far enough away from Brooklyn that she wouldn't have to keep looking over her shoulder or duck out of sight when spotting someone who could possibly recognize her.

Dropping her bag on the floor near the closet, Adina hung the Do Not Disturb sign outside the door, closed it, then slid the security latch into place. She hadn't slipped the backpack off her shoulders when the telephone rang. Going completely still, she stared at the instrument, her heart pounding painfully against her ribs. Had someone followed her from Brooklyn to Irvington?

The backpack hit the carpeted floor with a soft thud. Moving over to the bedside table, she picked up the receiver. "Yes?" Her query was a whisper.

"Ms. Jenkins, this is Ravi at the front desk. Do you find the room to your liking?"

An audible sigh escaped her as she sat on the side of the bed. "Yes—yes. It's very nice."

"Remember, if you need anything, just call the front desk."

"Thank you. Good night, Ravi." She hung up, smiling.

The woman covering the front desk when she'd arrived had refused to rent her a room because she didn't have a credit card. Short of making a scene, Adina had asked to speak to the night supervisor. She became the consummate actress when she told Ravi that she was running from an abusive boyfriend, that she hadn't taken her credit cards because he would've been able to trace her whereabouts and that she'd left everything behind except money she'd hidden from him and a week's change of clothes.

It was only after she offered to show him the burns on her thighs where the abusive monster had put out his cigarettes that the manager took over and checked her in. She paid a weekly single-room rate—in cash. Of course, there were no burns or boyfriend, but she'd counted on not having to substantiate her passionate lie with physical proof.

She'd spent the bus ride from New York to New Jersey reinventing Adina Jenkins and rehearsing her script: she was a battered woman who'd finally gathered enough courage to flee her abusive drug-addicted boyfriend after he kicked her in the belly and she miscarried. She'd told the police and emergency room doctor that she'd fallen down a flight of stairs because he'd threatened to kill her. After leaving the hospital she knew she had to leave because the beatings were becoming more frequent and brutal.

Lying came easy to Adina. Most times the lies rolled off her tongue without thought or hesitation. After a while she'd acknowledged that she was a pathological liar, but it was quick thinking and falsehoods that'd kept her alive for the past decade and she knew she would tell more lies before she achieved her lifelong dream.

She didn't need a psychologist to tell her why she'd taken to hustling men with the ease of a duck taking to water: every man she hustled became her father, and it gave her extreme pleasure to set him up to be stripped of his worldly goods.

Adina had envied the girls who held the hands of their fathers when walking along the sidewalks, those who escorted their children to the ice cream trucks and paid for whatever they wanted. She'd hated Father's Day because if she made a handmade card with her favorite crayon colors, she had no one to give it to. The men who'd come to *visit* her mother and who'd occasionally spent the night were always Uncle So-and-So but never Daddy.

Even when she'd sought to seduce flamboyant hustler Terence Yancey she'd known he eclipsed her tender age of thirteen by fifteen years. At twenty-eight, he would've been charged with statutory rape for sleeping with her, but Adina had refused to tell her mother or grandmother his name.

A wry smile twisted her mouth as she stared up at the swirling designs on the stucco ceiling. Unknowingly

Terence had given her life *and* had saved her life. She lay across the bed until her breathing deepened and her eyelids fluttered as she struggled not to fall asleep. Reluctantly she sat up and prepared herself for bed.

Tomorrow was another day—the first day of her new life.

Chapter 2

Adina stared out the train window each time it made a different stop before reaching her destination. Before boarding the train, she'd dropped the PDA down a sewer, severing all communication with Payne Jefferson.

It had taken only three days of hiding out in Irvington for her to devise a plan that would eliminate Adina Jenkins—forever. The idea had come to her after countless hours of television viewing. Aside from taking her meals at a diner half a mile from the motel, she'd spent all of her time dozing and half watching late-night infomercials, news and talk shows, soap operas, documentaries and cartoons.

A documentary on the History Channel chronicling American gangsters captured her undivided attention. It was footage of a mobster who'd cooperated with federal authorities where he'd identified members of his syndicate, giving up names and dates of robberies, murders and contract hits. His reward for selling out his former cohorts was a new identity in the Witness Protection Program. The government relocated him to an undisclosed location and set him up with a new name, birth certificate, driver's license and social security number.

It had taken hours to search through telephone books

to find a law firm willing to give her an appointment to talk to an attorney about a "personal matter." The one willing to grant her a consultation was based in Trenton. The only thing she knew about the Jersey capital was that it wasn't far from Philadelphia, a city she'd visited several times as mistress to a man who operated a prostitution ring in Atlantic City and Philadelphia.

Adina got off the train in Trenton and took a taxi to the address she'd programmed into her BlackBerry. When the driver pulled up outside the law offices of Siddell, Kane, Merrill and King, housed in a two-story stucco building painted a soft sand color with black shutters, she was prepared for the performance of her life. She'd rehearsed what she intended to say over and over until she could repeat it verbatim.

The building was one of several along a bucolic tree-lined street claiming a post office, a florist, a sweet shop, a bank, a dry cleaner, a mom-and-pop-type luncheonette and a gift shop. There was no litter in the gutters, abandoned cars, boarded-up storefronts or vagrants sitting on parked cars, lounging against buildings or loitering on street corners. Those wishing to linger sat at tables shaded by umbrellas outside awning-covered businesses.

And what affected Adina more than seeing young mothers pushing baby strollers and elderly couples greeting each other was the dearth of loud noise. There were no honking horns from passing vehicles or raised voices. Even the dogs on leashes walking along the immaculate sidewalks stopped frequently to sniff at a tree or shrub. She noted from the smiling faces and serene expressions on those who either lived or worked in the hamlet that the lack of noise, dirt and pollution—and, no doubt, a low crime rate—attributed to a comfortable existence.

She hadn't been living but existing; an existence that included ear-shattering decibels of loud voices and music, dirt, grime and the stench of rotting garbage, weed, crack, discarded baby diapers and unwashed human bodies. Most times she prayed for colder weather so she wouldn't have to navigate the residents hanging out in and around the projects where she lived. It was only during the frigid weather that most of them stayed indoors. The exception was the dealers selling their illegal shit to addicts who believed they couldn't survive without their drugs.

Adina walked up to the gleaming black door and opened it. An attractive brunette sitting behind a cherry-wood workstation smiled at her. "Good morning. I'm Adina Jenkins and I have an appointment to see Mrs. King."

The receptionist glanced at a telephone console on her desk. "Mrs. King is on a call, but I'll let her know you're here as soon as she hangs up. Please have a seat, Ms. Jenkins."

She sat and glanced around the reception area. Recessed lighting cast a soft glow on walls covered with a wheat-colored fabric. The black leather love seat on which she sat was like butter. The rosewood table cradling a large bouquet of fresh flowers was exquisite. The furnishings in the law office's reception area were more tasteful than what she'd seen in some living rooms.

The receptionist had addressed her as *Ms. Jenkins.* Adina couldn't remember the last time someone had referred her as Ms. or Miss. But, if luck was with her, then she wouldn't be Adina Jenkins much longer.

Chapter 3

Karla King drew interconnecting circles on the legal pad in front of her, half listening to the whining of a client she'd inherited from an older senior partner. The voice was akin to fingernails on a chalkboard. Now she knew why she'd been given the case. The client, whose grandfather had set up a trust for her, wanted to give her latest boyfriend a quarter of a million dollars to start up his own business.

"I'm sorry, Miss Evans, but your grandfather's agreement stipulates you can only invest in Wall Street–traded companies." She rolled her eyes when the woman started to cry. "Yes, I know it's not fair, but…" Her voice trailed off as she waited for the woman to compose herself. It took all of a minute. "I'm sorry, but I'm going to have to hang up because I have another client waiting for me."

As soon as Karla ended the call, her intercom buzzed. "Yes, Valerie."

"Ms. Jenkins is here to see you."

"Please send her in."

Reaching for her suit jacket draped over the back of a nearby chair, Karla stood up, slipping her arms into the sleeves. She'd moved over to the door and opened it at the same time she watched Adina Jenkins approach.

Her sharp gaze took in everything about the woman in one sweeping gaze.

She was young; Karla doubted whether she was thirty. Adina Jenkins was blessed with a beauty that most men, regardless of their age or race, would find attractive. Her petite figure was shown to its best advantage in a black pencil skirt, tailored white silk blouse and a pair of high-heeled sandals. As she came closer, Karla saw that her raven-black wavy hair, secured in a ponytail with a narrow black grosgrain ribbon, ended inches above her tiny waist.

Karla hadn't made it a practice before she consulted with a prospective client to prejudge them but a sixth sense told her that Adina was unlike most clients represented by Siddell, Kane, Merrill and King because Valerie had reported that Ms. Jenkins had been very evasive when she'd called for a consultation. Yet she'd set aside time to see her.

She extended her hand, studying the tiny woman. Up close, Adina's bare face made her appear as if she were barely out of her teens. "Good morning, Ms. Jenkins. I'm Karla King."

Adina grasped the slender, well-groomed hand of the tall woman with flawless sable-brown skin, prominent cheekbones and blunt-cut, chemically straightened chin-length hair. Karla King's penetrating dark brown eyes glowed with an intensity that appeared to miss nothing. The lawyer's grip was firm and confident.

Adina's smile was slow in coming. She took a quick glance at the rings on the lawyer's left hand. "Good morning, Mrs. King. I'm hoping you'll be able to help me."

Karla pointed to a round table with several pull-up

chairs. "Let's sit down. After you tell me what you want, I'll let you know whether I'll be able to help you."

Adina sat down, placing her purse on the table. Leaning over, she left a shopping bag on the floor beside her chair. She'd gone to a mall to buy an outfit she felt suitable for discussing business with an attorney. While there, she'd stopped at a nail salon and had the silk wraps removed. Colorful airbrushed nails no longer figured in her future.

Sitting opposite Adina, Karla reached for a legal pad and a pencil from a supply on the table. "Would you like something to drink before we begin?"

"No, thank you," Adina said, shaking her head. Crossing her bare legs at the ankles, she took a deep breath, held it, and then let it out slowly. She had to play it just right to get Mrs. King to believe her.

"I need to change my name from Adina Jenkins to Dina Gordon."

The pencil in Karla's hand was poised over the blank page. "You need to change your name." The question came out like a statement.

Adina nodded, her gaze fixed on a tray cradling bottled water and cellophane-covered glasses. "I need a new identity because I'm hiding from my boyfriend." She glanced up, her gaze meeting and fusing with Karla's. "I'm tired of him using me as a punching bag. If I say something he doesn't like, he slaps me. If I cook something and it doesn't come out the way he thinks it should, he punches me. And if I don't let him…touch me, then he rapes me. The last time, he beat me so badly that I couldn't get out of bed for a week. It was when I lost my baby that I realized I had to get away before he got me pregnant again. I waited until he went to visit his mother and left with whatever I could carry with me."

Everything she'd said was a lie, including miscarrying a baby. After giving birth to one child, she'd made certain it would never happen again. She'd had a procedure that assured her that she would never conceive again. This was not to say that she didn't practice safe sex. Getting pregnant was preferable to contracting an STD or, even worse, HIV. No matter how much the men she slept with professed to be disease-free, she didn't trust them enough to engage in unprotected sex. And her distrust of the opposite sex forced her to use her own condoms.

Karla leaned closer. "Where does your boyfriend live?"

"Brooklyn."

"Have you reported him to the police?"

Adina paused. "I can't."

"Why not?"

"Because he said he'd kill me." Adina saw Karla King jot down *O.P.* on the pad, deciding it was time she go on the offensive. "I get an order of protection and then what, Mrs. King? Once he's released for violating the order, then he'll beat me again."

Karla sat up straighter. "I'd like to help you, Ms. Jenkins, but I can't. What I can do is refer you to someone I know in New York City who'd be willing to take your case."

"Why can't you take it? You're a lawyer, aren't you?"

A lifting of her eyebrows was the only indication of Karla's reaction to the younger woman's acerbic query. "I am an attorney, but you've come to a firm specializing in wills, taxes and estate planning."

"If that's the case, then why did you agree to see me?"

"I didn't know if I'd be able to help you. When you called the office you didn't disclose your reason for a consultation."

Adina glared at the conservatively dressed woman. Although understated, the cut of her navy-blue linen gabardine suit was as exquisite as the diamond solitaire and eternity band giving off blue-white sparks on her left hand.

"That's because I was afraid to say anything over the phone. I'm still afraid and I don't know when I'll ever stop being afraid." Tears filled Adina's eyes and trickled down her cheeks; she swiped angrily at them.

Karla's closed expression didn't change. She didn't know why, but she felt Adina Jenkins's pain. "Does he know where you are?"

"No."

"When did you leave him?"

"Friday."

"Where are you staying?"

Adina peered at Karla through moisture-spiked lashes. She said a silent prayer that the attorney would change her mind. "I'm staying at a motel in Irvington."

"How long do you plan to be there?"

"Until I run out of money."

"When do you predict you'll run out of money?"

Biting down on her lower lip, Adina mentally calculated how much it would cost to spend a month at the motel. "I have enough for at least another month," she lied. How much money she had would remain her secret. "I'm going to need a new identity so I can get a job and rent an apartment. I have to start over, and that's not going to happen unless I change my…my name." The last word came out in a sob and the floodgates opened.

Heart-wrenching sobs shook Adina as she buried her face in her trembling hands. A full minute passed before her hands came down and she stared at Karla. The tears had turned her brilliant eyes a mossy green. "I'm sorry," she apologized before biting on her trembling lower lip. "May I use your restroom?"

Pushing back her chair, Karla came to her feet and rounded the table. She'd witnessed domestic abuse first-hand as an adolescent when she walked into a neighbor's apartment to find it ransacked and her best friend's mother on the floor in a fetal position after she'd been beaten by her son looking for money to support his drug habit.

Anchoring a hand under Adina's elbow, she eased her from the chair. "Of course you may. It's down the hall, on your left. Meanwhile, I'll call someone I believe can help you."

Adina gathered her purse, sniffling as she walked out of the office; she hid a smile that mirrored supreme triumph. She'd rolled the dice and had come up a winner yet again. Despite her protests, Karla King was going to help Adina to not only change her name but also her life.

Chapter 4

Karla, waiting until Adina left her office, moved over to her computer; she pulled up her mailing list and scrolled through the names until she found what she wanted. Pushing the speaker feature on her phone, she dialed the number. Unfortunately the person to whom she wanted to speak was in court. She left a message on his voice mail to return her call. No one had saved her friend's mother, who'd eventually been murdered by her son. But if she could, then she would do all she could to help Adina Jenkins.

Leaning back in the leather executive chair, Karla stared at a wall filled with diplomas and citations chronicling her life as a tax attorney. She'd earned degrees from New York University in accounting and law and an MBA. At forty-one, she'd come a long way; she grew up in a low-income Newark neighborhood as an only child of a single mother who'd worked two jobs because she hadn't wanted her daughter's life to mirror hers.

Karla didn't want to think of what she'd sacrificed to get what she wanted from life; but she differed from her mother because now she was able to give back. She'd accepted personal cases pro bono, volunteered her services to organizations serving at-risk youth. And if she couldn't get a former fellow law school student to take on Adina Jenkins's case, then she would do what she could to help the young woman.

Glancing at the clock on her desk, she noted the time. Adina had been gone more than fifteen minutes. She buzzed the receptionist. "Valerie, could you please check on Ms. Jenkins. She's in the ladies' room."

"No, she isn't," said Valerie.

A slight frown creased Karla's forehead. "No, she isn't what?"

"She isn't in the ladies' room. She left about ten minutes ago."

"Are you certain she left?"

"Yes. In fact, she thanked me on her way out."

Karla's dark eyebrows slanted in a frown. "Thank you, Valerie."

Perplexed, she hung up wondering if Adina had changed her mind and decided going back to her abusive lover was preferable to being on the run. Or perhaps she hadn't believed Karla when she said she would get someone to help her. Expelling a soft breath, she closed her eyes. It would stand to reason that trusting wasn't easy for a battered woman and that Adina was wary of everyone she met or confided in; after all, she hadn't trusted the receptionist who'd taken her call to let her know why she was seeking legal counsel.

Karla swiveled on her chair—and then she saw it. Adina had left without taking her shopping bag. She got up and picked up the bag. "Dammit," she swore softly. She hadn't gotten the name of the motel in Irvington where Adina was staying, so how could she return it to her?

Sitting down in the chair her elusive client had occupied, she opened the bag and removed several sheets of decorative tissue paper. Her jaw dropped as she stared at the bag's contents, her heart pounding a runaway rhythm. It took Karla several minutes before she was able to reach into the bag again. This time she took out a single sheet of paper addressed to her with Adina Jenkins's contact information. She'd written down the name and telephone number to the hotel. She'd also included a cell phone number with a nine-one-seven area code and her proposed new name. Ignoring the stacks of bills bundled in denominations of tens, twenties and fifties in plastic Ziploc bags, she removed a large white envelope. Inside the envelope was an official copy of Adina's birth certificate.

A slow smile softened her wide mouth. "Why, the sneaky little minx," she whispered. Adina Jenkins had come prepared to bribe her.

Rising to her feet, Karla walked over to the door to her office and locked it. She returned to her desk and buzzed the receptionist. "Valerie, please hold all of my calls until further notice."

Her step was resolute, her hands steady as she entered her private bathroom, locking the door behind her. The corner office and private bathroom was only one of the perks that came from making partner. She'd worked hard, harder than any of her male counterparts at the firm, but the results were more profitable than mentally rewarding.

She'd decided to take on Adina as a private client even before discovering the money; however, despite her passion for luxury, she wasn't about to let greed jeopardize her license to practice law.

The hands on the clock had made a full revolution by the time Karla had counted the cash and put it back in the bag. She'd been given ten thousand dollars to make Adina Jenkins disappear. Methodically, as if preparing to take a case to trial, she stored the money in a cabinet under the vanity, unlocked the door to her office, then returned to her desk to make a telephone call.

A broad smile softened her round face when she heard a familiar greeting coming through the earpiece. "I need a favor, darling."

A deep chuckle caressed her ear. "Does your husband know you're flirting with strange men?"

Reaching for a pencil, Karla made squiggly lines on the pad filled with other doodling shapes. "No, but Ronald doesn't have to worry about us."

"Are you sure about that, Karla? Surely you've told the poor man that I've been lusting after you since the first day we walked into the lecture hall at law school."

"I told him, but he knows nothing will come of it."

There was a pause before the ADA at the Mercer County prosecutor's office said, "I know you didn't call to talk about Ronald. What's up, darling?"

"I need you to run a trace on a potential client."

"Has he been indicted?"

"No. I'm talking about a woman who's hiding from her abusive boyfriend."

"Give me her name and address and I'll call you back."

Karla gave him the information she'd gleaned on Adina. "Please run her through the Bureau's database while you're at it."

"What do I get for this?"

"Are you trying to bribe me, counselor?" she teased.

"Damn straight, counselor. How about dinner?"

She smiled. "You're on."

"I'm paying this time, Karla."

"Remember, Henry, that I'm the one with the expense account."

"That's because civil servants don't have the luxury of expense accounts."

"That's why I'm paying."

There came another pause on the other end of the line. "I'll call you when I get the info on your client, then we'll set up a time to reconnect."

"Thanks, Henry."

Karla hung up, tucking several strands of hair behind her right ear, her mouth tightening into a hard, unattractive line. Henry had continued to come on to her even though she'd been married to Ronald for the past six years. Perhaps if she hadn't admitted, when she'd had too much to drink, that she and Ronald were swingers, then perhaps Henry would have given up his relentless pursuit.

She occasionally slept with other men and Ronald other women, but only with the other's consent. Even if she wanted to sleep with Henry, she wouldn't because she didn't want to shit where she had to eat. She'd learned a long time ago to never mistake business for pleasure.

The phone rang, startling Karla. She picked up the receiver when she saw the display. "What do you have, Henry?"

"She's clean."

She resisted the urge to jump up and cut a dance step. "Thank you, Henry."

He chuckled softly. "You're quite welcome, Karla. I'll be in touch."

"You know where to find me." She ended the call, then retrieved her cell phone and punched in the numbers on speed dial. The man who answered her call was one

Ronald would approve of her sharing his bed. It took less than five minutes to tell him what she needed.

All she had to do was messenger the birth certificate to make the impossible possible with a single telephone call. Adina Jenkins was about to become Dina Gordon.

Chapter 5

Adina closed her eyes, feigning sleep when an elderly man attempted to initiate conversation. She didn't want to talk—especially not with a stranger. All she wanted was to return to Irvington and the motel room that had become a safe haven. And she wouldn't feel safe until she closed and locked the door behind her.

The rocking of the train and the click-clacking sound of the rails lulled her into an almost hypnotic state and she was able to recall every detail of her last night in Brooklyn. It'd begun the instant she called a car service to take her to Chez Tangerine.

She'd leaned forward on the worn rear seat of the livery taxi, tapped the Plexiglas partition with a set of silk-wrapped, airbrushed fingernails.

"Put us out in the middle of the block."

The driver maneuvered alongside the curb in front of Chez Tangerine. The line for those waiting to get inside the trendy Brooklyn nightspot snaked down the block and around the corner.

"Oh, hell no," mumbled the young woman sitting next to Adina. "I told you before that I ain't fixin' to stand in no line just to get into a club."

Reaching into her tiny leather shoulder purse slung

over her chest, Adina pulled out a twenty-dollar bill and pushed it through the slot in the partition. Shifting slightly, she rolled her eyes at her friend. She and LaKeisha Robinson had grown up in the same public housing project but hadn't begun hanging out together until the year before.

"Have *we* ever had to stand on line?"

Even though LaKeisha was her girl, Adina didn't understand why she complained all the time. In fact, there wasn't anything in LaKeisha's life that was *that* critical to make her a chronic whiner. She'd just closed on a condo in a Park Slope town house complex, worked as a loan officer in a downtown Brooklyn bank, was only fourteen credits away from earning an MBA and, unlike herself, she wasn't a baby mama. Although educated, her friend lapsed easily into street jargon depending with whom she interacted.

What LaKeisha didn't know was that Adina envied her because not only did she know who her father was but also that Adina's grandmother had had her mother at sixteen, her mother had her at fifteen and she'd given birth to her own daughter, whom she passed off as her sister, at fourteen. And her grandmother still lived in the same housing project where she'd been raised, raised her daughter, granddaughter and now, at fifty-seven, her great-granddaughter.

Even though she'd dropped out of high school, Adina managed to earn her GED before her twenty-first birthday. She'd never been gainfully employed, and what haunted her most was that she hadn't seen her alcoholic, drug-addicted mother in ten years.

"No," LaKeisha mumbled.

"Then stop bitchin'."

"It's just that I'm due to get my period in a couple of days and my back bothers me if I stand too long."

Adina didn't respond to LaKeisha's reference to her period because her attention was directed at a man dressed entirely in black. His smirk widened until it became a full dazzling grin. Bending slightly, he opened the rear door to the sedan.

Within seconds she went into seduction mode, parting her full lips just enough to appear as if she were attempting to catch her breath; she tossed her long black braid over her shoulder as she slid forward on the seat to give him an unobstructed view of her legs and thighs under a short, tight skirt. Placing her hand on the broad outstretched palm, she felt the power in the strong fingers when he pulled her to her feet.

"Hey, baby. How you doin'?" crooned a deep voice that matched the man's massive bulk.

Adina rose on tiptoe and looped her arms around Jermaine Werner's neck. "Better now that I've seen you," she said, pressing her cheek to his clean-shaven one.

She was flirting with Jermaine because she was counting on him to get her and LaKeisha into the club without having to wait in line. The tall, dark-brown-skinned man was one of the finest brothers in all of Brooklyn, but for Adina he was off-limits. In fact, any man to whom she'd found herself attracted was strictly taboo. However, there were exceptions—the men Payne Jefferson set up for her to hustle.

At twenty-seven, she'd lost count of the number of men she'd seduced for her elusive boss. Payne referred to himself as a "commercial manager," but to Adina he was nothing more than a pimp. Payne always gave her a percentage of what he stole from the unsuspecting marks, but what she never disclosed to her boss was her own con, where she received special gifts that included money, designer clothes and an occasional fur coat or jacket. One mark had even given her a pair of calfskin thigh-high, mink-lined boots.

Earlier that morning she'd received an alpha-numeric text on her PDA from Payne, instructing her to attend a private party at Chez Tangerine. The guest of honor had been paroled after doing a bid for robbing and assaulting an elderly diamond merchant. Closed-circuit cameras had recorded the crime, and because of several priors for petty infractions, he was given a sentence of fifteen-to-twenty years at an upstate New York prison. The case baffled police because the uncut diamonds, appraised for more than five million dollars, were never recovered. Her mission was to seduce the guest of honor and uncover whether he still had the gemstones and, if he did, where he'd hidden them.

Jermaine gently removed Adina's arms from his neck and took a step backward so she wouldn't detect his hard-on. Her silk halter top was an exact match for the pinpoints of green in her large hazel eyes. Adina Jenkins was the sexiest woman he'd ever encountered, and as a normal man, he wanted to do her.

He found her incredibly beautiful; she had long, wavy black hair, a curvy body and perfect legs and feet. Although she identified African-American, she could've easily passed for Latina, Native American or someone from the South Pacific. Her olive coloring, exotic features, low, throaty voice and seductive walk had him thinking of her when he least expected. And whenever he found himself in bed with other women, it was Adina he fantasized making love with.

"When are we going to get together, beautiful?"

Adina's practiced sensual smile slipped, but within seconds it was back. Jermaine didn't know that she would never go out with him because with a wife, three children *and* a baby mama he couldn't afford her. Although he worked a nine-to-five and moonlighted as a bouncer at different clubs on the weekends, he definitely wasn't in her league.

She winked at him. "I'll let you know, Jermaine." Extending her left hand, she waited as he removed a plastic orange wristband stamped with the club's name and logo from the breast pocket of his jacket and fastened it around her wrist. "Please take care of my girl LaKeisha, and we'll talk later about when we can hook up."

Minutes later, a band circled LaKeisha's wrist and the two women strutted in stilettos over to the velvet rope suspended between sturdy stanchions. Raising their hands to display the bands of neon orange, Adina and LaKeisha batted their mascara-coated lashes at the man removing the rope as another opened a door for them.

They made their way down a narrow hallway with painted black walls, then into a large space with lights flashing a kaleidoscope of color against a background of orange. A balcony overlooked a U-shaped bar and dance floor. Scantily dressed women and their men in casual urban attire lined up at the bar ordering outrageously overpriced drinks, while others gyrated to the infectious hip-hop flowing from powerful speakers.

Adina glanced at the upper level. A procession of waitstaff made their way up the winding wrought-iron staircase carrying trays of food. A knowing smile tilted the corners of her mouth. Like a heat-seeking missile locked in on a target, her plan was to crash the private party.

"Let's split up," she said to LaKeisha.

LaKeisha grabbed her arm. "Where are you goin'?"

"Why do we go through the same shit every time we go out together?" Adina spat out. "We're never going to meet anybody if we look as if were joined at the hip. Now let go of my arm."

LaKeisha lowered her hand; her dark brown eyes in an equally dark, round face grew large. "You don't plan to cut out on me like you did last week?"

An expression of hardness settled over Adina's delicate features as she forcibly swallowed the curses poised on the tip of her tongue. "Look, La," she said, shortening her friend's name, "I told you I was sorry about that. I hadn't seen my friend in a long time, and he just wanted to go somewhere and talk."

What she hadn't told LaKeisha was that even though Payne had robbed the man responsible for running illegal numbers in Bed-Stuy, East Flatbush and Brownsville, she'd continued to see him because she didn't want to arouse his suspicions that she and Payne were somehow connected.

She and the number banker had had several trysts at a motel near JFK Airport, then she hit the jackpot when he invited her to spend the night at a Bushwick apartment he'd set up as his base of operation. Stored under the king-size bed were several strong boxes filled with cash. Two weeks later, three masked men broke down the door, held the workers at gunpoint and walked away with the cash.

LaKeisha gave Adina a wary look as she tucked several strands of freshly braided hair behind her ears. Large gold hoops dangled from her pierced lobes. She wished Adina had a cell phone—that way they could communicate with each other. She didn't like having to search the club looking for her. "If you need to find me, then wait by the bar. I'll come back every fifteen minutes."

Adina nodded. "I'll see you later."

"Later, 'Dina."

It wasn't until LaKeisha disappeared in the throng that Adina forced herself to relax as she tried to still the rush of nerves that came whenever she began a new *assignment*. That's what Payne called it, when in reality it was a new hustle.

If arrested, she'd be charged with grand larceny, which translated into an attempt to deprive a rightful owner of their personal property. However, she wanted to know if it was a crime to rob criminals when the so-called victims were themselves criminals?

Payne only stole from those selling drugs or running illegal numbers and pimps dealing prostitution. He'd set up a network where none of the break-ins and/or occasional assaults could be traced to him.

Payne Jefferson was smart enough to become CEO of a major corporation, but the seductive allure of street crime held him firmly within its clutches.

Chapter 6

Adina made her way up the staircase with the assured-ness of an invited guest. She stepped off the last step, and the scene unfolding before her rendered her temporarily paralyzed. The guest of honor was someone she'd never forget because he'd changed her and her life—forever. Those standing around with flutes of champagne raised in a toast didn't see her shocked expression or the natural color drain from her face.

Unknowingly she'd come to Chez Tangerine to meet Terence Yancey, a man she'd slept with *once* at the age of thirteen, and he'd gotten her pregnant. She'd gone in search of Terence to tell him that she'd had his baby, but he'd disappeared without a trace. Now she knew where he'd been.

Payne, the consummate gambler, rolled the dice over and over, but this time he'd crapped out; there was no way she could get away with seducing and setting up her baby's daddy.

Turning on her heels, she made it down the staircase on shaking legs, praying with each step that she wouldn't fall and call attention to herself. Moisture pricked her armpits and dotted her forehead. Heat, then chills, washed over her as she navigated the crowded dance floor, not seeing the angry glares thrown at her when she nearly lost her footing in the four-inch heels before managing to regain her balance.

The crush of human bodies, the ear-shattering din of music and voices raised to be heard, closed around Adina like an overheated lead blanket. She'd never developed a fondness for alcohol because she'd seen firsthand how it ravaged her mother's life, but this was one time she needed a drink to mellow her out. Those waiting at the bar to be served were three-deep, so she saw it as a sign to try to find LaKeisha and bounce.

"I told you that was her," a woman whispered behind Adina. "She's that ho who set up my cousin."

"Girl, it don't have to be her," said another woman.

"But it is. Alphonso told me what she looked like. How many bitches do you know with good hair down to they ass that ain't no weave?"

"That still don't have to be her. There's a lot of girls in BK who have they own long hair."

"He told me a short, bright ho with long black hair and green eyes knew where he stashed his shit. Next thing you know, it's gone and a couple of months later the police charge him with possession with intent to sell. And after he was sent up, he ran into Rhames Daniels, who's also doing a bid, and he said the same thing happened to him. When I seen him last week, he told me that they gonna git someone from 'round the way to cap the sneaky bitch."

Adina didn't want to turn around to see who was talking about her, but she knew she couldn't remain in the club. The acrid taste of fear burned the back of her throat as she left the bar area. She couldn't think straight as she replayed the threat that someone was going to take out a contract on her life. She shoved her way through the line waiting outside the ladies' room and down a hallway to a rear exit. The bouncer sitting on a chair near the door came to his feet with her approach.

"You can't use this door," he announced in a no-nonsense tone. "It's for emergencies only."

"Please," Adina pleaded. "I need some air or I'm going to throw up right here."

The man moved back as if she'd just announced that she'd come down with a contagious disease. He opened the door and she ran, not stopping until she made it to the corner.

The humid night air was only a few degrees cooler than inside the club, but Adina didn't notice. Flagging down a passing livery car, she got in and gave the driver her address. Closing her eyes, she literally collapsed against the seatback. She didn't know what it was, but fate had intervened on her behalf. If her mark hadn't been Terence, she wouldn't have known of the threat. Always the ultimate hustler, she viewed life as a game that had to be full of fresh moves and continuous entertainment and free of labor and routine. And given her wiles, there was no doubt she would've successfully crashed the private party.

A chill shook her. She knew people who'd shoot her for twenty dollars of crack and she'd become another crime statistic accredited to street violence.

In seeing Terence again, she'd come face-to-face with her past and in doing so she'd come to the realization that she had to run and to start over.

And if she was going to start over, then it couldn't be in Brooklyn, New York.

Chapter 7

Adina paid the fare and got out a block from the public housing complex with views of the Brooklyn Bridge and Wall Street. Whenever she came home by car she always directed the driver to drop her off a block or two from the towering brick building where she shared an apartment with her grandmother and daughter. And she'd made it a practice to flag down a passing car rather than call several car services in the neighborhood because she didn't want anyone to monitor or track her whereabouts.

It was Friday night, early May, and nighttime temperatures were in the low seventies, and that translated into residents—old and young alike—hanging out until exhaustion forced them inside their stuffy, crowded apartments. It wasn't unusual to see infants sleeping in strollers or in the arms of mothers lounging on benches well beyond midnight, hoping to catch either a breeze coming off the East River or the latest neighborhood gossip.

Adina remembered when she used to hang out on the benches; but it stopped when she woke up one morning with excruciating back pains. It was one of the few times Bernice Jenkins was sober enough to realize her daughter needed emergency medical assistance. Not waiting for an ambulance, Bernice took Adina in a livery cab to a hospital, where five hours later the fourteen-year-old gave birth to a two-pound, six-ounce baby girl.

Adina hadn't known she was pregnant because her period had come every month like clockwork; she'd worn the same school uniform throughout the year and her weight had remained the same. She left the hospital, leaving her baby behind in the neonatal unit. Three months later Jameeka Jenkins was discharged, and when Bernice carried the infant girl home, she'd loudly invited everyone to come and see her new baby daughter. Ironically Jameeka looked exactly like her grandmother, so the only gossip circulating throughout the projects had been who'd fathered Bernice's child.

My mother left me, and now I'm going to have to leave my daughter, Adina mused as she pressed the elevator button. Bernice hadn't had a maternal bone in her body, and neither did Adina. From the moment Jameeka arrived she'd found herself completely detached from the tiny infant she'd carried inside her. How could she bond with a baby when she hated the dolls her grandmother had bought her?

The elevator arrived. She stood off to the side to let a trio of teenage boys dressed in baggy clothes stumble out; they were laughing uncontrollably. The lingering stench of stale urine mingling with freshly smoked marijuana forced her to take a backward step. Holding her breath, she was grateful—and not for the first time—that she lived on the fourth floor in the fifteen-story building.

The sound of the door opening didn't faze Dora and Jameeka Jenkins; they lay on an oversize sectional sofa that dwarfed the living room, their gazes fixed on the flat-screen television Adina had given her grandmother as a gift the prior Christmas. Only self-stick squares of mirrored glass on the walls made the space appear larger. Dora, who wasn't much for visiting her neighbors, now rarely left the apartment except to shop for food and on occasion to purchase clothes for herself and her great-granddaughter.

"I'm going to make a quick run," Adina called out as she headed in the direction of her bedroom.

"That's what you said an hour ago," Dora countered. Moving slightly, she peered over her shoulder at her granddaughter.

"This time I'm really going out, Mama." She called Dora Jenkins "Mama" because she'd assumed the role as mother—because Bernice wasn't able to take care of herself, let alone a child. Jameeka, on the other hand, called her great-grandmother Nana.

Shaking her head, Dora grunted softly before turning her attention back to a close-up of Gene Hackman and Willem Dafoe screaming at each other in *Mississippi Burning*. Even though Adina looked nothing like Bernice, she was just like her mother. It was always a *quick run* here or there; whenever they left, days, and at times weeks, would go by before she'd see them again.

The last time Bernice made a *quick run* she hadn't come back. After a month Dora contacted the police, who'd turned the case over to the FBI's Missing Persons division. And that was ten years ago. She was left to care for not only her granddaughter but also her great-granddaughter. She was only fifty-seven, and even if she didn't look her age, she felt much older.

Dora didn't know where Adina got her money; she was past caring. She'd asked her once whether she was selling drugs, but Adina swore up and down that she wouldn't have anything to do with drugs because of Bernice's addiction. She'd heard of too many folks being evicted from the projects if a family member was charged with dealing drugs.

And where would she go with a teenage girl?

She definitely didn't want to go to a welfare hotel or a homeless shelter.

Chapter 8

Adina opened the closet in the bedroom she'd once shared with her mother. Not only had they shared the room but also the same bed—a bed where Bernice would lie with any man willing to pay her a few dollars so she could buy drugs and booze.

After Payne Jefferson paid her for her first hustle, Adina didn't spend the money on clothes or electronic gadgets but on a new bed. A week before the scheduled delivery she threw out the old mattress and frame, sleeping on the floor, which was preferable to the rancid odors clinging to the ticking covered with urine, semen and bloodstains.

The threat against her life replayed over and over in her head like a needle stuck in the groove of a record as she removed articles of clothing from hangers and opened drawers to pack what she considered essential items. Ignoring the boxes filled with designer shoes and shelves with designer handbags, she filled a carry-on with underwear, T-shirts, jeans, slacks, sandals, running shoes and personal toiletries. Pulling over a chair, she stood on it and felt around a top shelf. Her hands were shaking so much it took several attempts for her to grasp the leather handles to a khaki-colored backpack. What she'd secreted in the backpack was her ticket out of Brooklyn.

For most of her life Adina heard black women talk about having their "F.U." money; it was when she discovered the family of one of her friends had moved out without telling anyone they were leaving that she understood the phrase. Her grandmother explained that the woman, having grown tired of her husband's abuse, withdrew the money she'd saved without his knowledge from her "Fuck You" account and moved to a state where he wouldn't be able to find her and his children. Dora's sage advice of *Never let a man know how much you have in case you have to leave his ass* was imprinted on her brain.

Although PJ gave her money, she never let him know how much her marks had given her. The men she'd befriended offered her designer clothes and accessories because they wanted to show her off, so there was never a time when Adina had to go to a boutique or specialty shop to purchase something to wear. She wasn't certain whether their "gifts" were knockoffs or swag, but it hadn't mattered because she hadn't had to put out a dime for them.

Now she would leave behind the haute couture she'd always referred to as "material shit," because her life was worth a lot more than Louis, Choo or Chanel. Jameeka would never wear her clothes or shoes because, at fourteen, she was four inches taller than Adina, her feet three sizes larger and she wore a size-nine dress to Adina's two. Either the clothes would rot in the closet or Dora could elect to sell or give them away.

She changed out of the stilettos, halter top and short skirt and into a pair of jeans, a T-shirt and running shoes. Staring at her reflection in the full-length mirror attached to the closet door, Adina saw something in her eyes that had never been there before: fear. Even when she'd embarked on her first hustle, she'd been apprehensive but not fearful that she'd be found out. She'd learned at a very young age how to seduce a man to get whatever she wanted. It'd begun with one of the men who'd slept with her mother, then escalated to those who'd found her attractive. It wasn't that she was vain about her looks, but she knew how to use what she'd been given.

Reaching for a baseball cap, she covered her head, pulling her braid through the back opening. There wasn't time to wash off her makeup. She had to leave before someone came looking for her. Emptying the small purse she'd carried with her to Chez Tangerine, Adina counted the small stack of bills. She had a little more than one hundred dollars. Now she had to decide where she wanted to go. Flying wasn't an option because she knew she would never make it past security with a backpack filled with cash that exceeded the amount for declaration. She'd never been gainfully employed, so no doubt the IRS would want to know where she'd gotten the money.

Pushing the bills into a pocket of her jeans, she reached for the PDA on her dresser. It was her direct contact with Payne Jefferson. Opening a drawer in a bedside table, she took out a BlackBerry and put it into the bag with her clothes. The cell phone was her direct contact with her grandmother. No one had ever seen her use the phone because, like the money in the backpack, the phone was a part of her F.U. stockpile. Slipping her arms through the straps of the backpack, Adina picked up her single piece of luggage. She wasn't certain where she was going, but it couldn't be anywhere within New York City's five boroughs.

Glancing around the bedroom for the last time, she flicked a wall switch, plunging the room into darkness. Dora and Jameeka were still in the same position as when she'd left them.

"Later."

Both waved without turning around, and Adina opened the door and left the apartment, the door locking automatically behind her. She had the elevator to herself, and the crowd that had gathered to witness two women fighting hadn't dispersed. Several were describing to police personnel what had happened. Walking in the opposite direction, she flagged down a distinctive black-and-red vehicle from a nearby car service.

"Where to, lady?" the driver asked when she sat down.

"Take me the Port Authority bus terminal." It was the first place she could think of. She could've easily said the Long Island Railroad or Grand Central Station, but somehow taking the bus was preferable to the train because she didn't like tunnels.

The driver quoted her a flat rate, to which she would've gladly paid double. Exhaling audibly, Adina sat back, closed her eyes while planning her next move.

"Irvington! The next stop is Irvington."

Adina opened her eyes when she heard the conductor calling her stop. Gathering her purse, she pushed to her feet. A chill swept over the back of her neck, and she refused to acknowledge it as a bad omen, because she couldn't afford to indulge in superstition when what she was facing was as real as it could get. She left the train and hailed a taxi, instructing the driver to take her to the motel. She wanted him to take her *home*.

Chapter 9

The BlackBerry chimed and Adina reached for it next to her head on the pillow. A light sleeper, she'd put the phone in the bed with her because she was still waiting to hear from Karla King.

It'd been two weeks since she'd gone to Trenton. She suspected the lawyer had found the bag she'd left in her office; she'd expected her to call, but when she hadn't, Adina had shifted into panic mode. Her anxiety meter reached a dangerous level until she forced herself to relax, release and let go.

After she calmed down enough to think rationally, she decided to give the lawyer another week. And if Mrs. King hadn't followed through on her promise to help her change her name, then she would be awash in controversy when she put the prissy attorney on the spot.

Adina planned to ask Karla about the bag, which she'd *inadvertently* left in her office. But if Karla denied seeing it, then she would play her trump card. The parking lot, the reception area, the hallways and Mrs. King's office were all installed with closed-circuit cameras, and that meant the entire building was wired. She may not get her money back, but she didn't think Karla King, Esquire, would want her good name smeared in an alleged scheme to defraud a client.

Mrs. King—or whoever had discovered the bag with the money—would be hard-pressed to disavow knowledge of the item in question if camera footage showed otherwise. Adina didn't want to dime-out the sister-girl lawyer, but if she had to, she would, because it all came down to survival. And she hadn't survived ten years of hustling because she was a *nice* girl.

Peering at the lighted display, she recognized her grandmother's number. Now wide-awake, she answered the call. "What's up, Mama?"

"That's what I was 'bout to ask yo ass."

Leaning over, Adina flicked on the lamp on the bedside table. The glowing numbers on the clock read 3:20 a.m. "You called me, Mama."

"Whatcha doin' hangin' around wit PJ?"

A lump formed in Adina's throat, making it almost impossible for her to swallow. "I'm not hanging around with him," she lied smoothly.

"If that's not the case, then why did he come by fo' day in the mornin' and bust up my place? He broke up the walls, coffee table and TV. My pressure's so high that I cain't breathe. I hope I ain't havin' a stroke."

Adina clapped her free hand over her mouth to stop the screams welling up in the back of her throat. The tears filling her eyes were real, not forced like the ones she'd shed for Karla and the motel manager.

"Mama, talk to me. Mama!" she screamed when encountering silence.

"I'm still here, grandbaby."

A shiver of fear—stark, vivid and very real—swept over Adina. She'd always managed not to involve her family in her work, but that had changed because Payne had confronted her grandmother. Before she'd agreed to work for him she'd extracted a promise from him that he'd never let anyone know of their association.

"What did he say, Mama?"

"He says you got two weeks to get back in touch with him or else he's coming back to break mo' than glass." Dora recited the number PJ had written on a business card.

Adina gripped the cell phone tight enough to leave a distinct impression on her palm, wishing it was Payne's scrawny neck. She picked up a pen next to the lamp and wrote down the telephone number. He'd given her grandmother a number with a DC area code.

"Where's Jameeka?"

"She ain't here. She at a sleepover."

Adina let out a deep sigh of relief. Even though she'd given birth to Jameeka, she'd never thought of herself as her mother. Maybe it was because Bernice had claimed the baby as hers; once Bernice disappeared, Dora assumed full responsibility for raising her great-granddaughter.

"Why that trifling bum-bitch lookin' fo' you?" Dora asked, her voice louder, stronger.

"A couple of weeks ago he asked me to put a dollar on a number for him. It came out and I forgot to give him the money."

The lie was so good that Adina believed it herself. There was no way she was going to tell her grandmother about her decade-long association with Payne Jefferson, that she set up men for him to rob, that he was the mastermind behind robberies, burglaries and other unsolved crimes in Brooklyn too numerous to mention.

"How much do you owe him?"

"About five hundred dollars."

"Do you have his money, Adina Jenkins?"

"Yeah, I do. But I just have to get it to him."

"When you gonna do that?"

"When I see him."

"You gonna call him?"

"Yes, Mama. I'll call him later on today."

"I hope you ain't lyin' to me."

"No, Mama. I will call him."

"When am I gonna see you, grandbaby?"

Adina closed her eyes and bit down hard on her lower lip. How could she tell her grandmother that she would never come back to Brooklyn because there were people out to kill her?

"I don't know. I'm going to send you some money orders so that you can pay someone to fix up the place. I'll include enough for you to buy another television."

"I ain't got to have no big-screen TV. The one in my bedroom will do fine."

"But you loved that TV, Mama."

"Because it was big and new. Save yo' money, baby. I've been thinkin'..." Dora said after a swollen pause.

"What about?"

"Moving. The projects ain't no place to raise Jameeka."

"You want to move?"

"Been thinkin' on it."

"Where do you want to live?"

"No mo' public housing. I don't want Jameeka windin' up like me and yo mama. I want her to go to college and make somethin' of herself. I ain't sayin' you didn't finish high school, but I always wanted you to go to college because you is smart as a whip."

A hint of a smile softened Adina's lush mouth. Her grandmother had dropped out of school to give birth to Bernice, and Bernice had dropped out to have her. She'd dropped out because she'd begun hanging out at night and couldn't get up in the morning to make it to school on time. Yet at twenty she'd made herself a promise to get her GED before her twenty-first birthday, and she had. It wasn't until she'd enrolled in the course to prepare her to take the exam that she'd realized she could retain most of what she'd learned, acing the test on her first attempt.

"Maybe we can move someplace nice if I get a job paying taxes." Dora believed she had a position working off the books totaling daily receipts for a businessman who owned family-style restaurants in Bay Ridge, Bensonhurst and Sunset Park.

"Fo' real?"

Adina smiled for the first time since answering the call. "For real, Mama," she said truthfully; there was no way she could continue hustling.

In fact, she'd played the game longer than planned. When Payne first approached her with his scheme, she'd told him she would do it for a year. One year became two, three and eventually ten. Working the streets was not only dangerous but short-lived, with options limited to incarceration or a coffin.

"I'll call PJ," she promised. "Remember to keep your door locked." Many project tenants left their doors unlocked during the day because they didn't want to keep getting up to let in their children. "I want you to call the police if PJ comes back."

"Ain't you gonna call him?"

"Yes. I said that in case he decides to start more shit."

"When are you comin' back?" Dora asked again.

"I don't know. I'm working on something right now, and as soon I finish up here I'll let you know."

"Okay, grandbaby."

"Look for the money orders in a couple of days."

"Thank you, baby."

"I love you, Mama."

There came a beat. "Love you back."

Depressing a button, Adina ended the call and stared at the fading wallpaper in the room that suddenly felt like a tomb.

Fleeing Brooklyn may have saved her life, but it'd put her grandmother's at risk.

Her world and everything in it was spinning out of control.

Chapter 10

Seventy-two hours after Payne had trashed her grand-mother's apartment Adina called him. Punching in the numbers on the disposable cell phone, she waited for a break in the connection. She hadn't wanted to use her cell phone because she didn't want him to track her. Payne Jefferson may have lived in the projects, but his criminal network stretched far beyond its boundaries.

"Speak." The single word was a whisper.

Her eyebrows lifted when hearing the unorthodox greeting. "You wanted me to call you."

"I want to talk to you."

"Isn't that why you gave me your number?" Adina countered.

"Bitch, you know I don't like phones."

A wave of fire burned its way into her face. "Call me a bitch again and I'm going to hang up." She still hadn't heard from Karla King and her mood swings vacillated from hope to rage, and when she'd gotten up earlier that morning it was to a haze of rage—that had made it difficult for her to draw a normal breath.

"You hang up on me and I'll do more than fuck up your grandmother's place."

"Fuck with my grandmother and I swear I'll dime

your ass out." She hadn't lied to Payne. Fear and concern for Dora made her reckless *and* vindictive enough to give Payne up to the police, but only if she'd be able to cut a deal.

Payne laughed softly. "You know what they say about snitches."

"Yeah, I know. Snitches get stitches," Adina drawled recklessly. "I ain't scared of you, Payne."

"I know you ain't, because you know too much about my business. We need a face-to-face. I want you to meet me in Jersey." His tone had softened considerably.

Her heart leaped in her chest. Did he know where she was? Had someone seen her and reported back to him? "When and where in New Jersey?" she asked, praying it wasn't Atlantic City.

"Sunday. Twelve noon. Meet me near the grandstand at the Old Bridge Township Raceway in Englishtown. Do you know how to get there by yourself?"

"I'll find it." She had gone there once with one of her marks to attend a car show.

Those were the last words she said, because Payne hung up on her. She didn't know why he wanted to see her but knew that if she didn't meet him, he would have his people hurt or kill her grandmother.

Adina understood Payne Jefferson better than anyone in the projects, with the possible exception of his mother. At thirty-seven, he stood five-three and weighed about one-twenty, and as a boy he'd been taunted relentlessly by the neighborhood children, who'd called him Tiny, Pee-Wee, Spud and Half-Pint. The taunting stopped after he'd hit a much larger boy with a baseball bat, opening his head like an overripe melon.

Although sixteen, he was tried as an adult and sen-

tenced to five years in a minimum-security prison. After
he was paroled, he came back to the projects, went into
semiseclusion and devised a master plan to exact revenge on every criminal who reminded him of the in-
mates who'd abused and shamed him to assuage their
sexual perversions.

Although Adina had heard the rumors about Payne's
celebrated temper, she'd found herself drawn to him because he was an older man. He liked her because, at five-
two and one hundred three pounds, she complemented
him physically. They were never seen together publicly
because he always arranged for them to meet outside their
Brooklyn neighborhood. Their relationship was advantageous to both because Payne got what he wanted and she
got what she wanted without having to sleep with him.

She'd agreed to meet him at the raceway because it
was a public place. There wasn't much he could do to her
in front of hundreds of witnesses.

Chapter 11

Adina arrived at the Old Bridge Township Raceway forty-five minutes before she was scheduled to meet Payne. She ignored the curious and admiring stares from men as she made her way to the grandstand area.

It was mid-May, early-morning temperatures were already in the seventies and it'd taken hours for her to travel from Irvington to Englishtown on public transportation. If she'd continued to work for Payne, she wouldn't have hesitated to hire a driver. But the reality was that she wasn't working *and* she'd given away almost half her savings.

Her eyes hidden behind the lenses of a pair of oversize sunglasses, Adina scanned the crowd. A secret smile parted her lips when she noticed a man standing a few feet away, staring directly at her. He hadn't been there before.

With wide eyes she catalogued everything about him in one sweeping glance. The first thing she noticed was his hands: no rings and no telltale lighter band of flesh on his ring finger. The freckles on the backs of his hands matched those dotting the slightly flaring nostrils in a smooth, round redbone face. She lifted her eyebrows, her smile widening when he flashed a friendly smile.

His light brown eyes were the same color as the receding sandy-brown hair he wore in a short, natural style.

Her admirer was average height with a stocky physique. The timepiece circling his wrist, the off-white silk shirt worn outside the waistband of a pair of beige linen slacks and imported Italian slip-ons silently communicated good taste and sophistication. Her gaze lingered briefly on his hands again before shifting to his thin-lipped smile. She saw him as an ordinary-looking, high-yellow brother.

"Hi." Adina was hard-pressed not to laugh out loud when she saw his reaction to her throaty greeting. If the stranger thought she was coming on to him, then he was mistaken. She needed him as a witness just in case Payne decided he wanted to do more than "talk" to her.

Lancelot Haynes went completely still. Had he imagined that the exotic-looking woman had actually spoken to him because that's what he wanted? Or was he hearing voices? The first thing he'd noticed was her hair. Parted off-center, it fell in heavy waves down her back. He couldn't see all of her face behind the sunglasses, but what he saw he liked: a small straight nose and a full pouting mouth. His admiring gaze caressed her off-the-shoulder black-and-white striped top and black cropped pants that hugged every delicious curve of her petite body. A pair of three-inch black patent leather wedge sandals showed off her small feet and shapely legs.

"Hello," he said, smiling and extending his hand. "Lance Haynes."

Adina took his hand, finding it soft and comforting. It was apparent Lance Haynes used his head rather than his hands to earn his living. "Dina Gordon."

There, she'd said it. She was no longer Adina Jenkins, and what she had to do was think of herself as Dina.

Lance moved closer, inhaling the sensual scent of her perfume. "Do you come here often?"

Dina shook her head. "No. This is only my second time."

"Can I get you something to drink?" he asked. What he wanted to ask was whether she'd come alone or was waiting for someone.

"Yes, please."

"What would you like?"

"A soft drink, please."

"Are you certain you wouldn't like something a little stronger?"

Dina smiled, exhibiting a set of straight white teeth. "I'm very certain."

Lance nodded. "I'll be right back."

She was still watching Lance's retreating back when she felt pressure on the nape of her neck. Payne had come up on her without making a sound. She let out a soft gasp as his fingers dug into the tender flesh; her hair concealed the savage grip holding her captive.

"No one runs out on Payne Jefferson," he whispered in her ear.

"I couldn't—"

"I don't want to hear shit from you," he rasped, cutting off her explanation. "Because you didn't complete our last deal, I'm going to let you off easy."

The initial shock of Payne coming up behind her subsided, replaced by false bravado. "What do you want, PJ?" she drawled. She knew he hated being called PJ, but she was past caring about what he wanted. She wanted out and she'd do anything he asked to be rid of him.

"You owe me."

"How much?" she asked.

"Twenty."

Dina knew he hadn't meant twenty dollars. He wanted her to give him twenty thousand dollars. She would've had it if she hadn't given Karla King ten thousand dollars. "I don't have it."

"That's your problem." Payne knew men gave Adina money—lots of money.

"I need time."

"How much?"

Dina saw Lance coming in their direction holding a plastic cup in each hand. "Give me until the Labor Day weekend. After that, we're through. I'm out, Payne."

Payne noticed the man heading toward them. He let go of Adina's neck. "Okay. Three and a half months, bitch. Call me when you have it." He shifted, facing Adina while pointing at her with his thumb and forefinger.

A momentary panic seized her when she recalled what she'd agreed to. How was she going to come up with twenty thousand dollars in three and a half months, short of robbing a bank? Even if she secured legitimate employment, there was no way she was going to earn that much money given her dearth of work experience.

"Are you all right?"

Lance's voice reached into her troubled thoughts as she turned to find him staring down at her. "No."

A frown of concern creased his smooth forehead. "What's the matter, Dina?"

She took a step, took off her sunglasses, rested her forehead on his chest and dissolved into a paroxysm of tears. Her weeping tugged at something inside Lance. He couldn't comfort her because his hands were full. Confused by emotions he didn't want to feel, he lowered his head and pressed a kiss to Dina's fragrant hair.

"Talk to me, Dina."

She eased back and lifted her chin, seeing an expression of shock replace the concern in Lance's eyes. "Just get me out of here."

Bending slightly, he set the cups on the ground, reached for her hand and led her to the parking lot.

Chapter 12

Lance handed Dina his handkerchief after they were seated in his car. He felt as if he'd been punched in the gut when he saw her tear-filled eyes, eyes that reminded him of a lush rain forest, with shadowy hues of browns and greens. She was hurting, in pain, and where he was able to cope with most things, he failed when it came to a woman's tears.

Dina blotted the corners of her eyes with the square of cotton, taking care not to smudge her carefully applied liner and mascara. She wanted to look her best because she needed Lance Haynes—not for someone she could hustle but as a friend.

"Thank you, Lance," she said, delicately blowing her nose into his handkerchief. Placing a hand on the door handle, she gripped it. "I…I have to go now." A deep sob choked her entreaty.

Lance panicked. Reaching over, he placed his hand over hers and stopped her from getting out of the car. "Where are you going?"

Dina affected a tortured expression when she turned to look at Lance. "I'm going home. Thanks for your help."

He faltered in the silence that filled the car. He didn't want Dina to leave. There was something about her that was different from the other women he'd known. She wasn't a child, but there was something childlike in her he couldn't resist. The fact that he knew nothing about her was of no importance, because he wanted to get to know her.

Lance forced a smile. "I did nothing, Dina."

Her moist lashes fluttered. "You helped me more than you know. Please let me go."

It was with great reluctance that he nodded. "Where did you park your car?"

"I don't have a car."

"How did you get here?"

"I took public transportation."

Vertical lines appeared between Lance's eyes. "Where do you live?"

"Irvington."

"You came all the way from Irvington by public transportation?"

A slow smile found its way over Dina's lips when she saw his shocked expression. "Why do you make it sound as if I'd walked across Death Valley in the middle of the summer?" A rush of color darkened Lance's face with her backhanded retort, she finding it endearing. "You're a snob, Lance Haynes."

His blush deepened. "No, I'm not! And why would you say that?"

"When was the last time you took public transportation?"

An expression of surprise froze his features. "I…I don't remember."

Dina pointed a finger at him. "See. I was right. You are a snob." She angled her head. "You're finicky and very particular about where you eat or sleep. You're probably so obsessive that you check out a chair before you sit down."

Lance didn't confirm or deny her assessment of him. "What about restaurants?"

She blinked once. "You only dine in the best restaurants."

He lifted a light brown eyebrow. "You think?"

Dina nodded. "I know."

His gaze beamed approval. Dina Gordon was a good judge of character. "If you say I helped you, then I want you to help me."

"Help you how?" She wasn't clairvoyant, but she could predict the words that would come out of Lance's mouth. He wanted to drive her back to Irvington.

"Let me drive you back to Irvington."

She gave herself a mental check. "What's the catch?"

"Why does there have to be a catch, Dina?"

"I've been told that men who offer to do something for a woman usually want something in return."

"Who told you that?"

"My grandmother."

"Well, your grandmother's wrong, because I won't ask for anything in return except dinner."

Her luminous eyes grew larger. "You want me to cook dinner for you?"

"No. I want you to share dinner with me at a *restaurant*."

"Are you sure that's all you want?"

Nodding slowly, Lance glanced down the handkerchief clutched in her hand. Dina was afraid of him, and he wondered whether her fear had anything to do with the man who'd left quickly when he'd returned with her soft drink.

"You don't trust men, do you?"

"No."

"Has a man ever hurt you?"

"No, but I've seen what they've done to other women."

Stretching out his right arm, he rested it over the back of her seat. "You're judging all men by a few you've known?"

"Yes."

"You're too young to be so cynical," he said softly.

She gave him a shy smile. "Spoken like a wise elder."

His hand slipped lower as he caressed her hair. "I want you to trust me enough to take you to dinner, then to make certain you get home safely."

Dina stared up at Lance through her lashes, totally aware of the seductiveness of the gesture when he exhaled audibly. "What guarantee can you give me that I'll be safe with you?"

The seconds ticked off as Lance and Dina regarded each other. "My word," he said.

She'd been with enough men to know if she could or couldn't trust them, but Lance Haynes was one she knew intuitively she *could* trust. "Do you have a cell phone on you?" He nodded. She held out her hand. "Give it to me."

His flaring nostrils opened wider. "Why?"

"I'll give it back after you bring me home."

Shifting slightly, Lance reached for the cell phone on his waist, handing it to Dina and watching as she slipped it into her purse. "What would you like to eat?"

She'd alternated eating at the diner and ordering from soul food and Chinese take-out restaurants. The meals, though staving off hunger, weren't fancy. "Surprise me."

Lance started up the car, putting it into gear. Dina wanted him to surprise her, and he would.

Chapter 13

Lance headed north on Route 9, maneuvering expertly in and out of slower-moving traffic. Concentrating on his driving was safer than taking furtive glances at the woman sitting next to him. When he'd gotten up that morning he'd planned to drive from West New York to Englishtown to look at the classic cars at the Old Bridge Township Raceway because he'd contemplated adding another vehicle to his growing collection.

However, all thoughts of cars were forgotten when he saw the tiny woman enter the grandstand area. He followed her as if pulled along by an invisible string. He didn't know whether it was her hair, her sexy walk or her tiny body, but Lancelot Londell Haynes's nose had been so wide open that a tractor-trailer could have fit with room to spare.

Reaching for a pair of sunglasses on the dashboard, he slipped them on. He felt rather than saw Dina move closer to the door. She'd admitted she didn't trust men, and he wasn't very trusting of women, yet that didn't explain why two strangers were traveling together.

"How old is this car?"

Lance smiled. He'd driven more than twenty miles in

silence, and Dina's first remark was about his car. "It's a lot older than you."

Dina turned to stare at Lance's profile. Upon closer examination she concluded that he wasn't as nondescript as she'd originally thought. He had very little facial hair. Whereas his face was soft, it was not the same with his body. He claimed a pair of broad shoulders, a thick neck and muscled forearms.

"How old do you think I am?" she asked.

He gave her a quick glance. "Twenty-five."

"Wrong. You missed by two years."

Lance took his gaze off the road, his expression mirroring shock. "You're twenty-three?" He'd dated younger women, but not those young enough to be thought of as his daughter.

Dina laughed softly. "No. I'm twenty-seven."

He breathed a sigh of relief. She was closer to thirty than twenty. "But I was close."

"Yeah, right," she teased. "How old are you, Lance?"

"Take a guess."

Leaning to her left, Dina peered closely at him. "Thirty-seven."

"Nah," he said, mimicking a goat.

"Thirty-nine?"

"Nah."

"Thirty-six? No…no, I got it. Forty…forty-one."

Smiling, Lance shook his head. "Nah, nah, nah."

Dina threw back her head and laughed, the warm, honeyed sound filling the confines of the car. She couldn't recall the last time she'd laughed—laughed with a spontaneity that wasn't forced or fake.

She placed her hand over his, then pulled it back quickly as if she'd touched a hot surface. She had to be careful, very, very careful not to appear too forward. "Please tell me," she pleaded, pushing out her lower lip like a petulant child.

"Later."

"Pretty please."

Lance gave her another quick glance. He didn't know what there was about Dina Gordon, but at that moment he couldn't deny her anything. "Forty-nine."

Her jaw dropped seconds before she clamped a hand over her mouth. "No!" she said through her fingers.

"Why no, Dina?"

She lowered her hand. "I can't believe you're almost fifty."

"I won't be fifty until December."

"You look incredible for your age."

Lance nodded, his chest swelling with pride. Dina had just made the reality of his turning fifty a lot more palatable. "Thank you. In answer your question about the car, it's a 1963 Cadillac DeVille."

Relaxing against the supple leather seat, Dina listened to Lance extol the beauty and quality of his restored convertible. One thing that made her so adept at what she did was that she was a good listener. She'd learned at a young age that men were guided by ego and that their self-worth was measured by the speed of their cars or the number of women they bedded. No matter their age, they were still boys who needed their toys.

She closed her eyes, giving in to the smooth motion of the moving automobile.

She was sleeping soundly by the time Lance entered Matawan's city limits.

Chapter 14

Lance maneuvered into one of the few remaining parking spaces at LUA, a Hoboken waterfront restaurant/lounge. He was partial to the dining establishment not only because of its location, with views of Manhattan and the cross-Hudson ferry terminal, but because of its Latin-fusion cuisine, more than twenty kinds of tequila and a side room with doorman-barred club for private parties. He'd exceeded the speed limit to arrive before brunch ended.

Glancing to his right, he stared at Dina. She was still asleep, her chest rising and falling gently, her lips parted and her head at an odd angle. Streams of sunlight fired the gold in her satiny skin. His gaze lingered on the shape of her small, firm breasts, outlined against the body-hugging striped fabric. He tore his gaze away, staring out the windshield.

A shadow of annoyance crossed his face. He was angry with himself for staring at Dina like a pervert. What, he mused, if she'd caught him? His staring, though unintentional, would only serve to increase her distrust of men.

As if he'd willed it, he felt her stir. Stretching gracefully like a lithe cat, she came awake, her gaze meeting

his. Long, thick lashes brushed the tops of high cheekbones when she sat up straighter. Combing her fingers
through her hair, she pushed the heavy waves off her
forehead.

Dina ran the tip of her tongue over her lower lip, bringing Lance's gaze to linger there. "I'm sorry I fell asleep
on you. I suppose I'm not much for keeping you company."

He put up a finger. "Remember, I was the one who
offered to take you home. So forget about keeping me
company. Are you ready to eat?" he asked, deftly changing the topic.

She gave him a warm, open smile. "Yes."

"Don't move," he warned when she made a motion to
get out of the car.

Dina sat motionless, wondering what he'd planned. It
didn't take long for her to realize he wanted to help her
out of the car when he opened the passenger-side door.
Bending slightly, Lance extended his hand and she placed
her palm on his, permitting him to pull her effortlessly
to her feet. Cradling her fingers, he tucked her hand into
the bend of his elbow. The only men who'd opened car
doors for her in the past were hotel doormen.

"Thank you," she whispered, giving him a demure
glance. "This looks like a very nice place." The luxury
cars in the restaurant's parking lot were a testament to
the restaurant's elegance.

Dina had said the first thing that had come to her
mind. She had to talk, say anything to hide her growing
apprehension. She was disturbed by Lance's behavior
because he was treating her as if she were a fancy lady.

"It is," Lance confirmed. Dina pulled back, forcing
him to stop. "What's the matter?"

"Is what I'm wearing okay?"

"Of course it's okay. Look, I'm not wearing a jacket. We're having brunch, not dinner."

She nodded, following him around to the front of the restaurant. How could she tell him the men she saw usually entertained at clubs or private rooms at hotels or in casinos. And if it was a restaurant, they usually paid the owner to take over the premises for the night. She'd become just another pretty face, smiling and laughing for the host's pleasure and entertainment.

What Dina hated most was coming home after a night of partying smelling of cigars, cigarettes and weed. She didn't drink, so she spent hours nursing a virgin cocktail until her "date" informed her he was ready to leave. Once she climbed into bed with him she became an actress in a role, giving an award-winning performance. None of them knew that her whispered words of passion, her grunts, groans or orgasms were faked. Afterward she went into the bathroom to discard the condom and wash away the smell of sex mingling with sweat, cologne and her perfume.

She'd lost count of the number of men who'd professed their love; none were aware that she'd never return their affection. She deemed them prey and, once caught, it was time to move on to the next creature to trap in her web of lies and deceit.

Lance was greeted by name by the maître d'. They exchanged handshakes and within minutes they were shown a table next to a window. Dina was overwhelmed by the architectural lines of the restaurant's design and the views of Hoboken's waterfront area and the Manhattan skyline on the other side of the Hudson River.

After Hours

Her eyes danced with excitement. "The views must be spectacular at night."

Lance nodded, smiling. Dina reminded him of a child opening gaily wrapped Christmas gifts. He found her spontaneity and enthusiasm contagious. "They are. Would you like to come back here one night?"

"Yes!" The word had tumbled from her lips before she could censor herself. A flush crept up her neck to her hairline as she lowered her gaze. "I'm sorry, I shouldn't have said that."

Reaching across the table, Lance captured her hands, tightening his grip when she attempted to pull away. "There's no need to apologize, Dina. Look at me," he urged softly. Waiting until her head lifted, he met her tortured eyes. "If you want to come back, I'll bring you."

"I don't want to impose upon you, nor do I want you to feel obligated to do more for me than you're already doing."

"I never do what I have to, only what I want to." He loosened his grip, staring down at the tiny hands with delicate fingers and perfect nails. Even without polish they were exquisite. It was with reluctance that he released his hold on her. "I'm going to order a mojito. Would you like one?"

Dina wrinkled her nose. "What's that?"

"It's a Cuban drink made with rum, lime juice, sparkling water and crushed mint leaves. They serve it here with chunks of shaved sugar cane."

She shook her head. "No, thank you. I don't drink."

His eyebrows lifted slightly. "Not at all?"

"Hardly ever," she said truthfully. "I saw what alcohol did to my mother, and it wasn't a pretty sight."

"Would you prefer that I don't drink?" Lance asked.

"No, please have your mojito. It doesn't bother me when other people drink."

"What if I order one for you without the rum?"

Dina gave him a bright smile. "I'd like that."

Lance signaled a waiter and gave him their drink order, then rounded the table to pull back Dina's chair, leading her over to the area where a buffet was set up. His arm slipped down her back and settled around her waist as they waited in line to sample the fusion of Latin cuisine comparable only to South Beach.

Chapter 15

Dina took a sip of her virgin mojito, peering over the rim of the glass at her dining partner. Surprisingly she enjoyed Lance's company. With him she was able to relax enough to enjoy her food and beverage. She didn't have to analyze everything he said with the hope that he would reveal a clue or clues which she would pass along to Payne. Sharing brunch with Lance was close to perfect until the topic of conversation shifted to Dina Gordon.

"What about Dina Gordon?" she asked, touching the corners of her mouth with a napkin.

"Who is she? What does she do? What does she like? Dislike?"

A veil dropped over her eyes when Dina glanced at a spot over his shoulder. "Why are you referring to me as if I'm not here?"

Lance leaned back in his chair, wondering if he'd stepped over the line with Dina. She was so open, vulnerable, then without warning she put on a shield that made him feel as if he'd become a bother, an annoyance.

"I'm trying not to get too personal. Now, if Dina Gordon doesn't want to answer my questions, then she can opt not to."

Dina's gaze swung back to Lance. He'd finished his

mojito, ordered another one but it sat untouched. "There's not much to tell."

Lance chose his words carefully. "Are you willing to tell me what little there is to tell?"

Nodding, she closed her eyes, and when she opened them she felt as if Lance could see beneath the tough-girl facade she'd erected to protect herself from pain and disappointment.

"I never knew my mother or my father."

Her delicate features tightened with her pronouncement. Her expression had changed so quickly that Lance thought he was looking at a stranger. Dina's transformation reminded him of a snake he'd seen at the zoo. It'd shed its skin and completely changed its appearance.

He reached for his drink, taking a deep swallow. "Were you put up for adoption?"

The seconds ticked off before Dina spoke again. "It should be that simple." There was an edge of hardness in her sultry voice, the timbre deepening with her dark mood. "I meant it when I said I never knew my father. My mother was an alcoholic, a drug addict and a prostitute. When I asked her about the man who'd fathered me, she said she couldn't remember whether he was white, Latino or Asian. Her claim was 'after a while they all look alike.' I can count on one hand the number of times I remember her sober. I don't think she was ever clean. If she couldn't get her drugs, then she drank until she passed out. She was away more than she was home, and if it hadn't been for my grandmother, I don't know where I'd be today. One day she went out and never came back."

Lance found himself drowning in compassion for Dina, but there wasn't anything he could do to help her. Her mistrust of men had begun at conception, and he wondered if she'd spent her childhood staring into the faces of strange men with the hope that she would find the one man she resembled.

"Did anyone report her as a missing person?"

Dina lowered her head and her gaze. "Yes, but she was never found. Or she didn't want to be found. My grandmother put her name on the prayer list of every church she visited. After a while she knew Bernice wasn't coming back and finally released her."

Lance gave Adina a penetrating look. "Do you have any brothers or sisters?"

Her head came up. "No." She emitted an unladylike snort. "I guess you'd say that was a blessing."

Picking up a fork from his place setting, he speared a sea scallop in a blood-orange marinade. He shook his head. "I can't agree with you on that."

"Are you speaking from experience?"

Lance's hand tightened on his fork. "Yes. I was six when my older sister was killed in a hit-and-run. Her death devastated my parents and eventually destroyed their marriage. My dad worshipped his little princess, and the day they buried her a part of him also died. I missed her then and I still miss her."

Dina curbed the urge to reach across the table and hold his hand. "Where are your parents?"

There was another swollen silence. "My father passed away three years ago and my mother now lives in a Charleston, South Carolina, retirement community."

She shifted on her chair, leaning over the table. "May I ask you a favor?"

Lance sat up straighter, his expression brightening. "Sure. What is it?"

"Can we talk about something else? I've never been comfortable talking about death and dying."

He successfully concealed his disappointment behind a too-bright smile. He'd hoped that Dina would ask to see him again. "Of course, ba…" He'd stopped himself before he called her baby. "Yes, let's talk about something else."

Propping an elbow on the table, Dina rested her chin on the heel of her hand. "What do you do for a living?"

"I'm a software engineer."

"You're into computers?" He nodded. "The only thing I know about a computer is how to turn it on and go on-line."

"There's a lot more to computers than the internet."

"So say you," she teased.

"Tinkering with computers helps pay the rent," Lance countered.

"Not only the rent but also buys classic cars."

"Oh, so you noticed I like old cars?"

"Of course I noticed." Dina wanted to tell Lance that she'd also noticed his Italian-made shoes and gold timepiece. It was apparent he didn't live from paycheck to paycheck. "Did you go to the raceway today to buy another car?"

"I was thinking about it. However, I only buy something if I truly like it."

"Do you need another car?"

"Nope."

"Then why buy another one?"

"I collect classic cars."

Her waxed eyebrows lifted with this disclosure. "How many do you have?"

"Three." There was a hint of pride in his voice.

"You have three and now you're looking for a fourth. Are you aware that you can only drive one car at a time?"

Throwing back his head, Lance laughed, the rich sound causing couples at other tables to turn in their direction. "Of course I'm aware of that. But that's not going to stop me from buying another one if I like it."

"Men and their toys," she whispered.

He winked at her. "That's because men are just big boys. I don't have a wife or children, so I compensate with big boy toys." He sobered, staring at the large eyes that changed color with Dina's mood. "Would you like to drive back to Irvington?"

"I can't."

"Why not?"

"I don't have a license."

"Do you know how to drive?"

"Yes."

She'd learned to drive but never taken the time to get a license. She hadn't needed a car when there were buses, the subway and car services readily available. And she hadn't wanted the responsibility of getting up early in the mornings to move a car from one side of the street to the other for alternate-side street parking.

Dina peered at Lance's watch. It was close to three-thirty and the restaurant's waitstaff had begun clearing away the buffet. "If you don't mind, I'd like to leave now." She'd left her cell phone back at the motel and she wanted to check her voice mail for Karla's call.

Reaching into the pocket of his slacks, Lance took out a large bill and left it on the table. Dina made no move to stand up until he rounded the table and pulled back her chair. Glancing over her shoulder, she smiled up at him, and she wasn't disappointed when he returned it with a thin-lipped smile that she found adorable.

They were still smiling when they left the restaurant.

Chapter 16

Lance's gaze shifted from the two-story building with peeling paint on the second-story balconies to the woman next to him. The place she called home wasn't much more than a flophouse.

Dina realized she'd made a faux pas when she'd directed Lance to turn down the block leading to the motel. She wasn't in Brooklyn, where she could get out and walk past apartment buildings, brownstones and town houses to reach her public housing development. The motel was in an industrial area five hundred feet from a Home Depot, a Staples and a Sam's Club. The nearest residential area was half a mile away.

"What are you doing living—"

She put up her hand in front of his face, cutting him off. "Please don't ask."

He glared at her until she lowered her hand. "Okay, Dina, I'll stay out of your business." He'd only conceded because he knew when to advance and when to retreat when it came to women. "May I at least walk you to your door?" The motel wasn't in the best neighborhood and probably wouldn't garner a half-star rating even with a new paint job.

Her smile was slow in coming. "Yes, you may."

Lance walked into the motel with Dina, following her down a hallway to her room, and waited until she unlocked the door. At least the lobby and halls were clean and well lighted. She handed him his cell phone.

"Thank you for everything and a memorable afternoon."

He stared at the back of Dina's head, wondering why she wouldn't look at him. He actually didn't know much more about her than her name, age and that she lived in Irvington, not in a house or apartment but in a seedy motel. He wanted to know her marital status, whether she had children or where she worked.

More questions bombarded him like missiles: who was the man at the track who'd walked away with his approach? What was his connection to Dina and what had he said to her to make her cry? Lance knew his questions would remain questions if this was to be the last time he saw Dina.

"It was my pleasure," he said to her back. Turning on his heel, he retraced his steps, walking away from a woman who'd stirred up protective instincts he hadn't known he had.

Dina stood motionless, watching Lance until he disappeared from her line of vision, then walked into the room and closed the door. The threat against her life had changed her. Two weeks ago she would've seen Lance Haynes as the perfect mark. It wouldn't have mattered if he was married or single because she would've pimped him for everything he had and walked away without a modicum of guilt. Her rationale would've been if he'd been dumb enough to let the head between his legs do the thinking for him, then he deserved whatever he got.

What she couldn't understand was that she liked

Lance. But, then again, she was Dina Gordon, not Adina Jenkins—who would've messed him over royally. Lance Haynes didn't know how lucky he was that he'd escaped Adina Jenkins's clutches unscathed.

She slipped out of her shoes, sat down and reached for the cell phone in the drawer of the bedside table.

She checked her voice mail.

Her heart sank.

No one had called.

Chapter 17

Karla lay on a chaise on the shaded patio of the Oldwick, New Jersey, home she shared with her husband,
Ronald, sipping from a glass of iced green tea. Ronald
had gotten up early to play doubles tennis with three of
his fraternity brothers. He'd invited her to come along
and hang out with the other wives, but she'd declined.

She probably would see the same women the following
day at a cookout hosted by mutual friends. Interacting
with some of the women for two consecutive days was not
what she thought of as entertainment. There were a few
women who didn't like her, and the feeling was mutual.

It felt good to sleep in late, lose track of time after
she'd lounged in the Jacuzzi before eating a cholesterol-
laden, calorie-filled breakfast—something she rarely
did. It was Sunday, a day of rest, and Karla intended to
do just that—rest.

Her gaze narrowing, she stared at a bird circling lazily
overhead. She sat up and watched as it appeared to stop in
midair, then fell out of the sky in a burst of speed, disappearing from sight. She waited, counting off the minutes,
a smile parting her lips. The bird reappeared with what
looked like a small rabbit in its talons. She wasn't a serious bird-watcher, but she recognized the bird as a hawk.

She loved the four-bedroom, four-bath house as much for its spaciousness as for the surrounding countryside. The million-dollar, forty-six-hundred-square-foot Colonial with an inground pool set on three acres of landscaped property with a nearby stream was surrounded by a wooded area that sloped down into a picturesque valley. She and Ronald lived far enough from their closest neighbor to walk around naked without anyone seeing them. Walking around without their clothes on was something they did often.

Reaching for her sunglasses off the table next to the chaise, Karla settled back on the cushions and closed her eyes. The cool breeze feathering over her body countered the strong rays of the sun. Ronald hadn't decided what he wanted to do later that evening, but if it were up to her, she would spend it at home.

She felt as if she'd just dozed off when she heard the chiming of the doorbell. Sitting up, she glanced at her watch. It was five-thirty. She'd been asleep for hours. Swinging her legs over the side of the chaise, she went inside.

She pushed a button on a closed-circuit screen built into a wall in the kitchen to see the face of a man dressed in a FedEx uniform. A slight frown furrowed her forehead. She wasn't expecting a delivery, so it had to be something for Ronald. Pressing another button, she activated a speaker device on the intercom. "May I help you?"

"FedEx, Mrs. King. I have a delivery for you from R. Weichert."

A wide grin split her face. "Please hold on and I'll be right with you."

He'd come through for her. Her former law professor,

Judge Weichert, had expedited Adina Jenkins's name change. Opening a drawer under the countertop, she picked up a five-dollar bill from her household petty cash and made her way to the front door.

She signed for the envelope, gave the messenger a tip, closing the door before he could thank her. Sitting on a needlepoint-covered chair in the expansive entry-way, Karla ripped open the envelope and examined the contents. She smiled. Rhys had given her three official copies of the birth certificate. It was apparent he was looking for something special from her, and she would give it to him.

Going into the space she'd set up as a home office, she picked up her cell phone and dialed the number to Adina—no, she thought, Dina Gordon's cell. The call was answered on the second ring.

"Hello."

Karla smiled when hearing the tentative greeting. "Dina Gordon, this is Karla King." She heard a soft gasp through the earpiece. "I need you to meet me in my office Tuesday morning. I have several documents to give you."

"What time Tuesday morning, Mrs. King?"

"Is ten too early?"

"No. Ten is fine. I don't know how to thank you, Mrs. King."

Leaning a hip against one of two rosewood-topped facing desks, Karla stared at the modular wall suite in a soft vanilla-bean color with shelves of books and photographs displayed behind glass doors.

"Now, you know, you've already thanked me, Ms. Gordon. I hadn't called you because I wanted to wait to see if my friend would come through for you. If he hadn't, then I would've returned your property to you."

"Was it enough, Mrs. King?"

"Yes. It was enough. Enjoy your weekend and I'll see you Tuesday at ten."

"Thank you again."

"You're quite welcome." A warm glow eddied through Karla when she ended the call. Ten thousand dollars was spare change to a woman living with the fear that each day might be her last.

Pressing a number on speed dial, she waited for Rhys to answer his cell. She wasn't disappointed when she heard his resonant greeting. His voice was like the man—powerful. "I got it a few minutes ago. Thank you, Rhys."

"When am I going to see you, Karla?"

"You're going to have to let me know when you're available."

"Let me check with my secretary on Tuesday to see what's on my calendar, then I'll call you."

"I'll be waiting."

"Who are you waiting for?"

Karla spun around to find her husband standing in the doorway, his white shirt and shorts a startling sensual contrast against his tanned honey-brown skin. He smiled at her, and like Pavlov's dog she felt the flutters followed by a gush of moisture between her legs. She pressed her knees together to still the sensations.

Ronald Thaddeus King had had that effect on her more than six years ago when she met his gaze across the room at a party, and it was still evident. They'd dated for five months, then married in a small private ceremony with Judge Rhys Weichert officiating.

The first time she slept with Ronald she knew she'd finally met her sexual soul mate. Not only did his sex drive match hers, but he wasn't timid when trying new positions or other methods of sex play that ended in indescribable pleasure.

Karla had openly admitted to her husband that she'd married him because of the sex; however, it wasn't the only reason she'd remained Mrs. Ronald King. Before they'd celebrated their first wedding anniversary she'd found herself inexorably in love with the man.

Chapter 18

A mysterious smile tipped the corners of Karla's mouth. "Rhys."

Smiling, dimples flashing in his chiseled cheeks, Ronald King walked into the room, his gaze fusing with his wife's. Dark brown deep-set eyes caressed her face, moving sensuously down to her chest before reversing direction. The shape of her full breasts was ardently on display under a wife beater.

"Oh, yes, the Honorable Judge Rhys Weichert," he whispered seconds before his mouth closed over hers. Capturing her lower lip between his teeth, Ronald suckled it. "Are you planning to see him?"

Karla put her arms around her husband's waist, pressing her breasts to his wide, deep chest. She didn't want to talk about Rhys. "Mmm!"

Ronald shifted his attention to her neck; he cupped her waist, wondering whether she had on panties under the blue-and-white-striped cotton drawstring pants. He ground his hips to hers when he felt the stirrings of an erection. "Is that a yes or a no?"

Karla threw back her head, baring her neck for his kiss. "It's an *eventually*." Her breathing deepened with the hardening flesh against her thigh. "I'll let you know when."

"You better," he threatened softly. Every woman he'd slept with since marrying Karla knew, and vice versa. Ronald stared at his wife. She looked nothing like the lawyer who favored tailored suits and a chic hairstyle. She'd pulled her hair off her face in a ponytail. Wayward strands had escaped the elastic band to fall around her neck and over her forehead. The epitome of high maintenance, Karla King had a standing weekly appointment for her hair, her hands, her feet and a massage, claiming the massages were the cure for her tension headaches.

He'd always thought her more attractive than beautiful, yet that hadn't stopped him from pursuing the woman with whom he planned to spend the rest of his life. Five-nine and weighing one forty-five, she claimed the most incredibly toned body he'd seen on a woman. And in thirty-eight years he'd seen *and* had his share of naked women. However, it was Karla who complemented him in and out of bed. Both had an insatiable lust for power, luxury and unlimited sexual pleasure. But it was her intelligence, ambition and her willingness to take risks that made her the perfect wife.

Karla lowered her head and buried her face against the strong column of Ronald's neck. He smelled of sweat, cologne and man! He worked out every day in their home gym, running miles on the treadmill, lifting weights and bench-pressing twice his body's weight of two hundred pounds that was evenly distributed over his six-foot, two-inch physique. His crooked dimpled smile, delicate refined features and black silky close-cropped hair, eyebrows, trimmed goatee and mustache had most women—if they were normal—giving him a second look. One of the female attorneys at her firm had remarked that Ronald King had the face and body of a god, to which Karla had politely thanked her, then crossed the room to loop her arm through her husband's in a proprietary gesture that definitely wasn't lost on the others at the social gathering.

"What are we going to do tonight, darling?"

Ronald's hands slipped lower. He lifted Karla effortlessly until her legs were anchored around his waist. "Fuck," he rasped close to her ear.

Holding on to his neck to keep her balance, she laughed softly. "I'm serious, darling."

"So am I," he countered. "Join me in the shower, and *if* you can still walk and talk, then we'll see about going out for dinner."

"I'll watch you shower, but I'm not going to join you." If Ronald was disappointed that she didn't want to share his shower, his expression gave no indication as he carried her out of the office, down a wide hallway and up the staircase to the second story as Karla rested her head on his shoulder. "I want to put in another fireplace."

"Don't we have enough fireplaces, Karla?"

"Not really." Her voice was soft, seductive. She didn't want to tell Ronald that she'd come into an unexpected windfall thanks to the generosity of the former Adina Jenkins. "I'd also like to host a July Fourth party this year now that we have the pool."

Ronald entered their bedroom suite and carried Karla into his bathroom. When they'd met with an architect to draw up the plans for the house, Karla had insisted on his-and-her bathroom suites. Hers contained a powder room, a garden tub, a bidet and a shower stall; his had a steam room, a freestanding shower and a urinal.

When they'd decided to build the house, Ronald told

his wife he wanted nothing to do with the design or decorating. This is not to say that Karla didn't confer with him beforehand, because he had to countersign checks for big-ticket items. His mantra of *Whatever Karla King wanted Karla King got* kept their marriage on an even keel.

Discussing the household budget with her was something he avoided at all costs because he and his three sisters grew up listening to their parents' incessant arguments about not being able to make ends meet on their salaries.

It was different for him and Karla because they'd decided not to have children. Another factor wherein both differed from their parents was that individually they earned six-figure salaries. They'd also invested well with stock portfolios worth several million dollars.

"If you want it, then go for it, baby," he said, setting her on her feet.

Karla sat on a padded bench, watching her husband undress. She'd had the contractor draw up plans to put in an outdoor stove/grill and a stainless-steel sink in the expansive backyard, but now she could indulge herself with an outdoor fireplace. She'd fantasized about sitting outdoors in front of a fire in the cooler weather, and now it would become a reality.

Her gaze lingered on the muscles in Ronald's back when he leaned down to pick up his discarded clothes. She smiled. It'd taken a while, but he'd learned to pick up after himself. She'd lost count of the number of times she'd told Ronald that she was his wife, not his maid, even though a cleaning service came to the house twice each week.

"What do you think of having an outdoor fireplace?" she asked as Ronald walked in the shower area.

He hesitated, turning a faucet with a programmable thermostat. "What?"

Unconsciously Karla tucked several strands of hair behind her right ear. "A fireplace," she repeated. "We can entertain outdoors until it gets real cold."

A frown marred Ronald's almost-too-pretty masculine face. "You spend years decorating the house where you like it, and now you want to entertain outside year-round?"

"Not year-round, darling. Having an outdoor fireplace extends the time for outdoor entertainment. It would also save us sending our rugs out to be cleaned." She'd covered her wood floors in the living and dining rooms with priceless hand-knotted Turkish rugs.

Ronald turned on the water, and streams of water from jets built into the tiled wall cascaded over his body from shoulders to legs. "Okay," he drawled noncommittally. He didn't know why Karla wanted to talk about things that didn't interest him when all he wanted to do was make love to her.

"Okay what, Ronald?"

His frustration and temper exploded. "Put in the fuckin' fireplace."

Karla froze, nothing moving except the rise and fall of her chest. "What the hell is the matter with you?" Her voice was low, ominous.

He glared at her. "I told you that I want to make love to you, but you keeping going on about inane bullshit!"

Rising slowly from the stool, she closed the distance between them, standing far enough back so she wouldn't get wet. Hands on hips, her eyes narrowed to mere slits. "If you didn't want to talk about it, then you should've said something."

Cupping his hands, Ronald filled them with water and flung it at Karla. Water pasted the cotton to her chest, the outline of her breasts showing through as if she were naked. She looked down at her chest before her gaze shifted back to her grinning husband. His large, even teeth showed whitely against the black of his mustache.

"I don't want to talk about it. Okay, Mrs. King?"

Reaching down, Karla relieved herself of the wet undershirt. "No, it's not okay, Mr. King."

"Whatcha gonna do 'bout it?" he said, lapsing into dialect.

"This."

Her right hand shot out, she grasping his penis at the same time she stepped out of her pants. Ronald had guessed right. She wasn't wearing panties. He hardened quickly as they sank down to the floor.

There was no time for foreplay when Karla opened her legs. Her hand covered Ronald's as he eased his enormous penis into her vagina. Even after six years she hadn't figured out whether he was too big or she too small, but once he was fully sheathed inside her, the pleasure was always exquisite. They shared a groan and a smile as water flowed over them. She hadn't wanted to get her hair wet, but it was too late. She was wet, her hair was wet and her body was on fire!

Ronald slid his hands under Karla's hips, lifting her off the large blocks of tile for deeper penetration. "This is what I want to talk about, baby."

Karla, closing her eyes, nodded. She forgot about the specs for her outdoor kitchen, the official documents she would hand over to Dina Gordon, the cash she'd secreted in a drawer in her walk-in closet and Rhys, whom she would meet at a Philadelphia hotel.

What she couldn't forget or ignore was the heat and then chills as Ronald's powerful thrusts swept her away to a place where nothing mattered except the two of them. She opened her eyes to find him staring down at her. Droplets of water shimmered on his hair and dripped off the end of his nose.

Passion pounded the blood through her heart as she struggled to breathe. Then, without warning, waves of ecstasy throbbed through her; she gasped as the pulsing between her legs swirled uncontrollably.

Cradling her hips with one broad hand, Ronald covered Karla's breasts with the other, squeezing them until her nipples hardened like plump berries. She was an inferno, her heat sweeping into him. He may have slept with other women, but it was his wife he always came back to. She wound her legs around his waist, her body meeting his in a savage bucking that sent shivers up his spine. He felt the familiar tightening in his scrotum. Throwing back his head, he bellowed as he ejaculated, the walls of her vagina milking him until he was close to fainting.

They lay motionless until their respiration slowed to a normal rate. As if on cue, they got up, washed each other's bodies, then retreated to the bedroom and fell into bed together. The sun had gone down and stars littered the sky when they got up and went down to the kitchen to prepare a light repast.

It was after midnight when they went back to bed to make love yet again.

Chapter 19

Karla touched Ronald's arm to get his attention. "I'm going inside to see if Sybil needs help." He nodded and went back to his conversation with his host and two other men.

Navigating her way through the small crowd gathered in the expansive backyard of the two-story house in a new upscale West Orange, New Jersey, suburb, she slid back the screen door and stepped into a stainless-steel kitchen. Sybil Cumberland, dressed in a white tunic over a pair of pin-striped pants, stood at a cooking island, tossing salad fixings in a large glass bowl. Classical music flowed from speakers concealed throughout the house.

"I came to see if you needed help with something."

Sybil's head came up. She smiled, her upper lip disappearing against the ridge of her teeth with the gesture. "Thanks, Karla, but I have everything under control."

Resting a hip against the cooking island, Karla took a sip of her sweet tea. "Do you mind if I hang out here and watch you?"

Sybil's wide-set, slanting brown eyes bore into Karla's. "Something the matter with the company outside?" she asked intuitively.

Karla twisted her mouth at the same time she rolled

her eyes. "You know Maxine Owens and I can't be within spitting distance of each other without shit goin' down."

"I'd never invite her to my home if her husband wasn't related to Cory, and you know how he hates drama. The horse-face bitch will go after anything with a *dick*." She'd spat out the word.

Nodding, Karla agreed with Sybil. The one time she'd seen Maxine with her hand near Ronald's crotch, she'd been up and out of her chair and heading toward the woman with the intent of kicking her ass but not before snatching every track of weave out of her basketball-size head. Ronald had managed to defuse the altercation when he forcibly removed Maxine's hand, and whatever he'd whispered in her ear, it hadn't been to her liking, because she'd told her henpecked, frock-tail, candy-ass husband they were leaving.

Consciously dismissing Maxine, she watched Sybil quickly and expertly put together an antipasto platter. Green and black olives, marinated artichokes, roasted red bell peppers cut into narrow strips, anchovy fillets and parmesan cheese broken into bite-size pieces were put into separate small bowls and plates, then on a large serving tray along with serving utensils. She then separated thinly sliced Italian cured prosciutto and bresaola and layered them attractively on a hand-painted platter.

Sybil, who operated her own catering business, moved around the kitchen without wasting a single motion. She removed a parchment-lined baking sheet from the oven. The tantalizing aroma of tiny golden parmesan shortbreads filled the kitchen. After cooling them on a rack, she topped them with roasted cherry tomatoes and feta, parsley pesto and goat cheese. She removed another tray, this one with cocktail corn cakes she topped with spicy mango salsa.

Karla was introduced to Sybil three years ago after their husbands met at a Vegas-based computer show. She felt a particular kinship with the chef because Sybil's ambition matched hers. At thirty-six, Sybil was five years younger, and although she ran a successful business, it wasn't enough for the talented chef.

Sybil had a nervous energy that at first wasn't discernible. It was on rare occasions that her black shoulder-length hair wasn't pulled off her oval face in a ponytail. The inky darkness of her hair made her light brown complexion with yellow undertones appear sallow unless she wore makeup. A small, straight nose and high cheekbones made for an overall attractive visage.

"Do you sample everything you cook?" Karla asked.

Sybil shook her head. "If I did, then I'd weigh more than I do now."

"You weigh less than I do."

"I doubt it. I'm five-seven and weigh one sixty-three."

"I—I don't believe it," Karla sputtered. She couldn't believe Sybil weighed almost twenty pounds more than she did. "Maybe you look thinner because you don't have a sister-girl booty."

"I'm built like my mother. But if you tell anyone how much I weigh, I'll deny it. Even Cory doesn't know."

Karla pantomimed zipping her mouth. "Your secret is safe with me. Are you sure I can't help bring something outside?"

"What I'd like for you to do is tell Cory to come and take these trays outside. If I cook, then he has to serve."

"Okay."

Karla returned to the patio. Cory had taken up a position behind a portable bar, pouring and mixing drinks. Tall, dark and slender with an athletic physique, he had soulful dark eyes, a square jaw and had recently begun growing a goatee. His easygoing personality made him the perfect host, and whenever she observed him with Sybil there was no doubt he was hopelessly in love with her.

A DJ had arrived and was setting up his equipment. The Cumberlands, who'd moved into the sprawling high ranch in early January, had invited friends and family members to join them in celebrating their new home.

Karla moved behind the bar with Cory. "I'll take over here. Your wife needs you in the kitchen."

Cory handed a chilled martini to one of his guests. "Are you sure you can handle the bar, counselor?"

Karla smiled as if she were hiding a secret—and she was. "I promise not to poison anyone." She turned her attention to a Botoxed woman with a short, stylish haircut. "I'm going to have to see some ID before I can serve you," she teased.

The woman blushed to the roots of her frosted hair. "Stop! I'm a grandmother."

"You'd never know. Grandmas come young nowadays."

The woman placed a hand over Karla's, the gems on her bejeweled fingers sparkling in the bright sunlight. "Do you know what?" she asked as if sharing a secret.

Karla leaned closer and the smell of scotch wafted over her face. It was apparent she wasn't ordering her first drink. "What?"

"I like you."

Karla winked at her. "I like you, too." She reached for a tumbler. "Scotch and soda on the rocks?"

"How did you know?"

Filling the glass with ice, she wrinkled her nose. "Lucky guess."

She wanted to laugh when Cory asked whether she could handle the bar. She was as knowledgeable about cocktails as an experienced mixologist.

She took orders for a Salty Dog, a Rusty Nail and an Old Fashioned before Cory returned to relieve her. When she went to look for Ronald among the three dozen people who'd come to eat, drink and listen to music, she found him staring at her with a strange expression on his face.

"Please don't say anything, Ronald."

His mouth thinned noticeably under his mustache as he averted his gaze. "I wasn't going to say anything." His gaze swung back to meet hers, holding it for a full minute. His hands slid down Karla's arms, pulling her to his chest. "When are you going to learn to trust me to keep your secret?"

"I do trust you, Ronald. I love *and* trust you, darling."

Ronald held his wife close, feeling the pumping of her heart against his chest. She loved him and he loved her so much that it frightened him. Karla had become his world, his life.

Dipping his head, he brushed a kiss over her parted lips. "I love and trust you, too."

Chapter 20

"Ms. Jenkins, Mrs. King will see you now."

Dina stood up and gave the receptionist a baleful look. She'd arrived at the offices of Siddell, Kane, Merrill and King at nine-thirty, yet the dour-faced woman had made her wait an hour before she'd announced her. There were times when she appeared to doze off but wake up whenever the telephone rang.

She walked to Karla's office, knocking lightly on the door. "Mrs. King?"

Karla glanced up from the document she'd read twice while waiting for Dina Gordon. "I expected you half an hour ago."

Dina didn't miss the censure in the attorney's voice. Karla had pulled her hair back, leaving a wisp of bangs over her forehead. "I've been here since nine-thirty," she countered.

"Why didn't the receptionist let me know?"

"You'll have to ask her that." Her tone was cryptic, but after waiting she didn't much care.

Karla nodded, waving a hand. "Please sit down, Dina."

Concealing a smile, Dina sat on a chair in front of the desk. She'd called her "Dina." "Thank you."

Picking up an envelope, Karla handed it to her. "Everything you need to secure documents with your new name is in there."

She opened it and examined a set of triplicate birth certificates in a glassine envelope. She was now legally Dina Gordon. Her birth date and everything else had remained the same. There was also a smaller envelope. A soft gasp escaped her when she opened it, her gaze shifting from the contents to Karla.

"What's up with the money?" The envelope was filled with one-hundred-dollar bills.

A hint of a smile touched Karla's generous mouth when she said, "That's the firm's hourly fee."

Dina's mouth opened, but nothing came out. "I—I don't understand," she stammered.

Pressing a button on her telephone, Karla buzzed the receptionist. "Mrs. Siddell, will you please bring the receipt book." Minutes later the receptionist entered the office, book in hand. Karla smiled sweetly at the elderly woman. Jane Siddell was the widow of the man who'd set up the firm sixty years ago to handle the finances of wealthy New Jersey residents. Her son, who took over after his father's death, humored his mother when she'd volunteered to act as receptionist Tuesday mornings. Most times the impeccably dressed octogenarian literally slept on the job.

"Miss Jenkins will give you our hourly fee of six hundred dollars in cash. I need you to give her a receipt."

Dina handed her the envelope. Jane Siddell counted the money and wrote out a receipt with a flowery cursive that harkened back to another era. Waiting until the door closed behind the receptionist, she gave Karla a questioning look. "Do you want me to give you six hundred dollars?"

"No, Dina. It's the firm's policy to waive the fee for the initial consult. However, you've come in twice, therefore I must show a billable hour."

She couldn't believe the attorney had put up the money for her, even if it had come out of the ten grand she'd given her. "Thank you." She leaned closer. "The money's not dirty," she said *sotto voce*. "I found out where the cheap bastard hid his stash and I stole every penny. It's a small price to pay for what I had to go through for ten years."

Karla now understood why Dina had given her the money. It equaled one thousand dollars for every year she'd been abused, and the flip side was that it'd bought her freedom to live her life without fear. "I suggest you apply for a social security card and driver's license in your new name as soon as you can."

Dina met her direct stare. "I can't apply for a social security card until I get an apartment. I need a legal address."

"Are you still staying at the motel?"

She inclined her head. "Yes."

"Have you looked for an apartment?"

"Not yet. I wanted to wait until I was legally Dina Gordon."

"I suppose you're going to need employment, too?"

"I need a job, like, yesterday."

Karla stared at the woman on the other side of the desk. She looked nothing like the frightened, anxious young woman who'd sat in her office three weeks before. She now appeared older, worldly. Subtly applied makeup, her long hair fashioned in a chignon, she wore an ice-blue linen pantsuit with a matching shell and black patent leather pumps. She appeared very much the young professional.

"Do you have experience waiting tables?"

"No, but I'm a quick study." Dina hadn't lied when she'd told Karla she needed a job yesterday, because there was still the matter of repaying Payne Jefferson. If she got a position waiting tables, then there was no doubt she would be able supplement her salary with tips.

"If I'm able to contact a friend who owns a catering establishment, would you be available to go on an interview?"

Dina sat up straighter. "Yes."

Picking up the telephone, Karla punched in a number. Her eyebrows lifted when she heard Sybil's greeting. "This is Karla."

"What's up?"

"Do you still need a waitress?" Sybil had told her that she'd had to fire a waitress who'd gotten into the habit of showing up late.

"No. I just hired someone this morning. Why?"

"I have someone looking for work. She doesn't have any experience, but she's willing to learn. She's just applied for her social security card." Karla winked at Dina. "Will that be a problem?"

"Not usually. I'd pay her like a contract worker where she'll be responsible for her taxes until I put her on the regular payroll. If the girl I just hired doesn't work out, then I'll let you know."

"Sybil, I really need you to help me out now." Karla had lowered her voice to a whisper.

There was a noticeable pause before Sybil said, "Is she one of your special clients?"

Karla smiled. "How did you know?"

"Because I know you well enough to know that you don't beg too often. Look, I have some free time tomorrow. If she can be here at six, then I'll see her."

Karla covered the mouthpiece. "She can see you tomorrow at six."

"I'll be there."

"She's available, Sybil. Her name is Dina Gordon."

"Tell Ms. Gordon that if she's going to be late, then she should forget about coming."

"I'll tell her. Thanks, Sybil."

"No problem, Karla."

Karla ended the call and reached for a pen. She wrote down the name, address and telephone number of SJC Catering on a legal pad. Tearing off the sheet, she handed it to Dina. "You'll have to go to West Orange. You're to see Sybil Cumberland. She said if you're late, then forget about coming."

Dina stared at the bold handwriting before she looked at Karla. "I'll be on time."

There was something in the hazel eyes that said that Dina Gordon had been given a second chance to live a normal life and she wasn't about to blow it by not making it to an interview on time.

Pushing to her feet, she extended her hand. "I'll let you know how everything works out."

Karla stood up and took her hand. "Please keep in touch. Good luck, Dina."

"Thank you, Mrs. King."

"You're welcome. I think it's time you call me Karla."

The glow of Dina's smile reached her luminous eyes. "Thank you again—Karla."

Dina was there, then she was gone, closing the door softly behind her. Karla admired and respected the former Adina Jenkins. She'd fled her abuser *and* taken his money.

She was a woman after her own heart.

Chapter 21

Dina felt as if she were walking on air. She couldn't remember the last time she'd felt free, free of the demons that'd haunted her for as long as she could remember.

She'd taken the train from Trenton with her prized birth certificates clutched to her chest and a silly grin on her face. A few times she'd caught other passengers staring at her with strange expressions on their faces. One woman who'd sat down next to her had kept inching farther and farther away until she'd finally changed her seat. Oblivious to everyone and everything going on around her, she'd closed her eyes and mentally planned her next move.

As soon as Dina returned to the motel she went through her closet for something to wear to her "interview." Even the word sounded foreign. She, who'd never worked a day in her life, was going to get a legitimate nine-to-five. Staring at the garments on the hangers, she reached for a pair of slacks and a blouse.

She'd added a few more garments to her meager wardrobe when she'd gone shopping, and, if hired, she probably would wear a uniform, but she still needed clothes if she was to become a working girl.

Flopping down on the bed, she picked up a pad and pen and wrote down her to-do list: *get a job, find an apartment and apply for a social security card.* A driver's license wasn't a priority because she couldn't afford a car. Even a hooptie wasn't an option. She'd kept a mental running total of how much money she had left, and it was a long way from the twenty thousand she owed Payne. Living at the motel was steadily draining her funds.

The phone rang, startling her. Reaching over, she picked up the receiver. The only time the phone rang was when someone at the front desk called. "Hello."

"Ms. Jenkins, this is the front desk. There is a delivery for you."

Her nerves tensed as acute panic held her captive. Did a delivery translate into someone had discovered her whereabouts? "Is there a name?" she asked the desk clerk.

"Let me check the card.... It's from L. Haynes."

She whispered a silent prayer. "Thank you. I'll come get it."

Retrieving her key, she left the room, nodding to the woman assigned to cleaning the rooms on her floor. The only upside of staying in the motel was that she didn't have to clean up after herself. Housekeeping made the bed, cleaned the bathroom, dusted and vacuumed. Each time she left and returned to the room she checked to see if anything was moved or missing. Her greatest fear was returning to find the contents of her backpack gone.

She entered the lobby and stopped short. Lance had sent her a large bouquet of pale pink roses in a tall vase filled with colorful marbles. Several people who were checking in stared at her as she attempted to carry the vase. It was a lot heavier than it looked. They stared, but not one offered to help her.

Struggling under the weight, Dina made it back to her room and plucked the card off the cellophane. Men had given her money, clothes, furs, but never flowers. She read Lance's neat print: *I'd be honored if you would have dinner with me tonight.—L. Haynes.* He'd included the telephone numbers to his office and cell phone. Smiling, she put the card to her nose. The scent of his cologne clung to the small vellum square. Even the card was of the finest quality paper. Her gaze shifted to the roses with petals that were beginning to open. The flowers were perfect, and Lance had been the perfect gentleman.

What, she told herself, did she have to lose going out with him? After all, it was a date, not a hustle. Reaching for her cell phone, she dialed the number to his office. A strong female voice answered.

"Mr. Haynes's office. This is Della. How may I help you?"

Dina hesitated. She'd expected him to answer his own phone. "May I please speak to Mr. Haynes?"

"Mr. Haynes is out of the office. Would you like to leave a message?"

"Yes."

"Yes what, miss?"

"This is Miss Gordon. Please tell Mr. Haynes yes."

"Ms. Gordon, Mr. Haynes said that if you called, I was to tell you that he would pick you up at six."

She was mute for several seconds. Lance was so certain she would call that he'd given his secretary a message to give to her. "Tell Mr. Haynes I'll be ready at six."

That said, she hung up. It was obvious that Mr. Lance Haynes was very confident, a trait she admired in a man.

Confident men were usually successful men.

Lance wanted to date her and she needed a male friend.

A liaison would prove advantageous for both.

Chapter 22

Lance saw Dina as soon as he swung into a parking space near the front of the motel. His smile mirrored delight in seeing her again. His gaze roved leisurely over her petite figure as he got out of his car. He saw an expression of surprise in her eyes before she shuttered them quickly.

He couldn't believe she could improve on perfection, yet she had. She wore a flattering jade-green dress with three-quarter cuffed sleeves, a stand-up collar and an oyster-white colored obi sash that emphasized her narrow waist. His gaze shifted to her tiny feet in a pair of high-heeled black patent leather pumps. His smile widened. She'd left her tanned legs bare. Instead of her dark hair flowing down her back, tonight she'd pinned it in a twist on the nape of her slender neck.

Reaching for her hand, he brought it to his mouth, kissing the back of it. "You look beautiful."

Dina blushed like an innocent girl unaccustomed to male attention and flattery. She'd lost count of the number of times men had complimented her on her looks, but coming from Lance Haynes, it was different. He was her first real date.

"Thank you, Lance." Her smoky voice had dropped an octave.

Lance stared at the woman staring up at him, his protective instincts surfacing quickly. There was something so pure and childlike about Dina Gordon that it made him feel like a lecherous old man about to seduce a virgin. As soon as the notion entered his head, he banished it. He doubted that, at the age of twenty-seven, Dina was still a virgin.

"You look very nice," Dina said truthfully. Lance wore a pair of dark gray trousers with a faint plum pinstripe. His crisp laundered shirt was a pale lilac he'd paired with an exquisite silk tie in a rich lapis-lazuli-blue. The cufflinks in the shirt's French cuffs, either sterling or white gold, bore his monogram. He appeared slimmer, fit in his tailored attire.

He kissed her hand again, then tucked it into the bend of his arm. "Thank you."

"Where are we going?"

Lance gave her a sidelong glance. "Atlantic City. I planned for us to have dinner before taking in a show."

Dina stumbled and would've fallen flat on her face if Lance hadn't tightened his hold on her hand. "We can't."

Waiting until they were seated together in the car, Lance turned to stare at the woman beside him. "Why can't we?"

She couldn't tell him that there were people in Atlantic City who knew her face, that she'd been seen with too many high rollers and that she'd pulled off too many scores to risk going back. "I don't…I don't go to places where there's gambling and fornication."

Lance stared at Dina as if she'd just dropped out of the sky. The last time he'd heard someone mention *fornication* it was his grandmother, who'd warned him about drinking, smoking drugs and fornicating with fast-ass young women who would try to saddle him with a baby because they knew a good catch when they saw one. He'd been four months shy of his eighteenth birthday when his grandmother had accompanied his parents when they'd driven him to Georgia to enroll in college.

"You don't drink, smoke or gamble." His question was a statement.

Dina nodded. "And I don't fornicate."

"You don't sleep with men?"

They regarded each other for a beat. "No."

"I'm going to ask you something, and you don't have to answer it if you don't want." She inclined her head. "Are you a virgin?"

Dina stared wordlessly, his query causing her reply to wedge in her throat. She couldn't tell him that she'd lost her virginity at eleven when one of her mother's many "friends" robbed her of her innocence, then gave her money not to tell anyone. She'd become his special girl and he her secret. What he didn't know was that she hated him, hated what he did to her, but had gotten used to the five or ten dollars he gave her after he finished sweating and grunting. He'd always said the same thing: *Baby, you have the sweetest pussy in the whole wide world.*

After he would stumble out of the apartment, she would get up and wash, but no matter how long she'd sit in the tub or linger under the shower, she never felt completely clean. He'd become the first of many who gave her money to lie with them. The only man she hadn't taken money from was Terence, but he'd given her something the others hadn't—a baby.

"Yes."

Lance was momentarily speechless in his shock. He hadn't realized he'd been holding his breath until he labored to exhale. Usually cautious and distrustful of women, he wanted nothing more than to protect and take care of the petite, exotic woman with the hypnotic hazel eyes with whom he shared the same space. He ran a hand over his face, then stared through the windshield.

Dina knew her false admission had shocked Lance. That had been her intent because she didn't want to sleep with him. More than anything she wanted friendship, someone she could trust not to use her for his own selfish motives.

"We don't have to go out."

"What!" Lance's head spun around as if suspended on a spring, his flaring nostrils opening wider. "What the hell are you talking about?" he shouted at her.

Dina flinched as if she'd been struck across the face. "I said we don't have to go out—see each other."

Lance struggled to contain his rising temper. "Did I say I didn't want to go out with you? That I didn't want to see you?"

Dropping her head, Dina shook her head like a chastised child. "No."

"Then why would you say that, Dina?" His voice had softened considerably.

Her head came up, eyes shimmering with unshed tears. "I may not have slept with a man, but I'm not stupid or naive. I know eventually you're going to want me in your bed, and that's when it's all going to come to an end. It's happened with me before, so I suggest we end it now." Dina knew she was giving a flawless performance, so much so that she almost believed herself. She suppressed the urge to laugh.

Shifting on the black leather seat of the top-of-the-line white BMW sedan, Lance ran the back of his hand over her cheek. "Don't cry, baby." Leaning to his right, he kissed her hair. "I promise not to ask you to sleep with me. If it happens, then that choice will be yours."

Dina sniffled, blinking back tears. She opened her small purse, searching for a tissue. Lance beat her to it when he handed her his handkerchief. "Thank you," she mumbled, pressing the square of cotton to the corners of her eyes before returning it him. "You must think I'm some sort of freak."

He shook his head. "That's where you're wrong, Dina. Whatever your reason, I respect your right to hold on to your virginity."

A heavy silence filled the car as she composed her thoughts. "I've always harbored a fear that I would end up like my mother, sleeping indiscriminately with any and every man I'd come in contact with. I'd rather take my life than end up like her."

"Has anyone told you that you're not your mother?"

She affected a sad smile. "Yes. My grandmother had for as long as I can remember."

"Had?"

Dina nodded. "She passed away a few years ago." She'd told yet another lie.

"Did you trust her, Dina?"

"Yes."

"Then you should believe her."

"It's not that easy, Lance."

"What if I help you?"

Dina stared at him as an expression of tenderness softened his gaze. "How, Lance? How can you help me?"

There was just the sound of their breathing as their chests rose and fell in unison. "Trust me, Dina. Trust me to protect and take care of you."

Her eyes filled again, and this time the tears weren't forced or staged. Dina had waited all her life to hear a man tell her what Lance had just proposed. He was old enough to be her father, yet she didn't see him as a father figure.

"How do you propose to do that?"

Running his forefinger down her nose, Lance winked at her. "Come home with me. I want you to pack a bag—"

"No," Dina interrupted.

Lance shook his head, his finger moving to her mouth. "Don't say no until you hear what I've got to say. Okay?" She nodded as he removed his thumb. "I want you to spend the night in my guest bedroom. We can either eat out, order in or I'll cook."

The skin around her eyes crinkled when she smiled. "You're playing with me, aren't you?"

"No, I'm not, Dina. I'm quite serious." And he was. Lance wanted to get her out of the run-down motel. "I don't want you staying here. It doesn't look safe." He'd spent sleepless hours thinking of her, wondering if she were okay. He hadn't rescued her in Englishtown to have her placed in harm's way in a run-down motel that was no better than a cheap boardinghouse.

Dina told Lance she planned to move out of the motel as soon as she secured employment. "I have a job interview tomorrow evening."

He gave her a skeptical look. "Where?"

"West Orange?"

"How are you getting there?"

"I'm walking, Lance." He shot her a warning look. "I'm taking the bus."

"I have a late-afternoon dinner meeting with a client, but I'll arrange for a driver to take you there and bring you back," he said with a finality that warned her not to challenge him.

She said if you're late, then forget about coming. Dina recalled Sybil Cumberland's warning. She didn't know exactly where she was going but knew she couldn't afford to be late; she'd be a fool to turn down Lance's offer.

"Okay."

"Okay to what?"

"Okay to everything you've proposed."

She sat while Lance got out, came around to assist her. He followed her into the motel and waited in the room while she packed a bag. At the last possible moment she reached for the backpack and placed it in the bag, handing it to him.

"I'm ready."

She'd told Lance she was ready when she was frightened that she wouldn't be able to morph into Dina Gordon with the same skill with which she'd become Adina Jenkins, streetwise hustler. Maybe it was because the blood of Bernice Jenkins ran in her veins. All Bernice had to do was smile at a man to get him to do anything for her. However, she'd raised the bar because she hustled men for money while Bernice did it for booze and drugs.

As they walked out of the motel together Dina did something she hadn't done in years.

She prayed.

Chapter 23

Dina lay on a cushioned rattan chair, her bare feet resting on a matching footstool on the terrace of Lance's three-bedroom West New York, New Jersey, apartment, staring out at the towering buildings across the Hudson River. He'd urged her to relax and enjoy the view while he cleaned up the remains of the dinner he'd ordered from an Italian restaurant in nearby Union City. The sun was setting, taking with it the day's heat as a cool breeze blew in off the river.

When Lance told her that he lived in an apartment, she couldn't have imagined the luxury high-rise with twenty-four-hour concierge, pool, fitness and business center and controlled-access parking. The property was steps from the ferry to New York City and minutes from the Holland Tunnel.

His apartment featured a washer/dryer, dishwasher, frost-free refrigerator, microwave and an intrusion alarm. It had all the convenience of a home without the ongoing landscape and pool maintenance. Recessed lights, marble and rosewood floors and impeccably chosen furnishings turned the expansive apartment into a showplace worthy of a magazine layout.

He'd turned the bedroom off the living room into an

office/library. Books in every genre lined built-in floor-to-ceiling shelves. A ladder suspended from a rod provided easy mobility and access to the upper shelves. The only place where Dina had seen that many books was in the local public library.

She'd stayed in opulent suites at hotels and casinos, but after a while she'd thought of the glittery show as nothing more than conspicuous consumption for the few hours she'd spent there. Lance's apartment was different because it was a home—a place where one could escape the stress of an oftentimes hostile world.

The bedroom where she would spend the night was a quiet retreat. An adjoining full bath and sitting room with a table and two cushioned pull-up chairs positioned near a window invited her to while away the hours. It was furnished with a large mahogany four-poster bed covered with heirloom linens and coverlets. When she'd remarked about the bed dressing, Lance had disclosed that the stemware, china, silver and the other heirloom pieces would've gone to his sister—if she'd lived.

Dina had changed from her dress and heels and into an extra-large tee and shorts and had taken her hair down from the elaborate twist to fashion it into a ponytail. Suddenly she felt very sleepy but loath to close her eyes; she didn't want to miss the sight of the rays of the setting sun throwing feathery orange streaks across the darkening sky.

"Awesome, isn't it?"

A sensual smile touched her full mouth when her lips parted. Lance stepped onto the terrace and took a chair opposite her. He'd replaced his suit with a pair of khakis and a short-sleeved black shirt. He wasn't wearing shoes and she noticed that he had very nice feet. They were a little pale but still nice.

She nodded. "It's definitely humbling."

Lance tried not to stare at the woman seated across from him but failed miserably. Barefoot and dressed in the shorts and tee, she appeared so delicate, fragile. What, he mused, was there about Dina Gordon that pulled at his heart? From the first time he saw her standing by herself at the raceway she'd appeared so lost. Then, when he'd returned with her soft drink and registered her expression of fear, he'd known he had to rescue her.

"I called the car service, and a driver will pick you up at four. He's been instructed to wait until you complete your interview, then drive you back to Irvington. Don't give him a tip because I've taken care of his gratuity."

Dina regarded Lance Haynes with a speculative look. He'd fed her, would put her up for the night and had arranged transportation for her to go to West Orange for her interview with Sybil Cumberland.

"Thank you, Lance."

He smiled. "You're welcome. What are you thinking about, Dina?" he asked when a kind of a veil dropped over her eyes.

Her eyebrows lifted. "What makes you believe I'm thinking of something?"

"You have a habit of biting down on your lower lip when you're concentrating on something."

"You're very perceptive."

Lance shook his head. "I'm not as perceptive as I am observant."

"Do you like watching me?"

"Just say it's hard *not* watching you."

"Why would you say that?"

"Come now, Dina," he crooned as if she were a small child. "You have to know what you look like. You're drop-dead gorgeous."

"Maybe to you, but my looks may not be every man's ideal."

He chuckled softly. "Perhaps not every man, yet I'd be willing to wager a year's salary that *most* men would agree with me."

A slight frown appeared between her eyes. "I told you that I don't like gambling."

She hated casinos, with their bright lights, sounds of shuffling cards, the click-clack of the roulette wheel, the dinging of slot machines and the shouts and groans from winners and losers. Even when given money to bet on the turn of a card or a number, she'd refused to gamble. Most times the money went into her purse.

"I'm sorry, Dina. I'll be more careful next time."

A hint of a smile played at the corners of her mouth. "Will there be a next time with us, Lance?" His expression brightened, reminding Dina of a little boy. Although in his late forties, there was something undeniably boyish about Lance Haynes.

"I'd hope there will be."

"There will be," she confirmed, smiling. She sobered, her mood changing like quicksilver. "I don't know how I'm going to repay you for all you've done for me."

"Have I asked you for anything?"

"No. But that's what bothers me, Lance. I keep thinking that you're going to want something from me."

He sat up straighter, sandwiching his hands between his knees. "Where does your distrust come from?"

"The man you saw me with on Sunday is the husband

of a woman he used as his personal punching bag. One day she'd had enough and she just bounced."

"Bounced?" Lance asked, frowning slightly.

"It means she left suddenly," Dina explained.

Lance's frown deepened. "I know what it means. I just didn't expect you to use that word."

"Why?"

"Because it's so…so not like you."

"So not like me?" Dina didn't care whether she sounded defensive. *What the hell does he know about me?* she thought. "Is the word too ghetto for you, Lance?"

Pressing a fist to his mouth, Lance shook his head. He truly didn't want to get into it with Dina. He'd called in his dinner order within minutes of leaving Irvington, and when they'd arrived in Union City it was packed and ready for him. They came to his apartment and ate dinner in the dining room with a backdrop of soft music and panoramic views of the river and the New York City skyline. Now Dina wanted to ruin what had become a wonderful evening with a debate on ghettoisms.

"I said nothing about ghetto, Dina. It's just that I've never heard you utter a slang term, so I was surprised. I meant no disrespect."

Dina closed her eyes for a moment. She had to be careful, very, very careful, or she would blow it. She had to remember that she was now Dina Gordon, not Adina Jenkins. If she wanted to reinvent herself, then the street slang and mannerisms would have to be relegated to her past.

And like LaKeisha Robinson, she was able to go from speaking colloquial English to street jargon effortlessly. The teachers at the Lutheran school that she'd attended, thanks to the money her grandmother had earned as a lunch lady in a nearby public school cafeteria before she was forced to go on disability because of a bad hip, insisted she learn to speak properly or she would never get a decent job. What Dora didn't know was that she didn't need to speak properly when interacting with people whose existence depended upon the next hustle. But what confused her was that the men she took up with liked her because she did know how to speak, which in turn raised their status among their peers.

"I know you didn't, Lance." Her voice and expression were contrite. "I'm sorry. I shouldn't have gone off on you."

He gave her a quick smile. "Forget it. Please finish with your story."

"My friend's husband had begun harassing her friends to tell him where she was. I've seen what he's done to her, so seeing him again just dredged up images of her black eyes and bruises."

"Do you know where she is?"

"No. And even if I did, I'd never tell anyone."

"I'm glad I happened along when I did." There was a hint of pride in Lance's voice.

"So am I," Dina said truthfully.

"So we agree on something," he teased.

"I think we may agree on a lot of things." Without warning, she became a siren, her lips parting as she stared at Lance through her lashes. "The view from your place is better than my motel room and sharing dinner with you is a lot more pleasant than eating alone."

Smiling, he said, "I concur, fair lady." Much to Lance's surprise, she threw back her head and laughed, the husky sound swirling up and around him like a cloaking fog. Moving off his chair, he sat down on the footstool, placing Dina's feet in his lap. The fiery rays of the setting sun created a halo around behind him. His gaze met and fused with hers. "What do you want, Dina?"

Dina blinked once, tiny shivers of gooseflesh rising on her arms and legs as Lance stared at her. She swallowed in an attempt to relieve the increasing constriction in her throat. She couldn't believe she had no response or comeback to his query.

"I don't know."

Lance leaned closer, his slight grip on her toes tightening. "You don't have dreams or aspirations?"

"I can't afford to think about tomorrows. I'm only concerned with today and right now. I need a job so I can get an apartment."

"Where were you living before you moved into the motel?"

"I lived with a girlfriend."

"Why did you move?"

For the tiniest fraction of a moment Dina hesitated. "I had to get away from a man who'd started coming on to me. We worked together," she added when Lance gave her an incredulous look.

"Why didn't you report him?"

"I couldn't because not only was he my boss but he also owned the business."

"So you left rather than slap his ass with a sexual-harassment suit?"

"Leaving was easier for me."

Suddenly she tired of lying and trying to keep her lies straight. She couldn't tell Lance that she was running from a nameless, faceless person who sought to take her life. That she'd managed to escape her phantom, but she still had to deal with Payne Jefferson.

"I didn't mean to imply that you're a coward—"

"I am a coward, Lance!" she shouted, cutting him off. "The man is scary. He's always bragging about whatever he wants he gets. I wasn't going to hang around to let him get me. I am not my mother and I don't want to be anything like her."

Reaching out, Lance pulled Dina from her chair and settled her on his lap, his arms going around her; he cradled her to his chest as if she were a child. "Don't worry about anything, baby girl. Lancelot Londell Haynes will take care of you."

Eyes wide, she lifted her chin and stared at him. "Lancelot Londell?" He nodded. "You're really named Lancelot like the knight?"

Lance nodded again. "Most of my friends call me LL."

Although she was smiling, Dina's eyes were serious. "May I call you LL?"

He wanted to tell her that she could call him anything she wanted if she continued to look at him the way she did. She had the eyes of an innocent child caught up in a world of fear and disappointment. It was as if her soul had remained untouched despite what she'd experienced as a child and now as an adult.

"Of course you may, Dina. After all, we are friends."

Resting her head on his chest, Dina melted into Lance's strength. Changing her name on a birth certificate had become an easy feat when she compared it to eradicating Adina Jenkins completely. All of her life she'd fought not to become Bernice Jenkins, only to learn that she'd been stamped indelibly by the blood that ran in her veins.

She was the daughter of a woman who sold her body for drugs and a man who'd paid her for sex. What kind of man was he to have unprotected sex with a woman who was obviously an IV drug user?

One arm moved up tentatively and went around Lance's neck. Like the brave knight whose name he claimed, he'd become her knight in shining armor. And because she was now Dina Gordon, she swore an oath that she wouldn't do to Lance what she'd done to the men in her past.

"Right now you're the *only* friend I have in the world."

Lowering his head, Lance pressed a kiss to her fragrant hair.

He'd promised to protect and take care of her, and he would.

Chapter 24

Dina sat in a deep armchair in Lance's library, reading. She was waiting for a call from the concierge that her driver had arrived to take her to West Orange for her interview. She'd decided to wear the same skirt and blouse she wore the first time she'd met with Karla King.

"What are you reading?"

Her head came up and she saw that Lance had come into the library. The plush pale gray carpeting had muffled the sounds of his footsteps. He hadn't gone into his office earlier that morning because of his dinner meeting. Much to her surprise, he'd prepared breakfast and served it on the terrace. As with the night before, there had been no conversation as they ate, for which she was grateful because it afforded her the opportunity to observe the man whom she regarded as her personal knight. He wouldn't let her clear away the dishes, insisting she relax. He'd suggested she watch television or listen to music, but she'd opted to read. Dina knew the above average grades she'd earned while in school had been because of her voracious appetite for reading. Whenever she opened a book, it was to escape and fantasize about the mothers and fathers who loved and protected their children.

She'd graduated from the chapter books to novels with glittering locales and glamorous people who loved and lived for the next thrill. She wanted to become one of the beautiful heroines dripping with furs and jewels who had men falling all over themselves to get to her. However, life didn't imitate art, because she'd become a "tricked-out ho" who pimped men for an ex-con with an ax to grind. She'd helped Payne Jefferson perpetuate his raison d'être but at the risk of losing her own life.

Placing the book on a side table, she rose to her feet. "It's one of your legal thrillers."

Lance walked over to Dina, his gaze lingering on her face. He'd found her a chameleon. Today she looked like a corporate sophisticate with her tailored shirt and skirt, but the night before she'd reminded him of a little girl with her baggy shirt and bare feet. Carefully applied makeup accentuated her luminous eyes and sexy mouth. The coral color on her lips complemented the sun-browned darkness of her olive face.

"You look very nice."

Dina's lids slipped down over her eyes. "Thank you. You look nice too, Lance, but…" Her words trailed off when she realized what she'd been about to say.

Lance glanced down at his tan shirt with a contrasting white collar and French cuffs. "What's the matter?"

She glanced up, her gaze softening. She tried imagining Lancelot Haynes as a little boy. She assumed he'd been warned to stay out of the sun because, instead of tanning, his redbone skin burned, turning him a lobster-red. And there was something about his perfectly round face that afforded him a soft, boyish look. But that's where it ended. When she'd sat on his lap the night before she'd felt the bulge between his thighs. It wasn't an

all-out hard-on, but it was obvious that he had no problem achieving an erection.

"The color of your suit," she explained. "It's wrong
for your complexion."

Lance glanced down at the trousers to his suit. The
custom-made tan suit was one of his favorites. Reaching for his hand, she laced her fingers through his. "You
look like a solid wall of taupe."

"Come with me."

Dina wasn't given time to react when Lance pulled her
along with him as they left the library and walked into his
bedroom. The Asian-designed master bedroom screamed
masculinity, from the California king platform bed with
black sheets and white comforter piped in black, to black,
white and gray silk pillows in varying shapes and sizes.
A rug repeated the color scheme with black Chinese sym-
bols in large squares on a background of white.

He slid back the doors to a walk-in closet. Recessed
lights illuminated the efficiently organized space. Laundered shirts in every hue occupied three shelves above
slanted shelves for shoes ranging from patent leather
dress to leather slip-ons. Suit and sports jackets were
arranged according to color, as were slacks and trousers.
Her gaze lingered on silk ties too numerous to count.

Lance extended his free hand. "Take your pick."

Easing her hand from his gentle grasp, Dina walked
over to the suits in shades of brown. She needed to select
a suit that would complement his shirt with the white collar and his silk tie dotted with minute chocolate-brown-
and-white checks.

Her fingers touched jacket after jacket until she turned
and smiled at Lance. "This one would look better on
you." She'd chosen one in a warm henna-brown.

He took the jacket off the rod and held it up close to his face. It was perfect for his coloring. Her smile was dazzling. "It looks wonderful."

"What do I do with the suit I'm wearing?"

"Give it to a men's shelter."

A smile spread across Lance's face at the same time a bell chimed throughout the apartment. His smile vanished quickly. "That's the concierge." He walked out of the closet and pressed a button on the wall in the bedroom. "Yes," he said into the small speaker. "Yes, thank you. Your driver's here," he said to Dina, who'd followed him. These were the times he regretted—having to leave her. She took a deep breath, causing his gaze to linger on the roundness of her breasts under her blouse.

"I'd better get my things and leave or I'll be late."

"Call me and let me know how it went."

She nodded. "I'll call you when I get back to the motel."

"You don't have a cell phone?"

"No," Dina said, lying yet again. She couldn't call Lance from her cell phone because her grandmother's name would come up on the display, and she didn't want to have to explain Dora Jenkins.

"Don't leave yet," Lance said cryptically as he left the bedroom, Adina in pursuit. He retrieved a cell phone and punched in a series of numbers. Picking up a charger, he handed both to her. "Use this one. I just programmed in the numbers where you can contact me."

"What will you use?"

He smiled a thin-lipped smile. "I have another one."

Her eyebrows lifted questioningly. "Are you sure you don't need it?"

"Take it, Dina." Leaning over, he kissed her cheek. "Good luck with your interview."

Resting a hand on his smooth cheek, Dina rose to tiptoe and kissed him. "Thanks for everything."

"Call me, Dina."

She stared up him. "I will."

Cupping her elbow, Lance walked her to the door, where she picked up her bag and purse. He stood with her in the elevator as it descended to the lobby; when the driver took her bag and escorted her to the car, he rode the elevator back to his apartment, closing the door softly behind him.

He'd spent almost twenty-four uninterrupted hours with Dina Gordon, and still it wasn't enough.

Chapter 25

Sybil Cumberland stood in the doorway to her private office, waiting for Dina Gordon. *I'm going to hire her as sure as my name is Sybil Bernadette Johnson-Cumberland,* she thought.

A knowing smile found its way across Sybil's face with Dina's approach. She didn't know what it was about the young woman who'd arrived—on time—for her interview, but instinctively Sybil knew she'd hit the mother lode. Her male clients would love Dina.

Maybe it was her sexy slightly bow-legged walk, her perfect legs in a pair of high-heel pumps, her tiny curvy body or the too beautiful exotic-looking face, but she knew adding the petite woman to her staff would impact the business appreciably. Whether it was food, decor, centerpieces or waitstaff, it all came down to one thing: presentation.

Everything had to be dramatic, eye-appealing, and there was no doubt that Dina Gordon was eye candy of the finest quality. Now, if she could present as well as she looked, then SJC Catering would have hit the jackpot.

Extending her hand, Sybil gave Dina a warm smile. "Hello, Dina, I'm Sybil Cumberland."

Dina returned the chef's smile with a friendly one of

her own. She took her hand. She didn't know what to expect or how a female chef was supposed to look because all those on the Food Network ranged from stick-thin to full and curvy. Sybil wore a black tunic over a pair of black pin-striped pants. She broke up the somber color with a pair of bright yellow leather clogs. Her hair, pulled off her face in a ponytail, was so blue-black it looked dyed. The light sprinkling of freckles across the bridge of her nose was the only color in her bare face. With a little makeup and a new do, Sybil Cumberland was certain to garner her share of male attention.

"Dina Gordon."

Sybil's smile vanished quickly as she eased her fingers from Dina's firm grip. Dina's voice was low, smoky, belying her age. She remembered her mother's voice, which was low enough for her to be mistaken for a man because of a two-pack-a-day cigarette habit. Her mother smoked and her father drank excessively—addictions she abhorred.

"Have you had dinner, Dina? I hope you don't mind if I call you Dina. I deal with enough formality when conferring with my clients."

Dina hesitated, staring at Sybil Cumberland in confusion. She'd come to interview for a position, not eat. "No, I don't mind. And, no, I haven't," she said truthfully. Lance had offered to prepare lunch for her, but she'd been too anxious to eat.

"What would you like?"

"What are my choices?"

Sybil's face was impassive. Dina's query told her a lot about her. She was cautious. "You can have fish, chicken, beef, lamb or pork."

Dina glanced at the chef's hands. She wasn't wearing any rings. "I'd like the fish, Ms. Cumberland."

"Will grilled red snapper do?" Sybil asked.

Dina nodded. "Yes, thank you."

Sybil extended her hand. "Please come with me."

Dina followed Sybil down a narrow hallway to a set of double doors and into an enormous gleaming stainless-steel industrial kitchen. Pots, pans and cooking utensils hung from overhead racks, while steam from a tall pot on a stove top filled the space with a mouthwatering aroma. A tall black man stood at a large double sink, spraying water from a retractable hose over a colander filled with spinach leaves.

Adina had never been interviewed, so she didn't know what to expect. Were all potential bosses as informal as Sybil Cumberland? Did she treat all applicants the same by offering to feed them? Or was she being tested? She waited while Sybil whispered something to the man; he nodded in agreement.

Sybil returned to Dina. "We'll eat and talk over there." She pointed to an alcove at the opposite end of the kitchen with a round table and four chairs.

"I'm sure you're wondering why I'm interviewing you in the kitchen," Sybil said once they were seated.

Dina gave her a direct look. "Yes, I am. I've never been interviewed in a kitchen. No, let me correct that— I've never been on an interview before."

A flicker of one black eyebrow was the only indication of Sybil's response to the younger woman's disclosure. "I interview all applicants in the kitchen because I want them to see up close and personal what they're going to have to deal with. The kitchen is the heartbeat of every restaurant and catering business. It's hot and it's noisy.

There are chefs screaming at one another, waitstaff and busboys. You'll have to be on your toes at all times. In other words, don't bother to come in if you don't intend to bring your A game. Do I make myself understood?"

Dina nodded. "I understand."

Sybil flashed what could pass for a smile. "It's against the law to ask you your age, but I'm going to do it anyway. How old are you, Dina?"

"I'm twenty-seven."

"You're twenty-seven and you don't have any work experience?"

"Yes, I've worked, but not at a traditional job."

"What I can ask is if you've ever been convicted of a felony?"

A smile stole its way across Dina's face. "No convictions *and* no arrests."

Sybil gave Dina a long, penetrating stare. "I'm going to need you to complete an application for employment. If what you put down is proven to be false, then I can and will let you go without warning."

Some basic instinct for self-preservation seized Dina. There was no way she could fast-talk or con Sybil Cumberland into hiring her. She had to be straight or get up and walk out.

"I need a job, Ms. Cumberland. I also need an apartment, a legal address so I can apply for a social security card and a driver's license. I'm currently living in a motel in Irvington, and although it's not the Waldorf-Astoria, the room rate is eating away my savings. I have no experience working in a restaurant, but I'm a quick learner and I work well with other people. You don't have to worry about me being late, because I'm always on time. I don't smoke or drink, so you—"

"Enough, Dina," Sybil said, cutting off her passionate plea. "I'd go to church if I wanted to hear a sermon." The brown color in the hazel eyes disappeared, leaving them a cold, frosty green. "Is that your hair or are you wearing a piece?" she asked, knowing she'd startled Dina when her eyes widened.

Dina touched the coil of hair she'd secured with pins on the nape of her neck. "It's mine."

Sybil nodded. "Good. When you come to work, I want you to wear it down and in a ponytail. The first time I see you with a matronly bun, you're out. I'm going to hire you to check coats because right now I have nothing else."

Biting down on her lower lip to still its trembling, Dina whispered a silent prayer of thanks. "But it's almost the summer, Ms. Cumberland. Will people still need coat check?"

Sybil's small mouth tightened into a hard line. "Do you or don't you want to work, Dina? Don't forget that you're meeting with me today because I'm doing it as a favor for Karla King."

"Yes," she said quickly. "Yes, I do want to work for you."

The seconds ticked off as the two women regarded each other. Dina was the first to drop her gaze. Sybil's glare softened noticeably. "Now that we've resolved that misunderstanding, I'll give you some background on SJC Catering."

Chapter 26

Sybil sat at the desk in her office, cradling the telephone between her chin and shoulder, waiting for a break in the connection. "This is Karla," said the familiar female voice through the earpiece.

"Where are you, Karla?" She could hardly make out what she was saying because of a clacking background sound.

"I'm on the train. It's just pulling into High Bridge. Give me a minute to get to the parking lot."

Sybil didn't envy Karla, who drove her car to the High Bridge station, parked, then got on the train for a two-and-a-half-hour ride to Trenton. The reason she'd urged Cory to relocate from Plainsboro to West Orange was the commute. At first he'd resisted, but he'd eventually relented.

"Sybil, I'm back. What's up?"

"I hired her."

"Thanks."

"No, Karla, thank *you*."

"Did she tell you that she has no experience?"

Sybil nodded although Karla couldn't see her. "Yes. That's okay because, as a diamond in the rough, I can train her to suit my needs."

"I'm glad you could help her. I hope you and Cory haven't made plans for the Fourth, because Ronald and I are hosting a cookout."

"Count us in."

"Don't forget to bring a swimsuit."

"Should I bring anything?" Sybil asked.

"Please don't. Come and relax."

She chatted with Karla for another few minutes, circling July fourth on her planner, then rang off. Tension knotted her stomach; she pressed a hand to her middle. Reaching into a drawer, she took out a bottle of antacids and placed two under her tongue.

Leaning back in her chair, Sybil closed her eyes, waiting for the antacids to counter the buildup of acid churning in her belly. She'd done it again—she'd skipped breakfast and lunch. And eating more than twenty hours after her last meal always played havoc with her digestive system.

She opened her eyes, picked up a marker and wrote in bold black letters: Do Not Skip Meals! on a Post-it.

The reason she'd met with Dina Gordon was because one of her elite clients had canceled on her earlier that morning. What had left her in a foul mood was that she'd rearranged her schedule to accommodate him. Her annoyance had surfaced during the interview, but Dina had appeared oblivious to it or chosen not to take notice of her mercurial moods. Her gaze shifted to the application bearing Dina's name. She'd filled in Pending on the lines for her address and social security number.

Sybil had hired two of Karla's special clients in the past, and with surprising results. One had become her best waiter and the other was now a first-year culinary student. What Dina didn't know was that she was going to be put to the test—and if she passed, then her reward would be incalculable.

Fifteen minutes later Sybil rang the kitchen to inform her assistant that she was leaving. She would return the following morning to prepare a banquet for a fiftieth wedding anniversary celebration. The couple's initial guest list had gone from fifty-eight to seventy-two, prompting Sybil to move the party from the first- to the second-floor ballroom.

She changed into a pair of well-washed jeans, a tank top and a pair of comfortable running shoes. Locking the door to her private office, Sybil headed out to the parking lot. Slipping behind the wheel of her late-model Toyota Sequoia, she drove out of the lot, taking a local road. It was a longer route, but there was no reason to rush home. Cory was working late, and she would probably be in bed by the time he returned home.

Sybil pressed a button on the device attached to her truck's visor. Her heart stopped, then started up again in a runaway pounding when she saw her husband's car parked in its usual spot in the two-car garage. What was he doing home so early? The most horrific thoughts swirled around in her head as she got out of the vehicle and raced into the house. A soft beeping sound reminded her that she'd forgotten to lower the garage door. Her fingers touched a pad and the door lowered automatically.

Setting her handbag down on a table in the dramatic two-story foyer, she headed for the family room. There were two places where she was certain to find Cory whenever he came home: the family room or the bedroom.

The reason Sybil had fallen in love with the nearly

completed house in the exclusive gated community was the two-story foyer and family room. The thirty-four-hundred-square-foot-high ranch had four bedrooms, three and a half baths, a two-car garage, a kitchen island with a nook, a formal dining room and a master suite with corner soaking tub and Jack-and-Jill bath suite.

The house, like her business, had become a great source of joy for Sybil. Her childhood yearnings to be perfect in bed, in the kitchen and in her career were manifested the day she and Cory closed on the West Orange property.

She found her husband sprawled across a sunny-yellow leather chaise, asleep, while images flickered on the large flat-screen mounted on the opposite wall. He wore a white T-shirt and a pair of threadbare jeans that she should've discarded years ago yet hadn't because Cory claimed they were his favorite pair. Her gaze lingered on his slender, athletic body. Light from a floor lamp bathed his composed face in a soft, flattering glow.

Leaning over, she touched his shoulder. His skin was cool under the cotton fabric. He came awake immediately, staring at her with a startled expression freezing his features until he recognized her face. "What are you doing here?"

Sybil leaned closer and kissed his forehead. "I live here."

Reaching up, Cory pulled his wife down to sit on his lap. "You know what I mean. I thought you were working late tonight."

Wrapping her arms around his neck, Sybil rested her head on Cory's shoulder. He smelled of soap and clean laundry. "My client canceled at the last minute."

What she couldn't tell him was that the aborted liaison

was only supposed to consist of a party of two: she and the client. Whenever she donned a black latex bodysuit and concealed her face behind a black mask to wield a whip better than Halle Berry's Catwoman, she was no longer Sybil, but Delectable the dominatrix.

"I remember you telling me that you were also working late tonight, darling."

Cory closed his eyes and drew in a deep breath, then let it out slowly. "I can't test the new aeronautical software until the programmers work out a few bugs." The company where he worked as a quality-assurance manager had been awarded a military government contract to write an aeronautical software program for a sophisticated spy drone.

"What do you do now?" Sybil asked.

"Sit around doing nothing or take some of my vacation days before I lose them."

He glanced down to find Sybil staring up at him. "Can I interest you to take a few days off and hang out with me?"

Sybil wrinkled her nose. "Cory, you know this is my busiest season."

His lids came down over his soulful-looking eyes. "When is it *not* your busy season, Sybil? Christmas, New Year's, Valentine's Day and let's not forget Memorial Day through Christmas again. I'm the only married guy at work who doesn't take a vacation with his wife."

"That's because they all have children."

"Ah, children," he drawled facetiously, "those wonderful little creatures that make a house a home." After four years of marriage he was more than ready to become a father.

"I thought we agreed to wait until we celebrated our fifth anniversary," Sybil said in a soft, but lethal tone.

Dipping his head, Cory pressed his lips to hers as he caressed her mouth. "Can't we pretend it's December?"

Sybil returned his kiss as her hand moved over his chest and down his flat belly. Her fingers searched between his thighs, finding him fully aroused. "No," she whispered in his ear, "but nothing says we can't practice baby-making." She moved off his lap, and she wasn't disappointed when he rose with her. Reaching for a remote device, Sybil turned off the television. Smiling at her husband, she said, "Can you wait for me to take a shower?"

"Show me what I'm going to get and I'll let you know."

In one smooth motion, Sybil lifted the tank top with a built-in bra, displaying a pair of full breasts that never failed to arouse her husband. Closing the distance between them, she placed a hand on Cory's chest and forcibly pushed him down to the chaise. She didn't give him time to react when she ripped open the fly to his jeans and eased his penis through the opening in his boxers. Less than a minute later she eased herself over his erection, her own jeans and bikini panties down around her knees.

She became Delectable sans latex, mask and whip. Bracing her hands on either side of Cory' head, she bounced up and down on the hardened flesh as she pushed her breasts to his face. Gurgling sounds came from his throat, he struggling to breathe. Sybil alternated, changing the cadence from deep, violent thrusts to a quickening that gave her a sense of power and complete domination. It all came to an end when she reached under her hips and captured his testicles. She applied the slightest pressure, eliciting the reaction she sought when

Cory groaned in pain. Her fingers tightened, and when his eyes rolled back in his head, she climaxed, whispering his name over and over as he released his passion inside her.

Cory closed his eyes, unable to believe the exquisite ecstasy Sybil had offered him. Just when he thought he knew everything about her, she surprised him with something new.

They didn't make love as much as he wanted, but he had to admit that their coming together was always passionate and satisfying.

Chapter 27

Dina climbed into the back of the Town Car, cell phone in hand, and barely glanced at the driver who held the door for her. She sat down and scrolled through the directory of the phone Lance had given her. The driver hadn't maneuvered out of the parking lot to the two-story building, with handmade brick end walls evocative of the early Dutch, where Sybil Cumberland had established her catering enterprise, when she pushed the Send button.

Sinking against the black leather seat, she smiled when hearing Lance's greeting. "I got it," she said softly. She heard other voices—male and female—then Lance excusing himself to take a "very important" call.

"You got it?" he asked after a noticeable pause.

"Yes, and I'm sorry if I interrupted your dinner meeting. I was just so excited I had to tell you."

"Don't you dare apologize. Why do you think I gave you the phone? You can call me anytime."

"Okay."

"I suppose this means we're going to have to celebrate," Lance crooned.

Dina felt a swell of joy fill her chest, making it difficult to draw a normal breath. "Yes, it does."

"When am I going to see you again?"

"I'll call and let you know. Tomorrow I'm going apartment hunting."

"If you need help or a reference, then let me know."

"I will. LL?"

There came a beat of silence. "What is it?"

"Thank you, thank you, thank you."

His chuckle caressed her ear. "You're welcome. Dina, baby, I have to get back to my clients. I'll talk to you later."

He ended the call, *Dina, baby* playing over and over in her head during the ride to Irvington. Had Lance called her baby because of the twenty-plus-years difference in their ages or was it because he viewed her as "his baby"? She prayed it was the latter because there was something about Lancelot Haynes she liked enough to want to see him again.

When the traffic signs pointing the way to Irvington came into view, she asked the driver to stop at a convenience store, where she purchased several newspapers. It wasn't until she opened the door to her motel room that she noticed the shabbiness for the first time.

She stared at the fading wallpaper, the threadbare rug and a spiderweb in a corner near the window. *This will be the last week I'll sleep here.* The silent vow was one she intended to keep.

Dina sat in the middle of the bed, reading every entry in the classified real-estate section in several dailies and a weekly. She'd circled one advertising a furnished one-bedroom apartment in a private house owned by a Christian couple. It was within her price range. Reaching for Lance's cell phone, she dialed the number.

It was the voice as much as the greeting that rendered

her temporarily mute. "Praise the Lord," she repeated. "I'm calling to ask if the apartment is still available."

"It is," said the man with a deep baritone voice. "The ad said no children and no pets."

"I'm the only one who'll live in the apartment. Is it possible to set up an appointment to see it?"

"I have someone coming in the mornin'—"

"What time tomorrow morning?" she asked quickly.

"I believe it's ten. Why?"

"Can I come at nine?"

"Ain't you got a job?"

Dina smiled. "I have a job, but I don't go to work until early evening."

"Okay, I guess it won't do no harm. Come at nine."

She gave the man her name, then wrote down his address. "Thank you, sir. All things are possible through Christ," she added.

"Amen, Ms. Gordon. Have a blessed evening."

"Thank you, Mr. Foster."

Falling back to the mattress, she stared up at the shadows on the ceiling. If anyone would've predicted the turn her life would take, she would've called them a liar. She was realistic enough to know she couldn't have spent all of her life hustling, but she never would've imagined having to leave Brooklyn and changing her name and holding down a *real* job all because of a proposed or real death threat.

After the dinner of stuffed grilled red snapper, a mixed green salad and garlic baby spinach prepared by the Buddha-like assistant chef, Sybil had given her an overview of the catering business. More than half of SJC Catering's reservations were corporate affairs and small private parties hosted by those on her elite client list, and the other half were the general public for wedding receptions, birthdays and anniversaries.

Sybil revealed that she took a hands-on approach when it came to training, establishing a strict protocol as to how she wanted her staff to relate to her clientele; this revelation told Dina that Sybil Cumberland not only micromanaged her business but was also a control freak.

How the uptight chef ran her business was not Dina's concern. Earning enough money to pay Payne Jefferson what he claimed she owed him had shifted to the top of her priority list.

Chapter 28

The taxi stopped in front of a row house in a working-class Irvington neighborhood. There were several young children sitting on the porch steps of a neighboring house, arguing over a handheld computer game, but other than that the block was quiet.

Dina paid the fare and stepped out of the cab. She noticed the curtain in one of the front rooms moved before settling into place. Pulling back her shoulders, she mounted the four steps leading to the porch and rang the doorbell. The door opened, and she came face-to-face with a woman who reminded her of her grandmother.

"Good morning, ma'am. I'm Dina Gordon."

The woman beckoned her inside. "Come, child, and rest yourself."

Forty minutes after meeting with Mr. and Mrs. Gideon Foster, Dina hailed a taxi to take her back to the motel. The Fosters had given her a one-year lease and a set of keys to her new apartment. They'd expected her to bring letters of reference, but after Mr. Foster spoke to Lance, he informed her that if she wanted the apartment, then it was hers.

The rooms were a far cry from those she saw on *MTV Cribs,* but they were hers. The freshly painted space was immaculate with small, cozy rooms and large, bulky, functionable furniture.

She liked that she had her own private entrance and washer/dryer privileges, and the monthly rent of nine hundred dollars was less than her forty-nine-dollar-a-night motel rate. A dreamy smile crossed her face when she thought of what she had to do to turn her first apartment into a home. She had to buy linens, towels and pots and pans. It would be another week before she began working at SJC Catering, which gave her time to adjust to her new crib.

Cradling the phone between her chin and shoulder, Dina listened as Karla read back the Irvington address she'd given her at the same time she checked dresser drawers to make certain she hadn't forgotten anything.

"I keep pinching myself to make certain I'm not dreaming."

"You're not dreaming, Dina. You're now experiencing what you should've had years ago."

"But I couldn't have done it without you, Karla."

"You would've done it without me, because always remember that you're a descendant of survivors. Your ancestors went through hell for you to be here today."

Dina halted zipping the carry-on. "I never thought of myself in that way. Thank you for making me aware of it."

"If you're not doing anything on the Fourth, I'd like to invite you to my place for a cookout."

A shock flew through her. "You...you want me to come to your house?"

"Yes, I do. You have a new job, a new apartment and now it's time you make some new friends. Take down my address and cell number." Dina moved over to the bedside table and wrote down Karla King's Oldwick address. "If you need transportation, then let me know."

Dina thought of Lance. She wouldn't have to impose on Karla if he drove her. "May I bring a friend with me?"

"Of course," Karla confirmed.

"He has a car."

Karla laughed softly. "I understand, Dina. Good luck with everything. I'll see you and your *friend* on the Fourth."

"Okay, Karla."

She ended the call, picked up her bag, took one final glance around the motel room and walked out. She had to check out before Lance arrived. He'd promised to drive her to a nearby mall to shop before they celebrated her new job *and* apartment.

Chapter 29

Judge Rhys Weichert watched Karla King walk down the hallway, his gaze widening appreciably. Like fine wine, he found that Karla improved with age. She'd been a bright-eyed, barely legal twenty-going-on-twenty-one-year-old when he first saw her race into his classroom at NYU Law School, out of breath and her hair falling over her forehead in sensual disarray. She'd been one of his brightest students, and before she completed her first year they'd become lovers, meeting discreetly once or twice a week. It hadn't mattered that she was his student or that he was married. He'd fallen in love with the aspiring attorney, and after twenty years he was still in love with her.

He smiled. She was casually dressed in a pair of black cropped pants and a sleeveless white blouse. Her groomed feet were pushed into a pair of black patent leather wedge-heel sandals that put her close to the six-foot mark.

Karla's freshly coiffed hair moved sensuously around her head with each step that took her closer to the man who'd been teacher, mentor, lover and now confidant. She'd told Rhys things she'd never told Ronald. It's not that she didn't trust her husband, but she knew it would probably put a crack in the foundation of their perfect marriage.

A smile tipped the corners of her generous mouth when she saw the minute lines around the still-bright blue eyes deepen when Rhys smiled. He extended a heavily blue-veined hand, pulling her gently into the hotel room and kissing her cheeks.

"You look wonderful, Rhys," Karla said softly. She hadn't lied. He'd gained some of the weight he'd lost when she last saw him.

The state supreme court judge who'd recently celebrated his seventieth birthday had made it known that he was leaving the bench at the end of the year, declaring it was time he kick back, go deep-sea fishing and become reacquainted with his many grandchildren, most of whom lived on the West Coast. What he hadn't disclosed to anyone, with the exception of his wife and Karla, was that he'd been diagnosed with inoperable pancreatic cancer.

Resting a hand on the small of Karla's back, Rhys shook his head. "You've always been the most beautiful liar I've ever had the delight in knowing. Have you eaten?" he asked, smoothly segueing to another topic. He'd told Karla he was dying, then exacted a promise from her that they would never discuss his illness again. "I've taken the liberty of ordering a light repast."

Karla permitted Rhys to seat her; she stared intently as he rounded the table to sit opposite her. The ruddy color that was always apparent in the lean face of the tall man with the deep voice and shock of white hair had returned. His hair wasn't as thick and bushy as it'd been before he'd begun chemotherapy. However, he was luckier than most patients because it hadn't fallen out completely. He was impeccably dressed, as usual, in a crisp white shirt, open at the throat, and a pair of midnight-blue tailored slacks. The subtle scent of his specially blended cologne wafted in her nose.

She wasn't certain why she'd been drawn to the man, because he wasn't what she thought of as her ideal. And if she were completely truthful then she would have to admit that she was only attracted to men in her own race. Rhys Weichert had become the exception because of his elegance, wealth and brilliant legal mind.

Karla had supplemented her partial undergraduate and law school scholarships waiting tables and swinging around a pole at men's clubs until Professor Weichert asked her to have dinner with him. The one encounter changed her life completely when she became his mistress; he gave her the money she needed to complete her education. What he hadn't known was, although she'd stopped waiting tables, she'd continued dancing because the craving for male attention was so great that it'd become an addiction. Instead of dancing at a club, she'd performed in hotel suites for discriminating men with fat wallets and even more discriminating tastes. Her private performances came to an abrupt end the day Ronald placed an engagement ring on her finger.

"I like the room," she said softly, her gaze sweeping around the opulent hotel suite.

Rhys nodded. "I'm practically living here." Reaching for a bottle of chilled champagne, he filled a flute, handing it to Karla while ignoring the expression of shock freezing her features. "Erika and I aren't getting along too well nowadays."

Karla grasped the delicate stem of the flute. "What's wrong, Rhys?"

"She's in denial, Karla. She can't accept the reality that I'm dying and that she's going to be left alone."

"But we're all mortal," she argued softly.

A sad smile parted the judge's pale lips. "My dear wife has lived a life of privilege that's insulated her from the ugliness of the world as you and I know it. I met her when I was nineteen and she fifteen. Three years later she'd become my wife. I was the first and only man she's ever known. Although—"

"Why are you telling me this?" Karla asked, interrupting him. She'd met Erika at social events, and Ronald was aware that she'd once been Rhys's mistress, but intimate details of their respective marriages were never discussed.

Rhys's hand shook slightly when he filled his flute. "I need to talk to someone, Karla. My wife has shut me out completely."

"I'm sorry," she said. "Please continue."

A frown creased the lined forehead as he returned the bottle to the crystal bowl filled with ice, the brilliant jurist appearing deep in thought. His expression brightened when he raised his glass. "I'd like for you to make the toast tonight."

"Are you sure, Judge Weichert?"

"Very sure, counselor," he teased, winking at her.

The smile that softened Karla's generous mouth did not reach her eyes. They were sad, filled with pain and the impending loss of her best friend. "I toast to us."

His bushy white eyebrows lifted. "That's it?"

She nodded. "That's it, Rhys." She touched her glass to his, then took a sip of the bubbly wine. "It's excellent."

It was Rhys's turn to nod. "Thank you. I wonder what our lives would've been like if we'd married each other."

Waves of shock slapped at Karla when she mentally replayed his statement. Even though she'd slept with the man, she never would've considered marrying him. "Why would you even say something like that? You've had a wonderful life with Erika, and my life with Ronald is better than I could've ever expected it to be."

Rhys drained his glass, then reached for the bottle to refill it. "That's because you and Ronald have an incredible sex life." He held up his free hand when Karla's jaw dropped. "You didn't have to tell me, Karla. I knew he was satisfying you when you stopped sleeping with me. I kept telling myself that you wanted to be a faithful wife because I didn't want to admit that I'd lost you to a better man."

I'm not a faithful wife because I still sleep with other men. The difference is my husband knows about them, Karla mused as she stared at the man with the crestfallen expression. What she wanted to tell Rhys was that he'd lost his appeal even before she'd met Ronald, that it had started to take him longer and longer to climax and that she'd been left more sexually frustrated than before their encounter.

"It's not that at all," she said in a quiet voice, hoping to soothe his wounded ego. "I'm not going to deny that I love Ronald. But what I want is to live a simple life without the complications or encumbrances that come with having an affair." Reaching across the table, she placed her hand over Rhys's. "I can't believe that after all these years that you'd question my feelings for you. It wasn't just about the sex, Rhys."

He reversed their hands, his fingers tightening gently. "Then what was it about, my sweet, sweet child?"

Karla felt a rush of tears prick the backs of her eyelids. She attempted to extricate her hand from his grip but couldn't when Rhys tightened it. "Please don't call me that."

"But you are my sweet child."

Sucking in a lungful of air, she willed the tears not to fall. She'd lost count of the number of times she'd sobbed herself to sleep in Rhys's comforting embrace—when an instructor didn't give her the grade she felt she deserved; when her father, who'd divorced her mother to take up with another woman, called to ask her to represent him when charged with kidnapping and raping his stepdaughter; and when her mother died suddenly a day before she was scheduled to take the bar exam. She'd come to Rhys because she had no one else. He'd offered her solace and she, in turn, offered him her body.

"I gave you what you needed and you gave me what I needed."

He nodded. "You're right, Karla. You gave me what Erika couldn't or wouldn't unless she wanted another child. The only time we ever shared a bed was when our parents stayed over. In public she presents as the perfect wife and hostess, but behind close doors she's cold and unfeeling. She'd told me enough times to go out and get a mistress until I finally did. I lost count of the names and faces of women that I slept with during my marriage until I met you. Once we slept together, I never looked at another woman. You'd become my wife in every way possible. I don't know why I didn't leave Erika and marry you."

"You didn't do it because you knew eventually I'd leave you for another man."

Rhys released her hand and removed the cover to a serving tray. "You're right, Karla. Spouses who cheat are usually doomed to cheat again. I suppose that's the reason I didn't leave Erika."

Karla stared at the scrumptious cold seafood feast of lobster, shrimp, clams on the half shell, oysters and mussels with a variety of dipping sauces. She could always count on Rhys to order what she liked.

She smiled at him. "Erika loves you, Rhys. If she didn't, then she wouldn't be so fearful of losing you." His blue eyes grew hard, reminding her of particles of chipped ice.

"Please don't try to bullshit a bullshitter, Karla. Erika married me because our fathers decided to merge not only their businesses but also their families. The merger of Simons and Weichert Pharmaceuticals made them one of the country's largest drug companies. She could never love me because she was in love with another boy, and she's spent the past fifty years reminding me of that by keeping me out of her bed. At first I thought she was frigid, but when I discovered her treasure trove of vibrators and other sex toys, I knew differently."

Karla felt pity, compassion and another emotion she was unable to identify with his passionate disclosure. Pushing back her chair, she came around the table and wrapped her arms around his neck. "Do you want me to sleep with you, Rhys?"

Tilting his chin, he smiled up at her. "You know I can't get it up anymore."

Resting her cheek on the top of his head, Karla kissed the wiry strands. "Even if you could I still wouldn't have sex with you."

Rhys reached up and touched the thick hair falling over his face. He'd always loved touching Karla's hair. He loved everything about her: her hair, her skin and her smell. There was something about her smell that was uniquely hers. After they'd made love, he'd loathed getting up to shower because he wanted her essence to linger long after she left.

"Yes, Karla. I'd *love* for you to sleep with me."

She released him and reached into her handbag to retrieve her cell phone. "I'm staying over," she said to Ronald when he answered her call.

"Don't forget to invite Rhys and Erika over on the Fourth."

"I won't," she told him. "I'll see you tomorrow, darling."

"I love you."

She closed her eyes, smiling. "I love you, too." Turning, she looked at Rhys. "Ronald and I are hosting a Fourth of July get-together. He'd like for you to come with Erika."

A look of determination shimmered in the steely blue eyes. "We'll be there." Rhys never wanted to miss an opportunity to see Karla again. They talked on the phone, but that wasn't enough. Seeing her, making love to her, always counteracted his guilt whenever he cheated on his wife.

Chapter 30

When Dina leaned over the left shoulder of a man to remove his plate before dessert was served, she felt him slip something in her pants pocket. "It's just a little something for you, sweetie," he whispered in a trembling voice.

She smiled at the elderly man with a network of lines crisscrossing his deeply tanned, weather-beaten face. "Thank you."

She'd been "sweetie," "darling," "baby" and "luscious" to the accountants sitting in the smaller of the two first-floor dining rooms for their quarterly dinner gathering. They'd barely touched their food, preferring instead to drink dinner. Her perception of the stereotypical accountant was shattered completely when the group of twenty men and six women shed their conservative vests and jackets, heading straight for the bar and ordering cocktails, some she'd never heard of—green demon, chi chi and ritz fizz—and the ubiquitous martini and gin and tonic. Dina would be anything they wanted her to be as long as they tipped her for bringing them drinks, refilling their water goblets or just smiling.

Sybil had changed her mind about training her for coat check when she said she would be better utilized waiting tables. It took more than two hours of intense instruction for her to learn to serve, pick up, pour water and hoist a tray without spilling its contents. She garnered a rare compliment from Sybil when she simulated taking meat, fish or chicken choices from a table of ten, remembering who would get which plate.

It was now her second week of work; although waiting tables paid ten dollars more per hour, and with tips, Dina knew she wouldn't be able save enough over the next three months to repay Payne. And there was one thing she knew about her former boss, and that was he didn't issue idle threats. Irrespective of gender, the depraved little cretin took pleasure inflicting the most intense pain on his victims.

She budgeted carefully when she calculated how much money she had to put aside each week for her rent and car fare. What she got in tips was added to the backpack, and she continued the practice of mailing postal money orders to Dora Jenkins.

Dina hadn't spoken to her grandmother since Dora had called her about Payne busting up her apartment. As long as she sent the money orders, then her grandmother knew she was still alive.

A smothered cry of surprise escaped her when she felt a hand on her behind. Turning around, Dina glared at a man who definitely had had too much to drink. Shock quickly gave way to fury when she leaned and positioned her mouth close to his ear.

"If you touch me again, I'll cut your balls off and stuff them down your motherfuckin' throat," she whispered, all the while smiling demurely.

He stared numbly at her, the pale coming up underneath his tan. His Adam's apple bobbed up and down his throat. "I'm sorry, miss."

"I'm not," Dina countered. "May I bring you some coffee?" she said loud enough for the others at the table to overhear.

An expression of surprised relief flooded across his face. "Yes, please."

Straightening, she walked across the room to the kitchen.

"Your new waitress is causing quite a stir."

Sybil glanced up from sifting powdered cocoa on ramekins filled with tiramisu. "What are you talking about?" she asked her assistant as he walked into the kitchen.

"Dina Gordon. I'm willing to bet those pencil pushers are jerkin' off under the table while fantasizing about stickin' it to her."

"Oh, really," she crooned, knowing exactly what Jake Collins was talking about.

"Yeah," Jake drawled, giving his boss a sidelong glance. "Isn't that why you hired her?"

Sybil resumed dusting the individual desserts. "I hired her for coat check."

"Yeah, and I've been mistaken for Prince's twin brother a time or two." Standing six-five and weighing in at two-sixty, ex-footballer Jacob "Black Buddha" Collins was physically the complete opposite of the renowned musician.

Sybil placed the ramekins on another tray, hiding a smile. Removing her apron, she placed it on the back of a stool. "I'm going out to check the floor." She pushed open the swinging door and made her way into the smaller of the two first-floor dining rooms to find Dina heading in her direction.

A black silk obi sash and bow tie set off the whiteness of a pleated-front, wing-collar tuxedo shirt. The curling ends of her ponytail blended into the black of the silk fabric around her tiny waist.

Dina slowed her pace when she saw Sybil watching her, wondering what was going on behind her closed expression. Had she lingered too long at the tables? Was she supposed to ignore questions put to her or refer them to the head waiter?

"Nice work, Dina," Sybil said when she saw countless pairs of eyes trained on her newest employee. Jake was right, and she hoped a few wouldn't go into cardiac arrest before leaving her establishment.

Dina flashed a shy smile. "Thank you."

"You can bring out dessert now."

Wrong, Sybil, Dina mused. *A dessert named Dina Gordon, not tiramisu, has been available for the past two hours.* She'd lost count of the number of times the men beckoned to her. Even those sitting at another table manned by another waiter sought her attention.

"There are a few who need to sober up before they leave here," she said to Sybil.

Sybil nodded. "I don't know what it is, but it's the conservative ones who always go buck-wild."

"I have something to tell you."

Dina had decided to tell Sybil about the pervert before she heard his version. When he'd touched her, it had brought back memories of the man who'd robbed her of her innocence. He'd come to the apartment whenever she was alone and touched her behind. It'd been his cue for her to undress and get into bed. It wasn't until years later, whenever she slept with other men, unable to feel desire or passion, that she realized she'd been scarred for life. She'd listened to other women talk about orgasms and a man hitting their G-spot, but for all she'd understood, they could've been speaking a foreign language.

"What is it, Dina?"

"I told one of the men that I was going to cut off his balls because he groped my ass."

There was a moment of silence, then Sybil spoke again. "Good for you. I hope you told him that you'd make him eat them."

A warm surge of relief swept over Dina. She knew she'd reacted on impulse, but she didn't want to lose her job. "I did."

"Good for you," Sybil repeated. "Now please serve dessert."

Chapter 31

"Yo, Dina, your taxi's here."

Dina waved to the college student who doubled as busboy and dishwasher. "Thanks, Kevin."

Kevin Donahue worked not because he needed money for tuition or books but to make payments on his car. The twenty-year-old had one up on her—he had a car, and she had to rely on buses and taxis for her transportation. Tonight was one of those nights, because she'd worked a double shift. If she missed a bus, then she'd have to wait an hour for another.

Dina hated that she had to watch every penny when that hadn't been the case in the past. All of her "dates" had paid for everything she wanted or needed. It'd boosted their street cred whenever they'd ordered magnums of the best champagne, entertained in the most lavish hotel suites and handed out twenty- and fifty-dollar tips to barmaids, valets and bellhops. The attitude of the street hustler was that because he'd worked hard to achieve a modicum of recognition and wealth, he believed his good luck would go on forever. She'd recognized early on that *forever* meant either death or prison—something that she definitely hadn't wanted.

Now that she was out of the hustling game, Dina realized overhearing the two women in the club talking about her had saved her life in more ways than one. Either someone would've walked up to her and shot or stabbed her or she could've been arrested and charged as an accomplice to racketeering or drug trafficking.

She'd heard and read about women who let gangsters set them up in apartments only to lose everything whenever the feds invoked the RICO statute. She'd accepted clothes and shoes as gifts but never jewelry, because she didn't know whether the pieces were "hot." Even though she knew the man who owned the local pawnshop and he looked the other way whenever someone came in to hock a piece of jewelry, she wasn't willing to take the risk and have the item traced back to her.

Dina knew the reason she'd lasted so long in the hustling game was because she hadn't moved out of the projects while managing to keep a low-profile status. Many of those who lived or hung out around the projects sported designer labels—whether authentic or bootleg—so she blended in with everyone else.

She walked out of the catering hall to see the taillights of her taxi fading into the night. Temperatures had dropped dramatically after a steadily falling all-day rain tapered off to a light drizzle. "Shit!" Now she would have to go back inside to call again.

"Shame on you, baby girl," crooned a familiar voice. "I didn't know you used four-letter words."

Dina spun around to find Lance smiling at her. He looked different in a pair of jeans, running shoes and a sweatshirt with a fading college logo. Her pulse quickening, she closed the distance between them and wrapped her arms around his waist. Going on to her toes, she brushed a light kiss over his mouth.

"Baby girl may not smoke or drink, but she does cuss on occasion. What are you doing here?"

Lance pulled her closer, enjoying the press of the feminine curves against his body. Everything about Dina Gordon was imprinted on his brain: her feminine scent, the long, dark hair with reddish highlights, the differing shades of brown and green in her large eyes, her perfectly proportioned petite body and the smoky timbre of her dulcet voice. Although they talked to each other by phone every day, it wasn't enough for him. He wanted to *see* her every day.

Lancelot Londell Hanes had waited forty-nine years to find himself totally enthralled with a woman who'd bewitched him with her independence and innocence. However, it was her innocence that had him off balance.

Never married, he was always straightforward in his relationships with other women, having been in love only once. He was conventional and in complete control of his sexual nature, but perhaps it'd been his grandmother's constant warnings about sneaky, shifty women that made him overly cautious and somewhat distrustful of the opposite sex.

However, the one woman with whom he'd fallen in love sent him a Dear John letter after a two-year liaison, claming he was too possessive. He was devastated because he'd been willing to give up an important position with a prestigious computer firm to relocate to Los Angeles to be with her. Again it was his grandmother who'd asked how possessive could he have been with three thousand miles between them? He'd been twenty-five, and that was the first and last time he'd come close to falling in love.

"I'm your car service tonight," Lance explained.

Easing back in his loose embrace, Dina stared up at his smiling face. "You sent my driver away?"

"Don't worry, Dina. I paid the man for your fare."

"But it's close to midnight, and by the time you drop me off in Irvington and make it back to West New York it'll be almost one. You're not going to get much sleep if you have to be in your office at eight."

Lance kissed her forehead. "Stop fretting, Dina," he said in a quiet voice. "I'm taking the rest of the week off to help a certain young lady get her driver's license."

"You're kidding?"

He shook his head. "No, I'm not. You told me you don't have to come back here until Saturday afternoon, so that means we have the next forty-eight hours to hone your driving skills. Once you get your license, I'll see about getting you a car."

Pulling out of his embrace, Dina shook her head. "No, Lance. I can't let you do that."

"Why not, Dina?"

"I can't repay you. Not now."

Reaching for her hand, he led her around the building to the parking lot. "Did I say anything about money?"

"No."

"Then stop talking about it." There was a thread of hardness in the command that dared her to challenge him.

Always the one who had to have the last word, Dina rounded on him. "I'm not going to stop. I'm not going to owe you, Lance. I can't."

Lance wanted to shake Dina until she was breathless but decided on another method. Lowering his head, he covered her mouth with his. She went stiff in his arms, then without warning became pliant, her body melting against his. "Yes, you can, Dina," he whispered, his lips brushing against hers. "You promised to let me protect and take care of you. Letting you drive one of my cars so that you don't have to wait for a bus or spend probably as much money as you earn in an hour on taxis *is* taking care of you."

Dina knew Lance was right. The nights she worked a double, the fare for the cab rides took a large bite out of her salary. And she knew she never would've gotten her apartment without his reference.

"Okay, LL. But as soon as I save some money I'm going to buy my own car."

Raising his mouth from hers, Lance gazed into her eyes. "You just don't know when to stop, do you?"

Her eyebrows lifted. "What's wrong now?"

"You don't know how to say thank you and leave it at that." He smiled. "Now, repeat after me—thank you, LL."

Something in Lance's condescending manner annoyed Dina, but it wasn't enough to turn her off him. She knew he liked her, which aroused her curiosity and her vanity. When he'd kissed her, she was repulsed, then came a tingling in the pit of her stomach and she didn't want to be anywhere else but in his arms, his mouth on hers. His kiss hadn't been threatening but warm, caressing. It wasn't as if he were vying for dominance but reconciliation.

His touch, his kiss, were so different from the men with whom she'd been involved. Their idea of passion was to take a woman and ram their penises inside her while banging her head against the headboard. It was as if they had to let her know who was large and in charge. She'd lost count of the number of times she'd been called "bitch" in the throes of so-called passion. It didn't matter to them if she was satisfied, if they'd hurt her because they hadn't taken the time to arouse her to where she was wet enough to be penetrated. All that mattered to them was getting head and bustin' a nut.

The man holding her to his heart was different. He was kind, generous and, above all, considerate. A slow smile spread over her face as she met his gaze. "Thank you, Big Daddy." Her sultry voice had dropped an octave.

Throwing back his head, Lance laughed, the sound floating up and lingering in the damp night air. Shaking his head, he pulled her closer. "What am I going to do with you, baby girl?"

Dina buried her face against his shoulder. He felt good and smelled even better. "Protect and take care of me, Big Daddy."

"And I will," he said. "I'm going to take you back to your place, where you can pick up enough clothes for the next few days. We can sleep in late, and after you get up, I'm going to take you to an industrial area where you can practice turns and parallel parking."

"Don't I have to take a written test?"

Lance nodded. "We'll go to the DMV and pick up the book tomorrow. Before you apply for your permit you're going to need certain documents, like your birth certificate, utility bill or original lease verifying your address. They may also require pay stubs, your social security card and a bank statement."

"I'll have everything by the time I'm ready to take the written test." And she would. As Dina Gordon, she'd applied for her social security card, and once she received it she planned to open a bank account. Then she wouldn't have to give a check-cashing business a hefty fee to cash her paycheck.

Moving closer to Lance, she leaned into his strength. "Let's go home, Big Daddy."

Chapter 32

Sybil kicked off her clogs, rested her sock-covered feet on a corner of her desk and took a deep drag from the freshly lighted cigarette. Holding the filtered tip between her fingers, she threw back her head and blew out a perfect smoke ring, watching with narrowed eyes as the blue-gray circle lost its shape and faded into nothingness. The ash grew longer as she fixed her gaze on one of the recessed lights in her office.

It was two in the morning, her favorite time of the day. Everyone was gone, the catering hall silent. It was also her private downtime when she was able to indulge in her only vice—well, one of her vices—without Cory giving her what she thought of as his hypocritical glare. She'd always been an occasional smoker, stopping and starting at will, but once she became involved with Cory she didn't smoke around him. The pack of cigarettes in her desk drawer had been there so long they were practically stale, and it was only when she was scheduled to meet with a private client that she smoked a single cigarette beforehand.

Sybil smiled, her thin top lip disappearing against the ridge of her teeth. The only thing she loved more than performing in her role as Delectable was concealing her alter ego from her husband. Not only would Cory Cumberland have a shit hemorrhage but probably a stroke if he discovered her clandestine alternative dominatrix lifestyle. However, he never complained when she assumed the dominant role and position whenever they made love. In fact, he'd encouraged her to get on top and "ride his johnson until he screamed like a bitch." It didn't take much to make Cory scream. What her dear, very conservative husband refused to accept was that he didn't enjoy sex until she assumed control.

Her gaze shifted to the clock on her desk. It would be another hour before she would meet with her client, and that would give her enough time to shower and prepare for an hour of unbelievable pleasure and pain—for her and for the sixty-something bank president.

Sybil maneuvered her low-slung, black-on-black Audi TT along the private road to the iron gates protecting the sprawling property from intruders. Batman had the Batmobile, and Delectable had the TT. She always garaged the sports car in the three-car garage behind SJC Catering, taking it out only when she trolled the night as Delectable.

Coming to a complete stop, she plucked a mask off the console. She placed it over her face, securing it with black silk ties at the back of her head. Shifting into gear, she continued up the road to the gate. Her finger touched a button, and the driver's-side window lowered as Sybil turned to face a camera mounted on a pole above a glowing red sensor.

"Delectable," she said, the microphone picking up her voice.

The red light disappeared, replaced by a green one at

the same time the massive iron gates opened with a soft buzzing. Sybil drove through, and as soon as her tires passed over a metal plate the gates closed behind her. Adrenaline shot through her as she increased her speed, coming to a stop behind a large stone cottage a mile from the castlelike main house. The house had *been* a castle in Ireland before the original owner had it dismantled and shipped the stones to America at the beginning of the prior century.

Sybil had no interest in the history of the house or its owners, but she'd been forced to listen the one time she'd met with the elegant bank president when he'd come to arrange a surprise sixtieth birthday party for his wife, who knew nothing of her husband's sexual predilection. Wives and same-sex partners were not important to Delectable. She only did what she was paid to do. And she didn't don the latex cat suit and mask because she needed the money. She did it because it was the only time she was in complete control— of herself and her surroundings.

She parked alongside the back of the cottage, put on a pair of supple black kidskin gloves and reached for a matching leather satchel on the seat beside her. Minutes later she walked into a large space illuminated by dozens of flickering candles in varying shapes and sizes. There were even a few phallic-shaped ones. There on a large bed in the middle of the room lay a pale, naked man facedown, arms and legs outstretched in supplication.

Sybil placed her satchel on a table, taking out lengths of black silk and an evil-looking black whip. Reaching deeper into the bag, she took out a box with a supply of clear rubber rings and a riding crop. And because he was lying on his belly, she wouldn't need the whip. Opening the box, she placed the rings on the mattress at the foot of the bed.

"I've been waiting for you, Mommy," said the man on the bed.

Raising her right hand, her fingers tightening around the handle of the crop, she brought it down against the top of her thigh-high black stiletto boots. The crack of leather on leather sliced the silence like a crack of lightning.

"Shut the fuck up!" Sybil ground out between her teeth. "Did I give you permission to talk to me?" The figure on the bed was silent. "Yes or no, Paulie!" she shouted.

"No," he answered, his reply muffled in the pillow under his head.

"No what?" she countered.

"No, Mommy."

Sybil smiled as she approached the bed. Using the tip of the crop, she drew it down the length of his spine. She reached between his legs to grab his penis. He was semierect. "That's a good boy."

The man lying prostrate before her had unresolved issues with his mother, and Sybil had unresolved issues with her own deceased parents. Memories of her childhood were fraught with the horrific images of a domineering father, a Vietnam vet with PTSD, and her submissive half-French, half-Vietnamese mother.

As a child, she'd lain in bed, listening through paper-thin walls as her father beat her mother, then raped her, his grunts mingling with her whimpers of pain and protest. She'd begun planning ways to exact revenge for his cruelty, but her plans were for naught when he died from the debilitating effects of Agent Orange. It took years for her to come to the realization that he was gone, that he wasn't coming back to torture her mother. It was only when Jasmine Cherault-Johnson lay dying that she revealed to her youngest daughter that she'd accepted her husband's abuse because her father had beaten her mother. Sybil swore another oath—one she'd kept to this day: the cycle of domestic violence would end with her. Her forty-two-year-old twin schoolteacher sisters had had several long-term relationships, but ended them abruptly whenever their lovers exhibited signs of violence.

Working quickly, silently, Sybil tied E. Paul Redding's ankles to the bedposts with long silk scarves, then moved up to tie his wrists. The odor of alcohol was redolent on his breath. "Tell Mommy if you've been good or bad."

"I've been bad, Mommy," he slurred.

"Why have you been a bad boy, Paulie?"

"I...I opened the liquor cabinet...." His words trailed off.

"You opened the liquor cabinet and did what?" Sybil asked, looming over the prone figure like an avenging angel.

"I opened the bottle of the fifty-year-old scotch and drank it."

Tightening her grip on the crop, Sybil leaned closer. "How much did you drink, Paulie?"

"I finished the bottle." The crop came down, cutting a swath of fire across his buttocks. "Argh!"

Whack, whack, whack! The crop left red streaks across his backside. Even though they stung, she made certain not to break the skin. Her skill with the crop and whip had become legendary because within hours the redness faded without leaving a welt. In all of her years as Delectable she'd never scarred a client.

Sybil felt between Paul's legs again, finding him rock-hard. Picking up one of the rubber rings, she slipped it down the length of his erection. It squeezed his shaft, intensifying and prolonging pleasure while preventing the emission of semen.

She'd learned the technique from a celebrated dominatrix and along the way had added a few personal tricks to her repertoire. Untying the trembling man, she turned him over.

Her dark eyes glittered wildly behind the mask. "Are you going to behave now, Paulie?"

Grabbing his penis, Paul smiled up at her. "Do you want to kiss Paulie's cock, Mommy?"

The crop sliced across his belly. "You're a nasty, nasty boy!"

Sybil played the game until the president of one of the state's largest banks ripped off the rubber band and ejaculated, semen spraying up and over his belly. She watched in disgust as he smeared it over his face and lips, smacking loudly.

It would be several months before she returned to service Paulie again. She only came to the guest cottage when his wife was away on vacation. The poor woman had no idea that her loving husband got his jollies off when whipped with a riding crop.

Turning away, she gathered her sex toys, put them back in the satchel and left as surreptitiously as she'd come. If the men took pleasure in her punishing them, then she also experienced pleasure in punishing them; every man she whipped became the sick man who'd derived pleasure from hurting her mother. What Sybil refused to acknowledge was that she was no better than Alan Johnson because, as Delectable, she inflicted pain before her men were able to achieve sexual gratification.

* * *

A dense fog slowed her return trip. She arrived at the catering hall, deactivated the alarm and made her way to her office, where she changed out of the black costume and boots, showered and slipped into a pair of sweatpants, a tee and running shoes. She exchanged the sports car for the SUV, and when she walked through the door of her home and climbed the steps to her bedroom she forgot all about the man she'd tied to the bed as she undressed and got into bed with her husband.

Cory stirred, reached over and pulled her close to his body. "I tried waiting up for you," he mumbled.

Sybil pressed her breasts against his chest, her moist breath sweeping over his throat. "That's okay, sweetheart. I'm not going to work tomorrow."

"Why?"

"We only have a bridge club luncheon, and Jake has offered to cover for me so I can spend some quality time with my husband."

Cory tightened his hold around her shoulders. "Thank you, baby."

Sybil smiled and closed her eyes. Whenever he complained that they didn't spend enough time together, she made adjustments in her busy schedule to oblige him. It was the least she could do for a man who'd promised on his wedding night to give his wife her heart's desire.

Chapter 33

Dina felt a shiver snake its way down her back when she held out her hand to take the envelope Fletcher Stafford offered her. She didn't like him or the shit-eating grin he gave her whenever she came to pick up her paycheck. He was SJC Catering's maître d' but acted as if he owned the place. Because Sybil couldn't be everywhere all the time, it was Fletcher who stepped in to make certain the business ran smoothly. He fielded complaints about seating, meal and music choices. He'd become mediator, negotiator and customer service all rolled into one.

Dina took the envelope and turned to leave when his gravelly voice stopped her retreat. "I had to cut your hours."

She went completely still. Slowly she turned to face the short, slender man with the perfectly round shaved head that reminded her of a Milk Dud. She would've found him quite attractive if not for the "buck-fifty" along the left side of his face. She'd heard talk that someone had attempted to cut Fletcher's throat because he'd been suspected of being an informant for the police. The keloid began under his left ear and ran across his cheekbone to the bridge of his nose.

Dina's eyes narrowed. "What do you mean you cut my hours?"

"Not by much. Look in your envelope and you'll see."

She opened the flap of the envelope and took out her schedule for the following week. "You call ten hours 'not by much'?"

"Lisa came to me asking for more hours, so I had to give them to her."

"You gave them to her but at my expense!" Dina asked, her voice rising in anger. Ten hours with tips meant at least two hundred dollars less in her pocket.

"I shouldn't have to remind you that she has seniority and *you* don't, Dina. I'm sure you've heard of last in, first out."

Dina rolled her eyes at Fletcher. *I know this son of a bitch ain't threatening to fire me,* she thought. He hadn't hired her and he couldn't fire her. That much she knew.

"If you want, we can talk about it after your shift ends," Fletcher said, unaware that his eyes had betrayed his lust.

"There will *never* be a need for us to talk." That said, Dina turned and walked away, leaving the man staring at the space where she'd been. She knew what he wanted and Dina Gordon wasn't giving up her panties. Even as Adina Jenkins she wouldn't have given the clown the time of day.

Her life now had some semblance of order because she had her own place, worked a legitimate job and was able to send money to her grandmother. She was doing everything right, but there was still the matter of Payne and the money he claimed she owed him. Running cons and turning tricks for Payne Jefferson had made him a rich man, but that still wasn't enough for the twisted little sociopath. He'd used her so he could rob other criminals, and now he wanted to rob her.

Dina had thought about making arrangements to move Dora and Jameeka out of Brooklyn, where Payne couldn't find them, but realized that wasn't possible because although Dora Jenkins wasn't opposed to moving out of public housing, she'd always said that she would *never* leave Brooklyn.

An expression of determination tightened her delicate jaw as she walked down the hall to Sybil's private office. Lisa had gone to Fletcher to increase her hours, and she would go to Sybil to plead her case.

She found Sybil sitting at her desk, writing on a colorful Post-it. What caught her attention whenever she walked into the office was the scheduling chart on the wall behind the desk and then the many colorful flags attached to a corkboard with minute pushpins in corresponding colors. There was no doubt psychologists would've identified Sybil Cumberland as having obsessive-compulsive disorder.

Dina knocked lightly on the open door. "Can you see me for a few minutes?" she asked when Sybil glanced up.

A slight frown appeared between Sybil's eyes. It was the first time since she'd hired Dina Gordon that she'd sought her out; she was hoping and praying that her most popular waitress hadn't come to tender her resignation.

She rose slightly. "Sure. Come in and close the door." She pointed to the small round table in a corner. "We'll talk over there." Sybil didn't want Dina to see the contracts and invoices on her desk. Her office and everything in it was for her eyes only. That's why she'd had the Private sign affixed to the door.

Dina wanted to ask Sybil why she favored a black

tunic and pin-striped pants when white would've been more flattering to her complexion. She'd even exchanged her yellow clogs for a pair in black. She stared at the chef when she sat down across from her. With her black hair pulled tightly off her bare face, all Sybil Cumberland needed was a pair of canincs and she could masquerade as a vampire on Halloween.

Sybil gave Dina a long stare. "What do you want to see me about?"

"I need to work more hours."

Sybil's raven-black eyebrows lifted. "I assume Fletcher told you that he had to cut your hours?"

"Yes, he did."

"He came to me with Lisa's request and I approved it. I'm sorry, but she has seniority and—"

"I know that," Dina countered angrily, interrupting Sybil. "He told me the same thing."

Lacing her fingers together atop the table, Sybil leaned over and glared at the young woman. "If he told you, then what's your problem?"

"I need to make more money, not have it taken away," Dina said recklessly. "I have a daughter…." The admission was out before she could edit herself.

Sybil's lips parted in surprise. "You have a daughter?"

Dina bit back the acerbic words poised on the tip of her tongue. She didn't know why, but people tended to believe a lie before believing the truth. "Yes, I have a daughter. She lives with my grandmother. I send them money every week, and if you cut my hours, then that's not going to be possible."

Sybil wanted to ask Dina what size she'd been before she'd had her baby—a zero? Because now she couldn't be more than a two. "I've already committed to increasing

Lisa's hours, so reversing my decision is not an option. But there may be something else you could consider." The seconds ticked off as the two women regarded each other.

"What is it?" Dina asked after a swollen silence.

"Do you dance?"

She went completely still. "Dance how?"

Sybil leaned closer. "Do you know how to dance like the girls in hip-hop music videos?"

Unconsciously Dina's brow furrowed. "Are you talking about a video ho?"

Sybil nodded. "I'd prefer to call them backup dancers."

It was Dina's turn to nod. "Yes, I can imitate their moves. Why?"

"I want to help you out, Dina, but I'm not certain whether you'll accept what I'm going to propose to you."

"What are you proposing?"

"Occasionally I host private bachelor parties for athletes, CEOs, politicians and entertainers, and they usually want exotic dancers as part of the entertainment. You can earn more from one party than you can from a week of waiting tables. Your identity will remain anonymous because you'll wear a mask."

A slight frown marred her smooth forehead before easing. Sybil's proposal had answered her prayer. "How often would I have to dance?"

"It varies. Maybe once a week, then it can be weeks before you perform again."

"How will I be paid?"

"I'll pay you. And it will always be in cash."

A flicker of apprehension rushed over Dina. Had she traded a male pimp for a female one? There was a lethal calmness in her eyes when she stared at Sybil. "How much of a cut do you want?"

"What are you talking about?" Sybil hadn't tried to hide her annoyance.

"Do I get a flat fee or are you going to take a cut of what I earn?"

The chef's expression was thunderous. "Are you suggesting that I'm trying to pimp you?"

Dina's impassive expression didn't change. "No, I'm not. I just want to know where we stand. If I didn't need to make more money, then we wouldn't be having this discussion."

Sybil sat up straighter. She'd underestimated *and* misjudged Dina Gordon. This was the second time she saw hardness in her that wasn't overtly apparent. The first time was when she'd threatened to castrate the man who'd touched her. Under the pretty face, demure demeanor and fragile femininity was a young woman who didn't scare or get easily intimidated.

There were only a few women Sybil truly respected, and Dina had just become one of them. What Dina didn't know was that she was dealing with someone who was as hard as she was. She had to be to survive her horrific childhood without going to jail for premeditated murder.

"You need money and I said I'd help you out. But you're going to have to do whatever it is I ask of you."

"I'll do it as long as it's legal."

Sybil smiled. "Don't worry—it's legal."

Dina nodded. "Okay."

"I'm going to send you to a friend of mine who's a dance instructor. I'll pay for your lessons and pay you at the same time. I'm also going to have a costume designer fit you for a costume that you'll wear during the parties."

"What kind of costume?"

"She'll decide that. Whenever you're not waiting tables, make certain you rest up, because Carlos is going to put you through an intense workout that will push your body to extremes."

"How many lessons will I need?"

"Carlos will determine that. I have a birthday party for a baseball pitcher that will be held during the All-Star break, so you don't have much time to get your routine together."

"When is it?"

"The game is the second Tuesday in July, so that leaves you about five weeks to get ready."

"Will the party be here?"

Sybil shook her head. "No. Whenever I contract for a private party, it's always off-site. The party will be held on an estate near the Chesapeake."

"Maryland?"

"Yes, Maryland, Dina. I've already made arrangements for a driver to take us down and back. Do you think you're up to the task?"

Dina wanted to tell Sybil that she didn't have much of a choice when she weighed her options because she knew Payne hadn't issued an idle threat. If he said he was going to take care of someone, he did. He knew enough miscreants who'd take out their mother for a price.

"Yes." She'd said the word with such conviction that Dina actually believed she was ready to do anything Sybil asked of her.

It was funny how life had thrown her a vicious curve. As Adina Jenkins, the street hustler with the too-bright seductive smile, she'd only thought of herself. Now she was Dina Gordon, trying to right all of the wrongs, and life was coming at her fast and furious.

You are a descendant of survivors. Your ancestors

went through hell for you to be here today. She didn't know why, but Karla's words were never far from her thoughts whenever she felt like giving up.

Two black women she never could've imagined had changed her life, and there was no way she was going to disappoint either of them.

Chapter 34

The flickering flame from candles on a low table on the terrace bathed Dina's face in a luminous glow that fired the gold in her eyes and skin. Lance, unable to pull his gaze away from her, took a swallow of his wine. He couldn't remember spending a more pleasurable evening with a woman.

Setting down the glass, he picked up a napkin and touched it to the corners of his mouth. "The dinner was wonderful, baby girl."

She smiled at him. "Thank you."

Dina had promised Lance she would cook for him, and with the decrease in her work hours she'd finally fulfilled her promise. When she asked him what he wanted to eat, his response had been *Surprise me*. She'd surprised him with rosemary roast Cornish hens, garlic mashed potatoes, sautéed green beans and homemade yeast rolls.

He winked at her. "I have a confession to make."

"What's that?"

"I didn't believe you when you said you could cook."

Dina traced the rim of a goblet of sweet tea. "Why?"

He lifted his shoulders under a loose-fitting white linen shirt. "You don't seem that domesticated."

Her gaze met his across the small space. "Do you care to explain what you mean by *domesticated*?"

Lance ran a hand over his face. "I think I just put my foot in my mouth. You know what I mean."

"No, I don't."

"Help me out, Dina."

Her mouth twitched as she tried not to smile. "Why should I? Are you interpreting *domesticated* as not house-broken or not fit for marriage?"

Pushing back his chair, Lance came around the table. He eased her from her chair, cradling her to his chest. "I don't ever want to hear you say that again. You're the perfect—"

Dina had placed her fingers over his mouth. "Don't say it, Lance."

His fingers circled her wrist, pulling her hand down. "Don't say what?"

Tilting her chin, she stared up at him. "I'm not who you think I am. And I'm certainly not perfect."

"I don't care who you are, Dina," Lance countered. "All I know is that I enjoy being with you because you're never boring. You make me laugh when I don't feel like laughing. I—"

Dina stopped his passionate entreaty when she kissed him. It began as a tentative joining, deepening when his tongue gently parted her lips. His hands came up, cradling her face as she arched toward him.

All of the men she'd known ceased to exist for Dina when she gave in to the delicious sensations taking her beyond herself. She was soaring, floating outside of her body to a place where she'd never been. His mouth moved lower to the column of her neck as she curved her arms under Lance's broad shoulders, holding on to him as if he were her lifeline.

"Stay with me tonight," he whispered hoarsely.

Hot tears sprang up behind her eyelids. She wanted to sleep with Lance and experience what it meant to be a woman—a real woman. When she told him she was a virgin she hadn't lied altogether. Yes, she'd slept with men, but she'd never felt passion, or experienced an orgasm.

Everything she knew had come from porno flicks: the moans, groans, screams and the different positions. Men never knew that she'd choreographed and faked every move because their egos wouldn't permit them to believe that they weren't the best lover she'd ever had. There were times when she got out of sleeping with them when she told him she was on her menses or she'd gotten them so drunk that they fell asleep as soon as their heads touched the pillow.

"I can't, Lance."

"Why not, baby?"

"You know what can happen if I stay over."

"I promise not to touch you."

Dina pulled away from him and presented him with her back. "But I can't promise not to stop you if you do decide to touch me."

Lance stepped around Dina and cupped her chin in his hand. Her eyes were shimmering with unshed tears. His gaze dropped to the fluttering pulse in her throat. She was frightened of him.

"I'll take you home."

Dina walked up the narrow staircase leading to her apartment, Lance following closely behind. He waited until she unlocked the door and stepped inside. She'd left on the light in the hallway between the kitchen and the living room.

Winding her arms around his waist, she pressed a kiss to his smooth cheek. "Thank you for a wonderful evening."

He smiled. "I should be the one thanking you."

Dina dropped her arms and took a backward step. "Good night, Big Daddy."

Lance chuckled under breath. "Good night, baby girl. Make sure you lock the door."

"I will."

She closed and locked the door, listening to the heavy footfalls until they faded completely, then she turned and made her way into her bedroom. Light from the street lamp spilled into the room through the lacy curtains at the tall windows. She lowered the shades before switching on a table lamp.

Everything in the apartment reminded her of Lance because he'd paid for the comforter, the matching dust ruffle, the shams, the throw pillows, the bathroom towels and accessories; he'd ignored her protests when he selected cookware, dishes and flatware, then informed her that they were housewarming gifts.

Lancelot Haynes was her friend, but he was also much more. He was a man she could trust. She knew he was attracted to her, and if she were honest with herself, then she'd admit that she was attracted to him. He was older, worldly—traits she sought in a man—and he was someone who made her feel safe whenever they were together.

Tonight signaled a turning point in her life because she'd experienced desire for the first time. She wasn't certain how long she and Lance would remain friends, but she wanted to be prepared if or when it changed. He was expecting a virgin, and she had to make certain she could back up her assertion that she was.

Chapter 35

Karla stared at the paving stones in contrasting shades of light and dark gray in the fading light that expanded the patio by an additional one hundred feet. The outdoor kitchen was nearing completion; the contractor had reassured her that he would finish in time for her to hold her Independence Day celebration.

She felt the warmth of a body, then a pair of strong arms around her waist over a flowing caftan as Ronald joined her. Leaning back, she rested her head against his shoulder. "What do you think?"

"It looks okay."

"Okay, Ronald?"

"All right, Karla. It looks very nice."

She smiled at him over her shoulder. "Thank you."

"I thought you'd be dressed by now." It'd been a while since he and Karla had gone to a party with the intent of sleeping with other men and women.

Turning in her husband's loose embrace, Karla brushed a light kiss over his mouth. Ronald was dressed entirely in black: shirt, slacks and shoes. The color was dramatic, flattering, and he breathtakingly virile. "I'll meet you out front in ten minutes." She'd showered, made up her face and styled her hair.

Ronald ran his hand over the nape of her neck. "I'm going to time you."

"You're going to lose, darling."

"No, I'm not," he said, watching his wife walk.

Ronald Thaddeus King was living a life he never would've imagined while growing up. He'd married a brilliant, beautiful wife with whom he shared the most incredible sex ever. Their passion for luxury, lust for power and unlimited sex drive had drawn and kept them together.

He'd had numerous affairs, but that stopped completely the first time he shared Karla's bed. What had surprised *and* shocked him was that she was insatiable. At first he thought her a nymphomaniac, but when he'd asked if she was, her reply had been *I want to get enough before you leave.* He finally left her apartment after an entire weekend in bed, but he returned the following weekend and every weekend after that until he asked her to marry him.

And as unconventional as Karla was in the bedroom, she was the opposite outside of it. She wouldn't give him a key to her apartment and refused his when offered. She'd sleep with him, but refused to live together unless married. They'd had their share of disagreements, but he always compromised in order to save his marriage.

Together he and Karla had become a super couple who were living the American dream with a multimillion-dollar mansion, luxury automobiles and investments worth millions. They worked hard and partied even harder. Life for the Kings couldn't be better.

He made his way to the garage, where he'd parked his truck. He started the engine when he saw Karla. Ronald glanced at his timepiece. She'd dressed in less than ten minutes.

Getting out of the Escalade, he came around to open the door for her. Karla was stunning in a pair of black stretch slacks, a matching tank top and high-heel zebra-striped mules.

"I've changed my mind about going out," he whispered softly.

Karla's eyes widened. "Are you serious?" Ronald nodded. "Why didn't you say something before?"

His teeth shone whitely under his mustache when he flashed a smile. "I just had a change of mind."

Unconsciously Karla pushed her hair behind her right ear, the light over the three-car garage reflecting off the diamond stud in her ear. The diamond earrings were a gift from Ronald for their fifth wedding anniversary. She'd also given him jewelry—a gold watch with a genuine alligator strap.

"Let's go and hang out for a while, then we can leave."

"Are you sure that's what you want?" Ronald asked.

"Yes, Ronald, that's what I want."

She wanted to be anywhere but home, watching and obsessing about whether the construction project would be finished by the projected date. She needed to interact with people who were the complete opposite of the uptight pricks at her firm, who tended to take themselves much too seriously. She'd stopped a heated discussion about the best way to handle a client's estate when she reminded them that they weren't talking about a cure for cancer and that they should stop wasting precious time and make a decision. The silence that followed her outburst was deafening. Two minutes later they agreed on a course of action, and the ruse to inflate billable hours came to an abrupt end.

Ronald assisted her getting into the vehicle, then slipped in beside her. He shifted into gear and maneuvered out of the circular drive to a private road lined on both sides with sprawling properties dotted with pools, tennis courts and a nine-hole golf course.

"Are you all right, Karla?"

"Yes. Why would you ask me that?"

"You seem a little on edge."

Karla rested her left hand over his thigh. "I don't know what is it, but lately the old gray suits annoy the hell out of me."

Ronald smiled. She always referred to the men at the boutique tax firm as "old gray suits" or "old heads." "Don't tell me that you cussed them out again."

"I was this close." She held up her thumb and forefinger. "If I hadn't worked so hard to make partner, I'd leave."

"You can still leave, baby."

Karla shook her head. "No, I can't, because I don't want to give them that satisfaction. Not when I'm the only female partner—and a black woman, to boot."

Ronald lifted thick, silky black eyebrows. "Your decision not to leave is based on gender and race?"

"It's more gender than race, because of their old-boys'-club bullshit. They get together to golf, go sailing and share drinks at the country club. If I were a black man I'd be included to join their social outings, but because I don't have a dick between my legs I'm excluded."

Ronald laughed while shaking his head. "I, for one, am glad that you don't have a dick. One dick in this family is enough." Karla's hand moved closer to his crotch and she massaged the bulge resting against his leg. "Dammit, Karla! Don't do that while I'm driving."

Leaning over, she caught his earlobe between her teeth. "Pull over."

Ronald gritted his teeth as the flesh between his legs hardened quickly. "Stop it, Karla."

"Pull over, Ronald." Her teeth and hand worked their magic until she felt him trembling.

Maneuvering off the road, he drove a short distance and parked behind a wooded area with an overgrowth of brushes and trees concealing them from passing motorists. He parked and turned off the engine.

Karla didn't give him enough time to prepare for her sexual onslaught when she unzipped his slacks, released his erection and took him into her mouth. Eyes closed, head pressed to the headrest, he gripped the steering wheel with both hands and gave in to the exquisite ecstasy that seemed to stop his heart before starting up again.

Karla's tongue and mouth communicated a silent, passionate message that said Ronald King belonged to her and it was only with her consent that other women could sample the small pieces that he handed out like priceless gems.

Her fingers tightened around the thick, blood-engorged length of flesh as she quickened her rhythm. The musky smell of him combined with the sensual scent of his cologne had become an aphrodisiac, heightening her desire. She struggled not to push her free hand between her own legs when she felt the gush of moisture bathe her core.

The harsh, uneven rhythm of Ronald's breathing echoed in the close confines of the SUV as he struggled not to come in Karla's mouth. He tried pulling her head away, but she wouldn't let him go.

Broad shoulders heaving, his heart pumping painfully in his chest, he rose slightly off the leather seat and freed himself from the intense pleasure that had no way to go but outward.

Karla moaned softly with the rush of semen filling her mouth. She waited until the pulsing under her fingers slowed, then stopped altogether before she released Ronald's still-hard penis. Straightening, she opened the glove box and took out a handful of tissues, spitting into the soft cotton. She took another handful and gave them to Ronald.

He cleaned himself, rolled up the tissues and flung the wad at his wife. His hands were shaking when he attempted to adjust his slacks. "Fuck you, Karla King," he ground out between clenched teeth.

Karla knew Ronald was angry because he hadn't wanted to ejaculate into her mouth. "That's exactly what I want you to do. Now turn this truck around and take me home."

He punched the start button and shifted savagely into gear, retracing the route.

Ronald hated when his wife took out her frustrations on him. She'd gone down on him because he was a man and right now she was angry with the men who worked with her. Sucking him until he came in her mouth had reaffirmed her power and control over all men who wouldn't acknowledge her as their equal.

What Karla couldn't or didn't want to understand was that he never viewed her as inferior. She'd earned three degrees to his two, spoke fluent French and made twice as much as he did. The only exception was physical strength. He was able to bench-press twice his body's weight, while Karla hadn't been able to lift more than fifty pounds. He thought he understood her, but it was apparent he didn't know her at all, because she'd become a creature of extremes—physically, mentally and emotionally.

Karla was out of the Escalade as soon as Ronald came to a complete stop. Quickening her pace, she made it to the front door. She was upstairs in the bedroom when he walked in.

They stood motionless, staring at each other like strangers. Although married for six years, they still were strangers. Ronald didn't understand his wife's unceasing drive to prove herself and he knew she would never accept the aberrant sexual fantasies that emerged when he least expected.

Reaching up, he unbuttoned his shirt, dropping it to the floor. He kicked off his shoes, then bent over to remove his socks. His gaze met and fused with hers when he removed his belt, slacks and boxers. He saw her gaze shift to the pile of clothes on the rug.

Ronald knew she wanted him to pick them up, but he wouldn't.

Not now.

Not tonight. His hand went to his groin, fingers caressing the heavy flesh between his thighs.

A hint of a smile softened Karla's wide mouth as she kicked off her mules. It had become a battle of wills, a dance of desire as she eased the tank top over her head, exposing her full breasts to Ronald's heated gaze. Slowly, as if she were on stage seducing a room of horny men, she unzipped her pants and pushed them down her hips without bending her knees. Wearing nothing but a black thong, she turned and presented her husband with her back as she anchored her hands between the narrow elastic band, pushing it slowly down her thighs and legs.

Ronald moved quickly, sweeping Karla up in his arms and carrying her to the bed. Holding her effortlessly in one arm, he swept back the comforter, placing her on the cool sheets, his body following hers down. Grasping her wrists, he anchored her hands against her body as he slid down the length of the bed to press his face to the apex of her thighs.

It was his turn to exact revenge, to assert his power and control when he alternated suckling with nipping gently at the sensitive folds around her vagina. She screamed and arched off the bed when he captured her clitoris between his teeth, applying enough pressure to make her climax.

Moving quickly, Ronald entered her and they breathed out a shared groan of pure pleasure. The walls of her vagina closed around him, pulling him in until he was mindless with the lust that imprisoned his mind *and* body. His hands were everywhere—her breasts, hips, face and hair.

A moan of ecstasy slipped through Karla's lips as she felt the onset of contractions that signaled she was going to climax. She tightened her vaginal muscles but to no avail. She couldn't stop what had begun in the front seat of the Escalade and she couldn't stop the screams of rapture building up in the back of throat; she opened her mouth when a spasm of erotic pleasure seized her, holding her prisoner for several seconds before she and Ronald climaxed simultaneously, their breathing coming in long, surrendering gasps.

Karla languished in the weight pressing her down to

the mattress, the smell of sex and an amazing sense of completeness. Her arms went around Ronald's head as he pressed his mouth to her moist neck. She loved Ronald. He'd become her partner, the other half that made her whole.

"I love you," she whispered softly.

A beat passed before he said, "I love you, too."

Chapter 36

"Wake up, Dina. Open your eyes, honey."

Dina felt as if she were underwater, struggling vainly to get to the surface. Her eyelids fluttered before they closed again. At the nurse's urging, she opened her eyes, and this time they remained open. A steady arm around her back assisted her sitting up.

"How are you feeling, Dina?"

She affected a lopsided smile for the nurse. "Okay."

A pair of friendly gray-blue eyes met hers. "Do you think you'll be able to dress yourself?"

"Yes-s-s," Dina slurred.

Anchoring a hand under her patient's knees, the nurse guided her off the bed until she could stand on her own. "I'll help you."

Dina responded like an automaton, raising her arms and lifting her feet when she permitted herself to be dressed as if she were a child. The day before she'd consulted a female OB-GYN, reporting that a difficult delivery of a large baby had left her stretched and torn during childbirth; a significant decrease in sexual pleasure had been the final result.

She was referred to a surgeon specializing in labia-plasty and vaginoplasty. The office manager of the thriving Upper Saddle Brook practice quoted a fee of fifty-five hundred for the vaginoplasty; she informed Dina that Dr. Howe had a cancellation and could fit her in the following day.

When Dina disclosed that she didn't have insurance because she'd changed jobs, the fee was lowered to forty-five hundred. Her first impulse was to hang up, but she changed her mind. Having the procedure meant she would have to come up with even more money to meet Payne's demand.

Dr. Louis Howe peered at Dina Gordon over his glasses. "The procedure went very well, Ms. Gordon. I tightened your vagina, perineum and the supporting muscles. Once the anesthesia wears off, you'll experience the same discomfort as if you'd had a vaginal delivery. There will be a little bleeding, but it shouldn't last more than a week." Reaching for a pen, he made notations on a pad and ripped off the page. "This is a prescription for Tylenol with codeine. Take one every six hours as needed for pain. I want you to abstain from sexual intercourse for at least a month."

Dina wanted to tell the doctor that she hadn't had sex or planned to have sex within the next four weeks. "Do you want to see me for a follow-up?"

He removed his glasses. "I'd like you to come back in two weeks just as a precaution. I want to check your sutures. They should dissolve on their own. Do you have someone to drive you home?"

"No."

He frowned. "Did you drive yourself?"

Dina shook her head. "No." She'd ridden a bus to Newark Pennsylvania Station, gotten on a Pascack Valley line train to Nanuet, where she'd taken a taxi to the doctor's office.

"You can't leave my office without assistance."

Dina didn't want to call Lance because then she would have to explain why she was at a doctor's office in northern New Jersey. "Can someone call a car service to take me back to Irvington? My boyfriend is out of town on business," she added.

Dr. Howe buzzed the receptionist and told her to contact a car service and schedule a follow-up appointment for Ms. Gordon. He stood up, extending his hand. "Good luck, Ms. Gordon."

Dina shook his hand. "Thank you."

She managed to stand and make her way to the reception area to wait for the car. She hadn't realized she'd dozed off until the receptionist shook her gently to let her know her driver had arrived.

Dina heard someone calling her name, this voice deeper than the nurse's. She opened her eyes to find Lance sitting on the side of her bed. Her landlady stood behind him. He wore a lightweight light gray suit, pale blue shirt and dark gray tie.

"What…what are you doing here?" she slurred.

Susie Foster moved closer. "I let him in, child. Mr. Haynes said he's been calling you and when you didn't answer your phone he came over."

Lance stared at the wealth of dark hair spread out on the pillow beneath Dina's head instead of the outline of her breasts under a cotton camisole. He and Dina spoke every day. If he didn't call her early morning, she called him early evening.

That morning he'd called her and gotten her voice

mail. He'd tried her again before noon and again the call had gone directly to voice mail.

Placing a hand over her forehead, Lance found it cool to the touch. "Are you feeling okay?"

Dina saw concern and another unidentified emotion in his eyes. "I have cramps."

"I have the perfect remedy for your monthly," Mrs. Foster announced.

Dina lifted a limp hand. "I've already taken something." She'd had the driver wait for her while she stopped at a local pharmacy to fill the prescription.

Lance glanced over his shoulder at Dina's landlady. "Thank you, Mrs. Foster, but I'll take care of her now." Waiting until the woman left, he gathered Dina in his arms. "I'm taking you home with me."

"No, Lance."

He tightened his grip under her knees as he settled her on his lap. "Yes, Dina. Don't fight with me, because I'm a lot bigger and stronger than you."

Her head fell limply on his shoulder. The anesthesia was wearing off, but the codeine had kicked in, making it virtually impossible for her to stay awake. "I have to get dressed."

"Where are your clothes?"

She pointed to a double dresser. "My other things are hanging in the closet."

"When are you scheduled to go to work again?"

"I think Friday. No, I remember I have to go in Thursday afternoon."

"How long do your cramps usually last?" Lance asked.

"A couple of days," she said truthfully. Her period, though scant, always came on time, accompanied by cramps that left her out of sorts for several days. She'd heard that having a baby usually alleviated menstrual cramps—but not hers. In fact, they'd intensified after she'd had the tubal ligation.

Lance eased her off his lap. "Can you dress yourself or do you want me to help you?"

It was the second time that day that someone had asked her the same question. Combing her fingers over her mussed hair, Dina pushed it off her forehead. "I can dress myself."

Lance stood up. "I'll wait for you in the living room."

She gave him a grateful smile. "Thank you, LL."

Leaning over, he dropped a kiss on her hair. "You're welcome, baby girl." He walked out of Dina's bedroom, smiling. She'd called him LL. What Dina didn't know was that when she called him Big Daddy, he was ready to give her anything she wanted—because Lancelot "LL" Haynes had fallen in love with Dina Gordon.

Chapter 37

Dina opened the door to the employees' entrance, nearly colliding with Fletcher Stafford. He licked his lips as if savoring a decadent dessert. "Don't bother to change. Sybil wants to see you." She brushed past without acknowledging him. "You could say thank you, Dina," he called out to her retreating back.

"Thank you, Fletcher," she drawled facetiously. She didn't want to deal with Fletcher and she hadn't wanted to come to work. Spending thirty-six hours convalescing from vaginal restoration definitely wasn't enough time to counter her standing on her feet for the next six or seven hours. The only consolation was Lance had dropped her off and promised to pick her up when her shift ended.

She'd slept in Lance's guest bedroom, dozing off and on, while he'd worked from home. If he wasn't on his computer, then it was the telephone. He'd ordered lunch from a local restaurant, then threatened to force-feed her when she told him that she wasn't hungry.

When she apologized to Lance for interfering with his work, he told her how he'd founded his own software company in 1999, earning five hundred thousand in revenue the first year, and sold it two years later for four million. In 2005 he produced a simple program that allowed just about anyone to create a website. The following year he grossed fifty-six million, and his software company was named one of *Inc.*'s top ten fastest-growing privately held firms that year. His investment banker had urged him to go public, but he pulled the plug on the widely anticipated IPO because he felt that market conditions weren't right. She hadn't suspected that the man who claimed tinkering with computers paid his rent had amassed a modest fortune.

Dina came to Sybil's office and knocked on the door. "You wanted to see me?"

Sybil stood up. Today she'd chosen to wear a rose-pink cotton tee with a pair of twill taupe walking shorts and running shoes instead of her ubiquitous tunic, loose-fitting pants and clogs.

"Lisa's going to fill in for you tonight," she said, reaching for her handbag and a set of car keys. "Let's go."

Dina gave her a confused look. "Where are we going?"

"I'm taking you to be fitted for your costume," she explained when they were seated in her SUV.

Dina secured her seat belt. "When do I start dancing lessons?"

Sybil drove out of the parking lot. "I don't know. Carlos is in Florida choreographing several music videos and he isn't expected back until next week, which leaves us less time than I'd originally planned."

Dina wanted to tell Sybil that she'd undergone a surgical procedure that might impede her flexibility but held her tongue. Carlos, not Sybil Cumberland, would be better able to determine her physical limitations.

Patrice Sigler rested her hands on her hips, peering closely at Dina Gordon, who'd stripped down to her bra and panties. The overhead spotlight revealed things that wouldn't have been apparent with an ordinary lightbulb.

Dina returned the stare of the middle-aged woman with graying red hair pulled into a severe bun, gray eyes and a long, narrow nose in an equally narrow face.

Sybil, perched on a stool in a back room of the small West Orange shop filled with racks of colorful and outlandish costumes, watched the two women. She found it hard to believe that Dina had delivered a child given her incredibly flat belly.

"What do you think, Patrice?" she asked the costume designer.

Patrice pursed her lips and angled her head. "I see her as a fairy—a sparkling, very delicate green fairy."

Clasping her hands together in a prayerful gesture, Sybil affected a bright smile. "That's it. Dina will be known as Sparkle." Delectable and Sparkle were about to become a dynamic duo, she mused.

She watched Patrice measure her protégé from head to toe. The designer selected strips of fabric in varying shades of green, placing them against Dina's cheek and shoulder, while she kept up a rambling monologue.

"I have to get the right shade of green because she has so much gold in her skin. If it's too light, then she'll look sallow, too dark and it'll appear murky under the lights. The emerald might work, but then the lime is better. Yes, the lime will do if covered with crystals." Patrice glanced at Sybil over her shoulder. "Lime-green embroidered silk tulle covered with emerald crystals. I'll make a satin mask in the same color as the leotard, and the ties and ostrich feathers in the contrasting emerald. The legs of the leotard will have a high cut to give the illusion that Sparkle's taller than she actually is."

Sybil nodded her approval. "What about her shoes?"

"I suggest ballet slippers with satin ankle ties." Patrice squinted at Dina. "What's your shoe size?"

"Five and a half."

"I'll order a five because it should be a tight fit." A slight frown creased her forehead. Then she snapped her fingers. "Wings! All fairies have wings. You will become an extraordinary fairy because I'll trim your wings with delicate, wispy feathers."

"When do you want us to come back for a fitting?" Sybil asked Patrice.

"I'll call you. I'm not busy right now, so I could conceivably put her costume together this weekend."

Sybil smiled. "That's good. I'd like a final fitting before the end of the month."

Patrice waved a hand. "I can complete two costumes by that time. How many do you need?"

"We'll start out with one." Reaching into her leather hobo bag, Sybil took out an envelope and handed it to Patrice. "Thank you."

Patrice took the envelope without opening it. "Thank you for thinking of me."

"May I get dressed now?" Dina asked.

"Yes," Patrice said.

Dina put her clothes back on, her movements slowed by pain that threatened to bring her to her knees. She should've listened to Lance. He'd urged her to take a few days off, but he had no way of knowing that her financial problems had become exacerbated. The Labor Day weekend was less than ten weeks away, and she needed ten thousand dollars to pay off an ex-con who'd threatened her grandmother with bodily harm.

Chapter 38

Dina secured her seat belt, reached for her cell phone and punched the speed dial for Lance's home number. He answered on the first ring. "Hey, baby girl."

She smiled at his greeting. "I'm getting off early."

"I'm on my way." The line suddenly went dead.

She knew Lance was still uneasy about her claim that she'd had to seek medical attention to alleviate her menstrual cramps. She'd only taken three doses of the pain medication before flushing the rest down the toilet; she hadn't liked the adverse side effects that caused dizziness and a slowdown in her reaction time. The images of her mother stumbling, falling and mumbling incoherently hadn't faded even after ten years.

"Are you getting a ride home?" Sybil asked, concentrating intently on the taillights of the car in front of hers. The driver was tapping his brake every three seconds.

"Yes. A friend is picking me up."

Dina turned and stared at her boss's profile. It was the first time she'd seen Sybil with makeup. Blush, mascara and a light coat of lipstick had transformed her from nondescript to glowing.

"Do you drive, Dina?"

"Yes, but I don't have my license. After I get it, then I'll consider buying a used car."

"How are you getting back and forth now?"

"I usually take public transportation during the day and a car service at night."

"The car service must be costly."

Dina nodded. "It is, but it's safer than waiting for a bus."

Sybil took a quick glance at her employee. "Money shouldn't become an issue once you begin working the private parties."

"How much do you estimate I'll earn for each party?"

A silence ensued as Sybil stared out the windshield. "I'm surprised you didn't ask me before."

"I wanted to," Dina confessed, "but I decided to wait and see if I could trust you to do right by me."

A rush of color darkened the older woman's face. "*You* were testing *me?*"

"No more than you test me." Dina ignored Sybil's slight gasp. "When Karla asked you to interview me, you had no idea whether I'd work out until I was put to the test. It's become a win-win for both of us because I have a job and you hired a dependable server."

Sybil smiled. "Modest, aren't you?"

"No, Sybil, just confident." Although last hired, she had become one of the better servers at SJC. She never forgot a request, hadn't dropped a tray or broken a single glass. She was always pleasant, quick to smile even when she didn't feel like smiling.

"You're right about being a dependable server. Fletcher tells me that you're one of the best. I didn't hire you because Karla asked me to."

"Why *did* you hire me?"

Decelerating and coming to a complete stop at a red light, Sybil's fingers tightened on the leather-wrapped steering wheel. "I hired you because of your face and body. You have an exotic look most men find appealing. And there's no doubt you're aware that most of my patrons are men who prefer dining and entertaining in a more private setting. That was the reason I set my business up in a former home with less than three thousand square feet. These same men also retain my services for more discreet gatherings in private homes or hotel suites."

"Services as in female entertainment?"

The light changed and Sybil took off in a burst of speed, maneuvering around a slower-moving car. Accelerating, she glanced up at the rearview mirror to see if the police car that had been parked alongside the road had taken off after her. Exhaling, she settled back against the seat. She'd gotten three speeding tickets in the past four years.

"Yes, Dina. And that's all you'll ever be to them—entertainment. The men know beforehand not to try to proposition you, and vice versa. Now that you're going to be joining me, I'll renegotiate my fee." She angled her head. "If they accept my price, then you'll earn at least two thousand dollars. And that's not counting tips."

"Sw-e-e-e-t!" Dina drawled.

"Yes, it's quite sweet," Sybil confirmed.

"Do you also dance, Sybil?" The chef shook her head. "Then what do you do?"

Sybil's expression changed as a look of withdrawal crossed her face. "You'll see."

Dina knew Sybil's cryptic reply meant she wasn't going to tell her. She would just have to wait to see for herself.

"Are you coming in?" Sybil asked Dina after she'd pulled into her reserved parking space.

"No. The weather's nice, so I'm going to wait out here for my friend."

Keys in hand, Sybil peered closely at Dina. "Are you okay?"

"Yes," Dina said much too quickly. "Why?"

"I noticed you wincing."

"Menstrual cramps."

"Do you take anything for them?"

"No."

"I have something in my office that should help take the edge off."

Dina shook her head, her ponytail swaying with the motion. "No, thank you. I don't take drugs."

"Ibuprofen isn't a controlled substance, Dina."

"Thanks for the offer, but I'll pass." Dina forced a smile. "I'll see you tomorrow."

She'd unceremoniously dismissed Sybil because she didn't want to field her questions. Whenever she lied, then she had to tell another one to cover the previous one. Her body hurt and she was still under the influence, and that attributed to her possibly contradicting herself.

The sutures were tightening, pulling her flesh taut, and whenever she moved too quickly she was reminded why she'd undergone the procedure. As Dina Gordon she needed and wanted a man's protection, and Lance Haynes had become the perfect candidate. He was solvent, kind, generous and *single*. There were no ex-wives or children with whom she had to compete or share him.

And it wasn't the first time that she wondered, had she remained Adina Jenkins and met Lance would she have messed over him? Would she have recognized his good qualities or just viewed him an easy mark?

She watched Sybil punch in the code on the keypad of the door that led directly into the kitchen. Alone at last, she went over and sat down on a sturdy plastic crate to wait for Lance.

Chapter 39

Dina pushed to her feet when she recognized the make and model of Lance's car. She waved to get his attention.

Lance approached Dina, cradling her face between his hands and kissing her. "Have you been waiting long?"

She shook her head. "Not too long."

Dropping his hands, he cupped her elbow and led her to his car. He noticed there were only a few cars in the lot. "It looks like a slow night."

"Very slow," Dina confirmed as Lance opened the passenger-side door for her. "One party canceled."

He closed the door. "How are you feeling?" he asked when he sat beside her.

"Okay."

Lance stared at Dina, his gaze lingering on her profile before moving lower to her fisted hands. The lights on the dashboard threw shadows across her delicate feature. "You're tense." His voice, though soft, was accusatory.

"You make me tense, LL."

He smiled. "You make me tense, too, but I'm not complaining." She turned to look at him. He sobered quickly. "Do I frighten you, Dina?"

"Not as much as I frighten myself."

"Talk to me, baby girl."

Even though she wasn't prone to tears, Dina felt like weeping. She wanted to fall into Lance's arms and unburden herself. Maybe it was the lingering effects from the anesthesia, the codeine or the ongoing pain, but she'd found herself drowning in a maelstrom of uncertainty. "I'm confused."

"What are you confused about?"

"You. Me. Us."

"What about us, Dina?"

"You say we are friends."

"We are friends. Dina," Lance insisted.

"Why is it I don't want us to be friends?"

A silence ensued as he replayed her query in his head. If she didn't want to be friends, then what did she want? "What *do* you want?"

"I don't know."

"You don't know? Do you want us to stop seeing each other?"

Dina shook her head. "No, Lance." She sucked in her breath and gritted her teeth. Pain ripped through her lower abdomen like a lighted fuse, tearing, burning in its intensity. Sybil had offered her something to take the edge off, and she'd refused it. "Take me home," she pleaded, fighting tears. "Please."

Lance followed Dina up the staircase to her apartment, waiting until she unlocked the door and stepped inside. She was confused as to their relationship, and he was even more confused. What did she want from him? Dare he pray she wanted more than friendship?

"Are you going to be all right?" he asked.

She affected a silly grin. "Call me in the morning to check whether I'm still alive."

His hand shot out, pulling her up close to his chest. "Cut the bullshit, Dina! What's the matter with you?" She went limp, and he caught her before she fell.

Tears she'd held in check during the drive from West Orange to Irvington rolled down her cheeks. "Please don't leave me, Big Daddy."

Lance felt as if someone had ripped out his heart. He kicked the door closed, locked it, then carried Dina into her bedroom. The street lamp and a three-quarter moon bathed the space in silvery light. Bending slightly, he placed her gently on the bed, removing her blouse, slacks and shoes. He stood motionless, watching her. Awash with indecision, Lance vacillated whether to stay or walk away from the woman who'd twisted him into knots.

Seconds turned into minutes as he stared. Eyes closed, her breathing deepened as her chest rose and fell in an even rhythm. She'd fallen asleep

Slowly, methodically, Lance undressed, leaving on his underwear, and got into bed. Dina had asked him not to leave her and he wouldn't.

Not now.

Not ever.

Dina woke to find Lance in bed, his head resting on a forearm, staring at her. She was in her own bed but didn't remember how she'd gotten there. A slight frown appeared between her eyes as she pulled the sheet up to her neck.

"What are you doing here?"

Sitting up, Lance pressed his back to the headboard. He wanted to pull Dina into his arms but knew if he did touch her, then he would break his promise not to make love to her without her consent. "Last night you asked me not to leave you."

A flash of humor softened Dina's face. "Do you always do everything someone asks?"

He winked at her. "It depends on who's asking."

"You undressed me." Her query was a statement.

"In the dark—and I swear I didn't look."

"What else did I say?" Dina prayed she hadn't said something that would jeopardize her new identity.

Lance gave her a smile parents usually reserved for their children. "Don't worry, baby girl, your skeletons are still in the closet."

Dina felt a momentary panic that gnawed away at her confidence, confidence she'd spent years developing. It'd been Adina Jenkins's quick mind, quicker tongue and duplicity that had gotten her out of situations others may have deemed impossible. But she had to remind herself that Lancelot Haynes knew nothing about Adina because Dina Gordon had assumed her identity to reinvent herself.

"I don't have skeletons in my closet," she said deadpan, "but I do have…"

Her explanation died on her lips as she observed Lance through lowered lashes. Pinpoints of light coming through the lacy window sheers fired the warm color in his eyes, reminding her of sparkling new pennies.

She'd always felt herself incapable of loving or caring for someone other than herself, but each time she saw Lance her attraction to him was stronger than it'd been before.

Dina hadn't known if it was passion because she couldn't acknowledge what she'd never experienced. Yet she reacted to him like a heroine in a romantic movie or novel who'd found herself completely taken by the hero.

Unknowingly he'd become her hero, protecting her from harm and all that was seen and unseen. He'd promised to take care of her while asking for nothing in return.

"If you don't have skeletons, then what is it you have?" Lance asked Dina after a comfortable silence.

"I have nightmares."

"Do you want to talk about them?"

She shook her head. "I can't, LL. It would be the same as reliving them."

She was six when she experienced the lurid scene for the first time, and she'd relived it every night until accepting the realization that her mother was gone and never coming back. She'd come home from school to find Bernice slumped over the bathtub with a hypodermic dangling from her arm. Her screams brought neighbors and eventually the paramedics, who'd revived Bernice before she was taken to the hospital. She'd thought her mother dead, but the rumors were that she'd "OD'd on some bad shit that had junkies dropping like flies."

Dina held the sheet against her breasts and reached for her slacks at the foot of the bed. She managed to slip into them without exposing too much flesh. Although her head was clearer than it'd been in days, the discomfort in her lower belly and between her legs persisted. The doctor had predicted that the pain would be similar to what she'd had following childbirth, but she didn't remember it being this extreme, making her question whether she should've had the procedure.

What if she didn't heal before she was to meet with the dance instructor?

What if she and Lance never became lovers?

What if she'd spent forty-five hundred dollars for nothing?

Swinging her legs over the side of the bed, she gritted her teeth and pressed her hand to her abdomen. She took a step, then another. All she wanted was to get to the bathroom without embarrassing herself.

"You're not going to work tonight."

Dina stopped but didn't turn around. "I have to."

Lance got out of bed, picked up his jeans and slipped into them. "Why do you have to?"

She turned and glared at him. "If I don't work, I don't get paid, and I need this weekend's pay for next month's rent."

"I'll pay your rent."

"You will not!" she countered. "You paying my rent will make me a kept woman."

Lance decided to try another approach. "How much do you make?"

"Why?"

"Just answer the question, Dina." His tone was cold, impersonal.

Lancelot Haynes had become a stranger. There was no softness in his gaze or warmth in his voice. She told him how much she made an hour. "I'll double it—no, I'll triple it if you take off this weekend and rest."

Dina's eyes widened as she shook her head. As Adina Jenkins, she would've taken his money, but Dina was different. "I can't take money from you."

"Why not?"

She dropped her gaze and pulled her lower lip between her teeth. "I just can't." Turning on her heels, she walked out of the bedroom.

Lance was rooted to the same spot until he heard the soft click when Dina closed the bathroom door across the hall. She didn't sleep, live with or take money from a man. Just when he thought he'd figured out Dina Gordon, she confounded him with her old-fashioned virtue. He shook his head. What was he going to do with her?

He wanted to curse her grandmother for shielding her from the realities of life to where her hell-and-brimstone sermons hadn't permitted her granddaughter to experience why she'd been born female.

He realized the older woman had wanted to protect Dina from the harsh realities of her mother's addictions, but in the end she'd done her a great disservice. There was a lot of ugliness in the world, but there was also a lot of good.

Lance went over to get his running shoes. It was time, he thought, to show Dina that life was wonderful, and it could be fun—if only she trusted him enough to let him make it happen for her.

Chapter 40

Why is it I don't want us to be friends? It took Lance four days to grasp what Dina had been trying to tell him. She'd communicated in a roundabout way that she wanted more than friendship. But it came at a price and on her terms: courtship and marriage, and that meant she wouldn't live with him or sleep with him without a commitment.

What Dina didn't know was that Lancelot Londell Haynes was committed to his software company, not a woman. He'd sacrificed a lot because of his commitment and drive for success. The payoff was sweet and he'd become a casualty of *by any means necessary* because he hadn't missed not having a wife and children.

The times he woke up in bed with strange women, he'd question why. Why her? What was it about the woman, other than they either wanted or needed sexual release, that drew him to her? And each time the answer was *I don't know.* His only rationale was that she was a consenting adult and available.

Now he found himself questioning his motives when he continued to pursue Dina Gordon. He'd found her an enigma, an anomaly and a chameleon. She was unlike any woman he'd ever met or known.

Bedding virgins wasn't in his sexual repertoire. He preferred sleeping with sexually experienced women because he didn't have to deal with the responsibility of being her *first*. Whenever he ended a relationship he made certain it stayed that way. He wasn't one to put up with call-and-hang-up scenarios or someone showing up unexpectedly in the middle of the night. Dina was the first woman he'd invited to his West New York apartment since he'd moved in, and he wanted her to be the last.

Swiveling on his chair, he stared out the window in his office with panoramic views of the Hudson River and the towering buildings that made up Manhattan's skyline. It was a sight that he never wanted to get used to. The intercom rang and he turned around to answer it, his gaze shifting to the planner on his desk.

A slight frown creased his forehead when he saw that he'd circled this past Sunday but hadn't put down a notation. Flipping back through the month, he went completely still. He smiled. It'd been a month since he'd met Dina for the first time. He'd circled the date because it was their one-month anniversary.

The intercom buzzed again. He touched the speaker feature. "Yes, Della?"

"Mr. Bellamy's secretary called to cancel because his wife just went into labor. She said the baby wasn't due for another two weeks."

"Keep in touch with her, and when Mrs. Bellamy delivers, I want you to send her a basket of fruit and flowers." Lance could count on his executive assistant to stay on top of every situation. He only had to tell her something once and it was done.

"I'm on it," she said with her signature confirmation.

"I'm going out for a couple of hours. If you need to reach me, then call me on my cell."

"I'm on it," Della repeated.

Chapter 41

Dina sat at the branch manager's desk, signing signature cards for her checking and savings accounts. Her social security card with her new name had come in the mail earlier that morning, along with a printed invitation from Karla King. Enclosed with the invitation was a response card with a self-addressed stamped envelope. Her first impression was, Oh, that's how they do it. Proper ladies living in upscale suburbs don't pick up the telephone and say come on over or send word by a cousin twice removed to "come by my spot for some links and ribs."

She'd worked a double shift on Saturday and one on Sunday, but it wouldn't have been possible if she hadn't taken over-the-counter pain medication. Miraculously it did dull the pain enough to where she'd almost forgotten about it. Lance had offered to pick her up but she lied and told him that the busboy had offered to drive her home Saturday and Sunday.

What Dina didn't want was a repeat of Thursday. She didn't want to wake up and find Lance Haynes in her bed. If or when they shared a bed again, it'd be because she'd invited him.

She handed the branch manager the cards, her paycheck and the cash she wanted to deposit. She'd decided to open her checking account with two thousand dollars and the savings with one. Three thousand dollars was hardly enough to raise a red flag with the IRS, which required banks to report deposits totaling ten thousand or more.

"Come with me, Ms. Gordon. You need to select a four-digit PIN—or personal identification number—for your bank card."

Half an hour after Dina had walked into a local bank on Nye Avenue she left with deposit receipts and an ATM card that gave her access to her money 24-7. She strolled leisurely along Irvington's business district, peering into store windows before going into a diner for lunch. She'd gotten so used to the gourmet meals prepared by Sybil and Jake Collins that she was reluctant to eat out.

The refrigerator and pantry in her apartment held only basic emergency staples: coffee, tea, powdered milk, bottled water, crackers, canned soups, peas, beans and peanut butter. Arriving home after midnight and waking up late mornings wasn't conducive to her eating three balanced meals each day. It was only when she didn't have to go to West Orange that she'd hoped to establish a routine where she did her laundry, cleaned the apartment and went food shopping. However, her plans were placed on hold because she was still convalescing from the vaginoplasty. It'd been a week since the procedure, and she had to go back to Upper Saddle Brook for a follow-up visit. Hopefully she would be pain-free by the time she began her dance lessons.

Dina looked forward to entertaining at the private parties for one specific purpose: to earn enough money to pay off Payne. His threat was akin to a bribe, but there wasn't much she could do with a contract out on her life.

It wasn't until she paid him that she truly would be able to enjoy being Dina Gordon.

She gave the waitress her order for a small Greek salad, then reached into her purse for Karla's invitation and the cell phone Lance had given her. His secretary answered the call, then forwarded it when she identified herself. Her eyebrows lifted in surprise. Had Lance told Della who she was?

"Good morning...I take that back—good afternoon, Ms. Gordon."

Dina smiled at his formal greeting. "Good afternoon, Mr. Haynes. How are you?"

"Wonderful. How are you?"

She wanted to say glorious but changed her mind. Everything wouldn't be glorious until after she gave Payne his blood money. "I'm good. I'm calling to ask if you would accompany me to a Fourth of July gathering in Oldwick."

"Give me the address. That's in Hunterdon County," he said after a pause.

Dina wanted to tell Lance she wasn't familiar with any of the New Jersey counties. "Are you coming with me or do I have to hire an escort for the day?"

"If that's your idea of a joke, then I'm definitely not laughing."

She clamped her teeth together. Dina wanted to tell him to lighten the fuck up but swallowed back the retort. "I'm waiting for your answer, Big Daddy," she crooned in a sultry whisper.

"Of course I'll take you. Did you know what Sunday was, baby girl?"

She smiled. He was back to calling her baby girl. "No."

"It was a month ago that we met for the first time."

"You're kidding?"

"Nope. How would you like to celebrate tonight?"

Dina felt a wave of heat suffuse her face and neck. She couldn't believe she was blushing like a flustered adolescent when seeing her first crush. "I'd like that very much."

"Where do you want to go?"

"You promised to take me back to LUA." She wanted to see the nighttime views of the river.

"I'll call and make a reservation. I'll pick you up at seven. Will that give you enough time to get ready?"

Dina glanced at the clock on the wall. It was almost one o'clock. She wanted to go shopping and buy a special outfit for their special night. "Yes. I should be ready by that time."

"I'll see you later, baby girl."

"Okay, Big Daddy."

Chapter 42

Dina opened the door and Lance went completely still. Nothing moved. He couldn't believe the woman standing before him was his. Yes, she was his; she was LL's woman.

Skillfully applied makeup accentuated her large, brilliant eyes and pouty mouth. Even her hairstyle was different. The waves were missing. She'd parted it in the middle and it hung straight down her back.

She wore a sleeveless red silk wrap dress with a black sash that emphasized a waist he could span with two hands. His gaze moved down to her bare, smooth legs and feet in a pair of black high-heel pumps before reversing itself.

"I don't believe it." His voice was filled with awe.

Dina lifted her waxed eyebrows. "What don't you believe?"

"What did you do to your hair?"

She spun around slowly, her hair swirling around her shoulders and back, spilling an ebony curtain around her sun-browned face. "I had it trimmed, roller-set, then blown out." Dina didn't tell Lance that the entire ordeal, including a manicure, pedicure and eyebrow wax, had taken more than four hours. She'd barely had time to go to a boutique for the dress and shoes.

Lance reached for Dina and turned her gently to face him. His free hand went to the breast pocket of his suit jacket. He handed her a small box wrapped in silver paper with a black velvet bow. "It's just a little something to commemorate our one-month anniversary."

Dina stared up at the man who made her feel like a fairy-tale princess. If she looked different, then so did he. He'd had his hair close cropped, leaving a hint of sideburns that slenderized his round, smooth face. Everything about him radiated elegance and breeding, from the exquisite tailoring of his dark suit to his imported footwear. He smiled and her gaze lingered on his perfect white teeth.

"I didn't get you anything."

"You didn't have to. You're my gift." Tears filled her eyes as Lance closed his. He couldn't bear to see her cry—even in joy. He pulled her to his chest. "Don't cry, baby girl."

Dina's arms went around his waist inside his jacket. She wanted to love him, but she didn't know how to love. She'd grown up believing although mothers had babies, they didn't love their babies, and the cycle was repeated when she'd had Jameeka. The closest she'd come to loving someone was Dora Jenkins. Her grandmother fed her, kept her clean and protected her from the harsh realities of life the best she could. However, it wasn't enough, because she'd cut school, slept with men for money while setting them up to be robbed. There were times when she wondered if she would ever be able to love a man.

"Why are you so good to me?"

Lance buried his face in her silky hair. "Don't you know?"

Easing back, she met his gaze. "Know what?"

"You're special, Dina. I love everything there is to love about you."

His confession set off warning bells in her head as Dina struggled with her conscience. He'd fallen in love with someone who wasn't who he thought her to be; he'd fallen in love with a fraud.

She hadn't been Dina Gordon a month yet knew it would take more than a month to leave her sordid past behind in order to start over. Every day was a struggle, an uphill battle not to revert to Adina Jenkins, to lapse into the fast-talking, potty-mouth, trick-turning ho.

Karla, Sybil and Lance had all offered Dina Gordon a second chance to put her past firmly behind her, and she prayed she would succeed. And if she failed, it wouldn't be because she hadn't tried.

"You have to give me time because everything between us has happened so quickly."

Lance ran his hand over her hair. "I'm not asking you for anything. Especially not love. Either you feel it or you don't."

Dina closed her eyes. "It's not that I don't like you, Lance."

"Hush, Dina. You don't have to explain yourself—at least not to me. If ever you come to love me the way I love you, you won't have to say a word."

"How will you know?" she asked in a quiet tone.

"I'll know because I'll be able to feel it. It won't be in what you'll say but what you'll do. Love is quiet, darling, not loud and boisterous. And love can be communicated in complete silence. One of these days we'll look across the room at each other and know exactly what the other's feeling or thinking."

"Do you think that'll happen with us?"

"I know it will," he said confidently. "Now open your gift because we have to leave."

Pulling away, Dina removed the bow and paper. She opened the box to find a pair of heart-shaped earrings. The princess-cut diamonds winked at her like stars in a dark sky. Her mouth opened and closed quickly. "They're beautiful. I'm going to wear them tonight."

Lance took them from her as she removed the gold hoops from her ears and replaced them with the diamond studs, tucking her hair behind her ears. His smile was one of supreme satisfaction. The gems were perfect for her.

He winked at her. "You were meant to wear diamonds."

Dina's lowered her gaze demurely. "Thank you."

She took several steps and picked up her small evening purse and a black silk jacket with a Mandarin collar piped in red. Lance waited while she locked the door, then hand in hand they made their way down the stairs and out into the warm spring night.

Chapter 43

I'm the princess in a fairy tale. Lancelot is my prince and his apartment is our castle.

"What are you thinking about, baby girl?"

Dina pulled her gaze away from the lights in the buildings across the Hudson River to look at the man who'd done exactly what he'd promised to do: protect and take care of her. The flames from the votive on the table at LUA caught the brilliance of the precious stones in her ears and the warm, sensual glow in her eyes.

"It's not what but who."

"Who?" he asked as a mysterious smile softened her lush mouth.

Running a fingertip along her hairline, she smoothed several strands of hair behind her ear. "I was thinking about us."

Lance studied his right hand resting next to his place setting rather than stare at Dina. If she was going to reject him, then he wanted to hear, not see it. He was more than familiar with rejection. But now that he'd opened himself up to offer his heart to a woman for the first time in twenty-five years, he was mature enough to accept the consequences.

What he'd asked himself over and over was what was

there about Dina Gordon that made him seek her out, made him want to spend time with her? And why would he continue to see her when there was the possibility they would never be intimate?

Sharing a bed with Dina and not making love to her had tested his resolve. He'd promised not to touch her unless she gave her permission. But, damn, there were just so many cold showers and porn flicks he could put up with before resorting to other measures to relieve his sexual frustration.

"What about us?"

Dina knew she had to choose her words carefully or Lance would misconstrue her intent. She didn't know why he'd come into her life, but she didn't want to lose him. Unwittingly he'd become the man she'd spent most of her life searching for. Although she didn't view him as a father figure, there was something about him that *was* paternal. Fathers protected and cared for their children in the same manner he took with her.

There was one thing that had to be resolved before she took their relationship to the next level. She'd dealt with her claim that she was a virgin with the surgical procedure, but now she had to devise a plan to keep Lance interested in her until she was medically cleared. "I want us to become more than friends." Her smoky voice was lower than usual.

Lance stared Dina as if she'd spoken a foreign language. Had she read his mind? Did she know how much he wanted her? Not just her wit and companionship but all of her?

"Are you saying that you're ready to sleep with me?"

Dina lowered her gaze, staring at Lance through her lashes as a blush swept from her chest up to her hairline.

"I want to sleep with you, but I'm still not ready." She looked directly at him. "I feel something with you that I've never felt with other men who've kissed me. You make me want you, LL."

She hadn't lied. Each time she saw Lance the pull was stronger than it'd been the time before. She felt comfortable enough with him to crawl up on his lap like a trusting child. Whenever they were together, her world took on the brightness and goodness he radiated effortlessly. He'd said she was perfect when she knew he was perfect—for her.

Exhaling inaudibly a sigh of relief, Lance slumped back against the blond, curved Scandinavian-style chair. He'd mentally prepared himself for her rejection. "And I want you, too, baby girl. Like I told you before, I'm willing to wait for you to come to me."

"What if it's three months?"

Reaching across the table, he patted her hand. "Then it will be three months. What you don't understand is three months ago I didn't know Dina Gordon existed, so what's another three months?"

That's because Dina Gordon didn't exist three months ago. At least not the Dina Gordon he knew. Reversing their hands, she laced their fingers. Lance Haynes radiated strength, self-confidence and power.

"You're right. And since meeting you, I'm not the same woman I was a month ago."

He lifted sandy-brown eyebrows. "Is that good or bad?"

"It's very good, Big Daddy," Dina crooned, winking at him.

Lance returned her wink, squeezing her fingers gently. "Are you ready to order?"

"Yes."

Reluctantly he withdrew his hand and picked up the menu.

He was hungry.

He needed to eat.

But what he wanted was not listed on the menu.

It was seated across the table.

Chapter 44

Cory Cumberland opened one eye, peering at the clock on the nightstand on his side of the bed. It was ten-ten. Rolling over, he placed a hand on his wife's shoulder, shaking her gently.

"Wake up, darling. It's after ten."

Sybil moaned softly, pressing her face deeper into the softness of the pillow under her head. "I'm not going in today."

Cory sat up quickly. "What's the matter?"

She moaned again. "Nothing's the matter, Cory. I'm just not going to work today."

Resting a hand on her bare back, he ran his fingertips up and down her spine. "Are you feeling okay?"

Sybil rolled over onto her back and glared up at her husband. "What don't you understand, Cory Cumberland? I told you that I'm not going to work today. You've been complaining that we don't spend enough time together, so I'm going to accommodate you and stay home."

Cory's soulful eyes widened slightly. "Accommodate me, Sybil? Is that how you view spending time with your husband? Thanks but no, thanks."

Mumbling an expletive under her breath, Sybil swept

back the sheet and swung her legs over the bed. "I just changed my mind. I'm going to work."

Cory panicked, springing off the bed to stop his wife. "I'm sorry, baby," he apologized, wrapping his arms around her body. "Stay home with me. Please."

Sybil's arms remained at her sides when she wanted to hug Cory, tell him that he was forgiven. But something wouldn't let her relent. "Why are you sending me double messages, Cory? You bitch and moan that we don't take vacations together, that we're like two ships passing in the night, and now when I decide to take two days off you interrogate me. Why can't you just accept whatever I say without analyzing it?"

Resting his chin on the top of Sybil's head, Cory rocked her from side to side. "I am sorry, sweetheart. I'm just a little tense."

"What are you tense about?"

"I've been sitting around the house doing nothing while I wait for the programmers to work out the kinks in the software for the spy plane."

Sybil's arms came up and she placed her palms on Cory's solid pectorals. "I thought you went out yesterday."

"I went for a drive to Red Bank, hung around a while and then came back."

What Cory Cumberland couldn't tell his wife was that he'd gone to Atlantic City. He'd spent hours at the black-jack table trying to win back the money he'd lost. In the end he'd walked away with twenty dollars. A mere, shitty twenty dollars that wasn't enough to pay for the gas it took to drive there and back.

He was gambling—heavily. If it wasn't the casino, then it was the horses or lottery tickets. He won some and lost some, but even when he broke even it was as if he couldn't stop. The truth was he didn't want to stop.

Gambling was like a fever in his blood, the heat threatening to incinerate him whole. He'd begun gambling because he was bored. His wife worked long, erratic hours, and whenever they weren't together he found himself at a loss.

Before he'd met Sybil, he'd spent his spare time hanging out with his fraternity brothers. But one by one they married and the focus shifted to their wives and children. Now it was on a rare occasion when they got together, and if they did, it was always a family affair.

"Well, today I'm going to make sure you're not bored. I'm going to prepare brunch and later on tonight I'm taking you out."

Cory smiled. "Where are you taking me?"

Pressing her naked body to his, Sybil kissed his throat. "It's a surprise."

He knew enough not to pressure Sybil into disclosing her surprise. He would be patient and wait. Bending slightly, he picked her up and carried her into the bathroom. "I'll wash your back if you wash mine."

Sybil looped her arms around Cory's neck. "You've got yourself a deal, Mr. Cumberland."

"No, you didn't," Cory said when Sybil maneuvered into the parking lot behind Shaken Not Stirred. Her surprise was what he needed to relax and forget about his gambling losses.

He'd met his future wife at the Plainfield café frequented by aging beatniks, hippies, bohemians and those disenchanted with the establishment. On any given night the patrons were treated to an art exhibit, jazz music or poetry readings. It was the poetry readings Cory liked best.

The first time he'd seen Sybil, she'd been with another man. Two weeks later he'd seen her again, and this time she'd been alone. He'd approached her, offering to buy her a glass of wine. She'd refused the wine, saying she much preferred a cappuccino. He'd never drunk cappuccino or espresso, but after several dates with Sybil he'd come to enjoy coffee, tea and different cuts of steaks. Sybil Johnson had resigned her position as a high school guidance counselor to become a chef.

"This place hasn't changed in seven years."

They got out of the truck, Sybil moving closer to Cory when he put an arm around her waist. "It hasn't changed in more than thirty years. Same owners, same ambience," she said, smiling up at him.

"I can't remember the last time I came here."

"Remember when I catered the kiddie party in Philly this past April?" Cory nodded. "Before heading back home, I stopped for coffee. It was as if time had stopped. I saw some of the same people who came here when we were dating."

Lowering his head, he brushed a kiss over her parted lips. "Thanks, baby. You can surprise me anytime you want." He'd stopped frequenting Shaken Not Stirred once he found another favorite hangout closer to Princeton, where he'd enrolled in a graduate engineering program. He and Sybil had dated for a year, lived together for another year before deciding to marry.

"I'm glad you like it," she whispered, deepening the kiss.

They walked into the dimly lit café with a stage, a bar and dozens of small round tables. In the past, a cloud of smoke from cigarettes would have hung heavily in the air, but it was now the fragrant aroma of brewing coffee that greeted them.

Sybil and Cory found seats not far from the stage, where a tall, thin man with salt-and-pepper dreadlocks rapped a passionate poem about finding and losing his Nubian princess as a prerecording of African drumming provided the musical backdrop for his sonorous chanting that ended amid thunderous applause.

Cory stared at the enthralled expression on Sybil's face. He knew she'd suggested coming to the café as much for herself as for him. She loved art, jazz and poetry, while he had no interest in art, read only technical magazines and was partial to hip-hop and R & B. However, poetry readings were the exception. There was something about the spoken word that held him transfixed.

He leaned closer. "Good evening, my sister, may I buy you a glass of wine?"

Sybil turned, gazing lovingly at her husband. Those were the exact words he'd said to her what now seemed aeons ago when in reality it'd only been seven years. "Good evening, my brother," she said, playing along with him. "I hope you don't mind, but I'd much prefer a cappuccino."

Cory leaned closer, staring intently at the woman with whom he'd fallen in love on sight. His gaze caressed her raven-black hair fashioned into a chignon, her small, straight nose and high cheekbones she'd inherited from her Asian-born mother.

"Promise me you won't run away," he teased.

"I promise." Sybil watched Cory as he made his way

to the coffee bar. For a fleeting moment she experienced guilt, guilt that she *hadn't* spent much time with him.

She'd married Cory because he was the complete opposite of her father. He was sociable, peaceable and incredibly gentle. He wanted children, and Sybil knew he would make a wonderful father because he talked about raising their children differently from how they'd been raised.

His father had abandoned his mother and their three children the year Cory turned fifteen. His younger brother, who'd joined a street gang, was now serving a life sentence for capital murder. And his sister, an unwed mother with three children from three different men, had sought counseling and had taken control of her life to turn it around.

Sybil had promised Cory that they would start a family when they celebrated their fifth wedding anniversary. And she had six months before making good on her promise.

She watched him make his way over to the coffee bar. A woman waiting in line in front of him turned and said something to Cory. He nodded, then turned and pointed in Sybil's direction.

"What was that all about?" Sybil asked when he returned with her coffee. He'd ordered a beer for himself.

"She wanted to know if I was here with someone."

Sybil's eyes narrowed. "Hell, yeah, you're here with someone."

"She knows that now."

"How often do women hit on you?" she asked after taking a sip of the creamy coffee.

"She wasn't hitting on me."

"You think not?"

Cory frowned. "I know not. And even if she was, I wasn't biting."

"I hope not."

His frown deepened. "Where's all of this jealousy coming from, Sybil?"

She gave him a steady look. "You say I don't spend enough time with you, so I thought maybe you were looking for attention from other women."

"I told you before that I don't cheat. I didn't cheat when I dated and I definitely won't now that I'm married."

Sybil took another sip. "I was just checking."

There came a beat. "Is that why you decided to take a couple of days off? What's up? Don't you trust me?"

"Of course I trust you, Cory. If I didn't, I wouldn't stay with you."

Sybil schooled her expression to not reveal what she was feeling, had been feeling for a while. She knew she and Cory were growing apart, but that was because she was trying to grow her business. He claimed he understood, but did he really? Not when he complained of her not spending time with him.

It was the first time since she'd married Cory Cumberland that she wondered whether her marriage would make the five-year mark.

Chapter 45

Dina stared at her reflection in a room of wall-to-wall mirrors. The dance instructor, who went by the single name of Carlos, stood behind her. Sybil had called to tell her that she didn't have to come to work for the next two weeks because Carlos had rearranged his calendar to put her through an intense workout. As promised, Sybil paid her for her regular hours and the days when she would be in the studio.

Carlos, only several inches taller than Dina, met her gaze in the mirror. When she'd walked into the studio he'd set up in a room in the rear of his house, his first impulse was to recommend that she become a music video backup dancer. She had what most video producers and directors wanted—the look. What he saw was a dancer's body.

His dark eyes met hers. "First we're going to see how flexible you are. Hold on to the bar and lift your right leg."

Dina hesitated. He was asking her to lift her leg when today was the first day she was completely pain-free. Dr. Howe had examined her, saying she was healing nicely. He also said she could resume sexual intercourse in two weeks.

"How high?" she asked.

"See if you can rest your heel on the bar."

Slowly, as if testing how high she could raise her leg without experiencing some discomfort, Dina held on to the bar, leaned back slightly and rested the heel of the ballet slipper atop it. She felt a slight pulling between her legs but no pain. She shared a smile with the short, muscular man with a perfectly conditioned compact body in a black leotard and footless tights. When she'd walked into his studio, she'd had to force herself not to stare at the large bulge between his thighs. She'd known men who stuffed their briefs in order to look bigger, but she suspected Carlos's package was all his.

"Very good," Carlos said. "Now try the other one."

Dina lost count of the number of times she raised and lowered her legs. She was put through a stretching routine that made her feel as if she'd been pulled in every direction. Her tendons and muscles in places she didn't know she had figuratively and literally screamed. She ached—everywhere. Once back in her apartment, she took a hot shower and collapsed into bed.

After more than a week of stretching exercises, Carlos put on a CD of dance music. He sat on a chair, watching as Dina danced freestyle. She was familiar with the latest steps, had a natural rhythm…but something was missing.

Pushing a button on the portable CD player, he stopped the music while clapping his hands together. "Enough!"

Dina complied, glaring at the man with a curly ponytail that was as long as hers. At first she'd thought him soft because of the stereotype that all male dancers were gay, but there was something in the way he stared at her breasts and legs that told her he was definitely straight.

"What's the matter?"

"Are you a nice girl or a naughty girl, Dina?"

She blinked once. "Say what?"

"Nice or naughty?" he repeated.

"I'd like to think of myself as nice."

Carlos closed the distance between them. "I'm a man, Dina, and I wouldn't give a dollar for that performance."

Hands on hips, Dina lifted her chin in a defiant gesture. "What's wrong with it?"

Resting his hands on her shoulders, Carlos pulled her close. "You're a very sexy woman, but you don't dance like a sexy woman. You're going to have to learn to use what you've been given."

"And that is?"

"Hair, tits, ass and legs." He ignored her soft gasp. "You've good rhythm because you feel the music. Remember—when you're up on stage you're no long Dina Gordon but Sparkle. What you want is for every man in the room to think that you're dancing solely for him. In other words, I want you to give them a lap dance without sitting on them. I want every dick in the room to be standing at attention when you bend over and shake your ass. Have you ever seen a booty clap?"

Dina nodded rather than say she had. Not only did she know what it looked like, but she'd also done it.

Carlos smiled at Dina. "I want you to do it again, this time putting your hair, tits and ass into it."

The driving, pumping bassline beat started up again, and Dina knew that if she didn't dance the way Carlos wanted, then she could forget about entertaining at Sybil's private parties. She'd do anything the relentless, overbearing dance instructor wanted her to do to get his approval. He'd told her that Carlos would discharge her only when she pleased Carlos.

She'd lost weight she couldn't afford to lose from the strenuous workouts and developed muscles in her legs and thighs that weren't visible before. What she didn't want to do was look as if she were lifting weights.

If Carlos wanted freak, then she was going to give him freak personified. She was no longer Dina Gordon but Adina Jenkins, popping, locking and dropping her ass in order to get a man's attention. She didn't see the smirk stealing its way over Carlos's face, but she heard his applause when the dance number ended. They shared a knowing smile.

Carlos kissed her on both cheeks. "You're ready."

Chapter 46

The morning of the Fourth, Karla slipped out of bed, leaving Ronald snoring loudly. She couldn't believe how loudly he snored until she woke before him. And it wasn't that he snored all the time —just when he'd been drinking.

He'd offered to act as bartender for the soiree and had mixed several new concoctions he wanted to try out on their guests. She'd been adamant about not getting anyone so drunk that they either passed out or ended up in a vehicular accident. It was the lawyer in Karla that had surfaced.

She showered quickly and threw on a sundress to go outside to survey the area where a tent had been erected. Eight round tables, each with seating for four, were set up around the brick patio.

All of her consternation as to whether the outdoor kitchen would be completed on time was alleviated when the contractor called to tell her he was finished and would send her a bill for the cost overruns. His crew had worked around the clock to put in the outdoor fireplace.

She put up a pot of coffee, then began the task of taking out individually wrapped bouquets of red and white flowers that would serve as centerpieces for each table.

In keeping with the holiday color scheme, Karla had decided on white tablecloths with the red and white flowers in blue glass vases.

She'd taken several days off to prepare for the cookout because she wanted to put her personal signature on the gathering. Ronald had insisted she hire a party planner, but she told him she could easily handle a party of less than fifty invitees. The butcher had cut the differing meats to her specifications, and her favorite bakery had delivered a half a sheet cake made up of fresh strawberries atop shortcake.

The night before, she'd made coleslaw and potato salad using her mother's recipes; she'd also cooked a large dish of baked beans and marinated all of the meat. The only thing on her agenda was to make a fruit and tossed salads. The many ears of fresh, sweet bread-and-butter corn were shucked and in the refrigerator.

What Karla wanted was a traditional menu. No professional bartender or servers, no foie gras, caviar or sushi. Those she usually offered for a small cocktail party. She wanted her guests to eat, drink and have fun while doing it.

"Everything looks smashing."

Karla turned around. Ronald had come out of the house completely naked. Her gaze went to his smiling face before lowering to the thick, heavy sex hanging between his muscled thighs.

She returned his smile. "What are you trying to do? Make me horny?"

He approached her, cradling his penis in one hand. "Bet you a dollar you're wet."

Karla shook her head. "Now you know that I'm going to lose."

Pulling up the hem of her dress, his free hand went between her legs. "Damn, baby, you're like Niagara Falls." He withdrew his hand, the dress falling back around her knees; he rubbed his fingers together before putting them into his mouth and sucking loudly. Ronald winked at Karla. "Sweet," he crooned.

Karla felt as if she were on fire. Ronald had started something only she could finish. Slipping the straps of the dress off her shoulders, she stepped out of it. "I need a big, fat link before our guests arrive."

Ronald achieved a full erection within seconds. He and Karla had made love the night before like starving people pouncing on food. It was as if they couldn't get enough of each other. His wife had complained of tenderness in her breasts, so he knew she was ovulating. It was during *that* time of the month that her sex drive kicked into an even higher gear. They always made certain to attend their swinger group whenever she ovulated because Karla always needed multiple partners. Even he had to get some sleep.

"How do you want it, baby?"

Karla moved over to the fireplace, bracing her hands against the solid stone structure. "Let's break in this baby," she crooned as she turned to present Ronald with her back.

Looping an arm around her waist, Ronald eased her forward and pushed his blood-engorged sex inside his wife. He closed his eyes and groaned deep in his throat. This was his favorite position, taking her doggie-style. He was able to watch his dick slide in and out of her sweet pussy while it also permitted him deeper penetration.

Each time he pulled out, he thrust deeper. The juices from Karla clung to the profusion of hair surrounding his shaft. And it wasn't the first time he was thankful that he'd met and married a woman who never complained that she was too tired for sex or that she had a headache or that she had cramps. Karla King was always willing and ready for sex.

He felt his balls tightening and tried thinking of anything else but the exquisite pleasure straining for release. He didn't want to come. Not now. Slowing his thrusts, he cradled her breasts in his hands, squeezing gently. Karla's soft moans had become his undoing. She pushed her hips back as he thrust forward, the slapping of flesh meeting flesh disturbing the early-morning silence.

He forced himself to think of another of his sex partners—someone he'd met during the last swinger party, someone who'd asked to see him without his wife. It'd taken Ronald all of two seconds to give his approval.

Just thinking of his next liaison made him harder, and then the dam broke. He pulled out, ejaculating all over Karla's firm, round ass. She wasn't finished, so he inserted his finger and masturbated her until she came all over his hand.

Moaning out the last of her passion, Karla turned and smiled over her shoulder at her husband. Wrapping both arms around her waist, he pulled her back against his chest. He buried his face in her hair. "There's nothing better than early-morning lovemaking with all of nature as a witness."

"You're right. Will you join me in the Jacuzzi?"

He kissed the side of her neck. "Yes."

They returned to the house and made their way up the staircase. Both knew they would make love at least once more before their guests arrived.

Chapter 47

"Are you sure you're not lost?"

Lance took a quick glance at the navigational screen. "I'm very sure, Dina. We should be there in less than two minutes."

The drive from Irvington to Oldwick had taken longer than he'd anticipated because of a horrific accident that had brought traffic to a virtual standstill along a major road. The words were barely off his tongue when he turned off the narrow winding road to see a large white house built on a rise behind an overgrowth of old and newly planted trees. The Kings lived in one of the most exclusive enclaves in Oldwick.

Dina stared in awe at the house coming into view. Karla King lived in a mansion. Everything silently screamed opulence—from the professionally maintained landscape to the many luxury cars in a parking area at the side of the imposing white Colonial. Karla's house was the one she'd read about in her novels, a house with grand staircases, towering ceilings and filled with price-less objects that turned a house into a home.

She'd sent back her response card indicating she was bringing a guest. She'd debated whether to call Karla and ask if she should bring something to eat or drink, but in the end decided not to. What she didn't want to do was appear gauche. If Karla wanted her to bring something, then there was no doubt she would've noted it on the invitation.

It was to become her first social outing as Dina Gordon, and she prayed she would come through it without embarrassing Lance, her hosts and herself. Although an informal outdoor gathering, Dina knew it would not be the same as the ones she'd attended in the past.

Lance stopped next to a late-model Lincoln, cut off the engine and came around to assist Dina. He wondered how Dina had come to garner an invitation from someone who obviously lived quite well but hadn't asked because their relationship hadn't progressed to where he felt *that* comfortable with her.

He still found her an enigma. Just when he thought he was breaking through to get her to open up to him, she put up an invisible shield. What, he wondered over and over, was she hiding? Who was she hiding from? He'd done everything possible to get her to trust him, but she continued to keep him at a distance.

He reached for her hand and they made their way around the back of the house, where a small crowd had gathered under a large white tent. The rear of the house was as spectacular as the front. A large shaded patio area held an outdoor kitchen with a sink and stove, an inground pool and an unlit fireplace. It was apparent the Kings had spared no expense on their home.

Dina saw Karla with a tall man with wiry white hair, the two talking quietly in a corner. "There's Karla," she said to Lance. She steered him in the direction of the woman responsible for changing her life.

* * *

Karla turned away from Rhys to see Dina Gordon and a man coming in her direction. She assumed the man was the friend she'd mentioned. "Excuse me, Rhys, but I must welcome another one of my guests."

She came forward to meet Dina, who'd captured the attention of most, if not all, the men in attendance. Smiling, she shook her head. There were men who claimed to be "chick magnets." Well, Dina Gordon was a "man magnet." A pair of navy stretch cropped pants, a navy-blue-and-white-striped tank top and white-and-blue-striped espadrilles showed off her compact body to its best advantage.

She extended her hands. "Dina, I'm so glad you could make it." She and the petite woman exchanged air kisses.

Dina returned Karla's warm smile. The attorney looked different. A pair of walking shorts, a loose-fitting blouse and sandals had replaced her tailored suit and pumps. Even her hair was styled differently. Today she wore it up in a ponytail.

"Thank you again for inviting me. I'd like to introduce you to my very good friend. Lance, this is Karla King. Karla, Lancelot Haynes."

Lance nodded to Karla. "It's nice meeting you. I have something in the trunk of my car I need to bring in."

Karla angled her head, studying the man. It was obvious he was older than Dina, but how old she wasn't able to discern. There was something about him that was familiar as she mused where she had met or seen him before. Was he, she wondered, responsible for Dina leaving her abusive boyfriend?

"You didn't have to bring anything, Lance. May I call you Lance?"

Lance smiled. "Of course I don't mind. As to bringing something, I was raised never to come to someone's home empty-handed."

"True," Karla drawled. "Then I thank you."

Lance smiled at Dina. "I'll be right back."

Karla waited until Lance walked away, then took Dina's hand. "I want to introduce you to my husband while we wait for your *friend*. Then I'll introduce the two of you to the others."

Dina picked up on her tone immediately. "Just in case you're wondering, we're only friends."

"I wasn't insinuating otherwise, Dina," Karla countered. "I didn't invite you to my home to get into your business," she countered.

"I'm sorry, but I suppose I still have a problem trusting people. It's not that I don't trust you," Dina added quickly, "but—"

"Don't apologize, Dina," Karla said, interrupting her. "I understand where you're coming from. Now come meet Ronald."

Ronald King, wearing a bibbed apron that had *Griller Killer* stamped on the front, checked pieces of chicken and other meats for doneness. He was as casually dressed as the others, in a pair of shorts, a T-shirt and sandals.

Karla tapped his shoulder to get his attention. "Darling, I'd like you to meet a friend."

Ronald turned, his eyes widening appreciably when he saw the woman with his wife. Her gold-brown skin, black hair and incredibly beautiful face called to mind the dolls sold in toy stores. Smiling, dimples winking in his chiseled cheeks, he put down a long-handled fork.

"Whom do I have the pleasure of meeting?" he asked in a deep voice that seemed to rumble in his chest.

Dina extended her hand. "Dina Gordon."

She'd figured out Ronald King in one sweeping glance because she'd met more Ronalds that she cared to remember. Tall, with unquestionably sensual masculine good looks and believing he was truly a gift to all women, he wasn't above using everything in his manly arsenal in his quest to seduce a woman. If she'd been Adina Jenkins, she would've taken special pleasure in bringing the cocky Ronald King to his knees. But she wasn't Adina, and Ronald was her friend's husband. And just as game recognized game, freak recognized freak, and she knew unequivocally that Ronald was a freak.

"Welcome to our home," Ronald said politely.

Dina smiled. "Thank you for inviting me."

Karla watched the exchange between Dina and her husband, reading his mind. She wanted to tell him that if he thought Dina would sleep with him, then he was sorely mistaken. There was no way she would agree to it.

"As soon as Dina's date comes back, I'll introduce her to the others," she told Ronald. The spark of interest in Ronald's hungry gaze dimmed when she mentioned *date*.

Lance returned carrying a case of imported champagne. "Where should I put this?" he asked Karla.

Ronald went completely still when he recognized the man holding the box of wine. "I'll take that," he offered, taking the box and placing it on the floor next to a built-in refrigerator. "Aren't you Lance Haynes?"

Lance's eyes narrowed slightly as he met Ronald's gaze. "Yes. Have we met before?"

Ronald shook his head. "We didn't meet personally, but I was in your seminar in Vegas at the computer show a couple of years back." He extended his hand. "Ronald King."

Lance shook his hand, smiling. "Well, Ronald, you certainly have me at a distinct disadvantage. I hope I didn't make a fool of myself while up there."

"No way, man. It was worth hanging out in Vegas in the middle of July just to hear you speak."

Karla patted Ronald's shoulder. "I hate to break up what I know is going to turn into computer talk, but I want to introduce Lance and Dina to the others before getting them something to drink."

Ronald acquiesced to his wife's suggestion, saying, "We'll talk later, Lance. And thanks for the champagne."

Lance nodded to Ronald. He didn't remember him, but it was apparent Ronald King knew him. What Lance found strange was that there hadn't been that many brothers at the computer show. It was possible that Ronald came to his seminar because he'd been the only African-American facilitator on the workshop schedule, so there was no doubt he'd wanted to hear what he had to say.

He'd spent two days in his hotel room writing, editing and rewriting his presentation. He'd been asked to talk to potential entrepreneurs who were contemplating going into business for themselves. His topic was "Begin small, think big." The session was heavily attended because most wanted to hear how a black man had grown his company of one into one that employed thousands worldwide. Most of his company's employees lived in Malaysia and India because it'd become more feasible and profitable to outsource his business.

Karla introduced him and Dina to her guests. All were married couples, the women older than Dina and their husbands closer to his age. He'd discovered the Kings' guest list was ethnically and racially balanced.

"I'll leave Dina to introduce you to her boss," Karla told Lance.

Sybil Cumberland turned when hearing Karla mention Dina's name. Her expression mirrored surprise when she saw her. "How are you? I didn't know Karla had invited you."

Dina smiled at her boss, who looked completely different from the chef who ran SJC Catering like a drill sergeant. Today she wore a red slip dress over a matching bathing suit. Her hair was loose, falling around her shoulders. She looked soft and very feminine.

"I didn't say anything because I didn't want to alert you. Maybe you didn't want to socialize with your employees." In another week, she and Sybil would not only work together but also socialize together.

Sybil waved her hand. "We're not at SJC Catering, so that doesn't apply today."

Dina felt completely relaxed with Sybil for the first time. "This is my friend Lance. Lance, Sybil Cumberland." The two exchanged handshakes.

"It's nice meeting you, Lance." Her gaze shifted, her expression noticeably softening. "Here's my husband." Cory Cumberland had returned carrying a plastic crate filled with glasses.

Dina thought him the perfect mate for Sybil. He claimed a nerdy type of conservative attractiveness that reminded her of her childhood friend Irving Gordon.

"The bartender returns," he announced loudly. He'd worked his way through college waiting tables and tending bar. Mixing drinks came as easy to him as turning on the tap for water. There was never a need to hire a professional mixologist when he was in attendance.

He hesitated putting down the crate when he recognized the man standing next to Sybil. "Lance Haynes?"

Lance gave him a do-I-know-you? look. "Yes."

Cory set down the crate. "Ronald and I sat in on your seminar in Vegas. Man, you were incredible."

Lance wondered about the odds of meeting two black men at a party who were in the same field as he. He flashed a modest smile. "Thank you."

Cory wiped his hands on the towel on the portable bar, then extended his right one. "Cory Cumberland."

"I guess you know who I am," Lance teased, shaking the proffered hand. His arm went around Dina's waist. "And this is Dina Gordon."

Cory nodded, barely glancing at the woman with Lance. He'd never told anyone, but he envied Lance Haynes. The man had started with practically nothing and now he was a multimillionaire. He knew he'd never achieve Lance's earning status until he ran his own company. Whenever he bet on a horse, the roll of the dice, the turn of a card or a purchased lottery ticket, his wish was always the same—to win big so he could set up his own business.

Blinking as if coming out of a trance, Cory looked at Dina Gordon for the first time. What he saw hit him like a punch to the gut. The woman with Lance Haynes was perfect, just as the software genius's life was perfect. Talk about hitting the jackpot big-time. He wondered, if Lance wasn't who he was, would Dina be with him?

"Hello, Dina. What can I get you to drink?"

"I'll have a club soda."

"A club soda with what?"

"Just a club soda."

Cory reached into the ice bin under the bar and shoveled ice into a glass, then opened a bottle of club soda and filled it with the clear sparkling liquid. He handed it to her. "What can I get you, Lance?"

Lance perused the many bottles of top-shelf liquor lined up on a shelf behind the bar. "I'll have a scotch neat."

Dina sipped her beverage, meeting Sybil's gaze over the rim. "It's strange not to see you cooking."

Sybil smiled. "I offered, but the grill-meister threatened me with bodily harm if I even breathed on his grill. You'd think I'd slapped his newborn."

Cory handed Lance his drink. "Lance, perhaps you can explain to the ladies that a man's grill is like his car—you don't touch it without permission."

Lance raised his glass, touching it to Cory's when he lifted his. "It's as easy as ABC. You don't touch a man's grill or a man's car, and please don't touch a knob on his home theater unless you have security clearance."

"Here, here, my brother," Cory chanted.

Sybil placed her wineglass on the bar and looped her arm through Dina's. "I don't know about you, but all this man talk is turning my stomach. Let's get something to eat."

Chapter 48

Ronald waited until everyone sat down at the tables under the tent to eat before he turned off the grill. He made his way over to the bar for a drink. "Wait up, Cory," he called out as Cory came out from behind the bar. "I need something to quench my thirst."

"What do you want?"

"Make me a double martini." Resting his elbow on the smooth surface, he turned and stared at the people who'd come to his home to eat, drink, relax and enjoy a day off from whatever it was they did. "I can't believe *the* Lance Haynes is sitting in my backyard."

Cory nodded, filling a shaker with ice. "No shit. I truly want to pick the man's brain to find out how he set up his own business."

"He told us how he did it in Vegas."

"No, he didn't, Ronald. The man's real slick. He alluded to it, but he never actually said how he did it. Don't get me wrong—I loved his presentation. But he didn't give up anything concrete."

"Why should he, Cory?"

"Why shouldn't he?"

Ronald leaned in closer. "Just because he's a brother you think he should spill his guts? The rest of the guys don't do it, so why should he? Walt Disney didn't let the cat out of the bag when it came to animation until he actually perfected it."

"What happened to helping a brother out?"

"Fuck a brother!" Ronald said angrily.

"Yo, man, lighten up," Cory said, shocked at Ronald's outburst. "I'm not saying he has to give away his secret for success."

"That's exactly what you're saying," Ronald insisted. "We all start out on equal footing, but it's the ones who go the extra step, work a little harder than the others, who become success-story heroes and heroines. Just look at you and Sybil. You've worked hard to get what you want. You didn't stand around with your hand out begging for scraps off someone else's table. You worked your ass off to put yourself through college. Cory, man, you made it because you wanted more than just enough to get by. You didn't become a baby daddy or piss away your money by snorting shit, like so many others do when they get more than two nickels to rub together."

What Cory wanted to tell Ronald was that he wanted his own business; he wanted to be in charge of his own destiny, like his wife. Sybil had the luxury of accepting or rejecting whatever client she chose. He wanted to deal with projected profit margins the way she did. It'd been Sybil's money that had purchased the West Orange property, not his.

He hadn't wanted to move to West Orange yet had relented because she held the purse strings. When it came to Sybil, it was never his money or her money but *their* money. But that didn't make things any more palatable because he believed the man should be the breadwinner. He knew his way of thinking was archaic, but Cory Cumberland had turned into Gavin Cumberland. His father had worked odd jobs while his mother had had a secure position in hotel management. In the end, because his father couldn't feel like a man, he left.

While Ronald admitted that he didn't mind that Karla had the greater earning power of the two, Cory didn't feel the same. Many thought he was living the American dream with a talented wife and a house in an upscale suburban community, but he was miserable. He wanted his own business and he wanted children. He didn't know why he'd agreed to the five-year stipulation to wait before starting a family, but he realized Sybil wouldn't have married him unless he went along with her carefully mapped-out plan as to how she wanted to run her life.

"I know you're right, Ronald, but—"

"If you know I'm right, then why are you whining like a bitch?" Ronald said, cutting him off.

Cory glared at his friend. "I am not a bitch." He'd enunciated each word.

Ronald knew he'd stepped over the line. "I'm sorry, man. I wasn't calling you a bitch. It's just that I've learned to be grateful for what I've been given and I think you should do the same. It's hard out here for our folks, especially in our field. Remember—we counted the number of brothers at that convention. There wasn't enough to make two teams for a baseball game."

Cory stirred the martini and poured it through a strainer into a chilled glass. "That's why I suggested setting up an organization of black software engineers like the black accountants and the other professions."

"I don't agree with you. This field is too new for us to isolate, alienate and segregate ourselves. How are we going to know what's going on if we're on the outside looking in? Lance Haynes is the exception, not the norm. Once there're more Lance Hayneses, then I'd be glad to step up and join up."

"Here's your drink."

Ronald raised the glass to his mouth and took a deep swallow. Iciness, then warmth, spread throughout his chest. "Damn, that's good." He took another sip. "What do you think of Haynes's woman?"

Cory gaze shifted to where Dina and Lance sat at a table with an older couple. "What about her?"

"Karla said they're just friends, but I find it very hard to believe he's not sleeping with her."

"Why can't you believe it, Ronald?"

Ronald shook his head. "She has a certain innocence about her, but I think it's all a facade. Did you see the way she walks?"

A smile found its way over Cory's face. "Who could miss it."

"I tell you, man, she's a freak. Every woman I've known with a nasty-ass walk is a freak."

"How can you tell?" Cory asked.

"I just know." He stared at Dina as she smiled at something Judge Weichert's wife had said to her. He felt the flesh between his legs stir restlessly. It'd been a long time since he'd wanted to make love to a woman he'd just met, and Dina Gordon definitely turned him on. The last woman who'd turned him on like that he married.

"Shut down the bar, Cory, and come eat."

Chapter 49

It was late afternoon when Dina found herself sitting next to Karla under the shade of a large white umbrella. Most of the other guests were either reclining or sleeping on lounge chairs set up around the pool. Several men, Lance included, had retreated to an area of the patio to watch an action movie on a large built-in screen in an enclosed alcove next to the pool house.

Karla ran the back of her hand over her forehead. "I think I drank too much. Did you get enough to eat and drink, Dina? Because if you didn't, then I'll—"

"I'm good," Dina said, cutting her off.

Karla stared at Dina under lowered lids. Her former client appeared totally relaxed, and no doubt having an incredibly wealthy *friend* made her life less stressful. Ronald had told her that Lance Haynes was known in the computer world as the black Bill Gates.

"How's work, Dina?"

Dina smiled at Karla. "It's good."

"How many hours a week do you put in?"

"Right now I'm clocking between ten and fifteen."

"Is that enough to pay your rent?"

"No. But I'm going to be working with Sybil when she hosts private parties, and what I'll earn from them will more than pay my rent for the month. If I work two or three times a month, then I can really save some money."

Karla sat up, her curiosity piqued. "Private parties?"

Dina also sat up, swinging her legs over the side of the lounge chair. "Yes. I'm going to work as an exotic dancer for bachelor parties." She'd lowered her voice so she wouldn't be overheard by another woman sitting close by.

Karla pushed off the chair. "Come into the house with me," she ordered Dina. "We need to talk."

Dina followed Karla into the spacious coolness of the opulent mansion filled with furnishings she'd only glimpsed in magazines, wondering if she would ever live as grand as Ronald and Karla King. And there was no doubt that Cory and Sybil Cumberland also lived well. She'd discovered that all of the Kings' guests were professionals: lawyers, doctors, college professors and a state judge. Several were CEOs of their own companies.

She made certain not to call attention to herself. She responded when spoken to, mouthing what she knew were the appropriate quips when women smiled while their men gave her lecherous stares. If Lance noticed their hungry gazes, he didn't reveal it. Most times she could find him nearby but not so close as to stifle her. Whenever she wanted something, he'd do her bidding. Publicly he was as attentive as he was whenever they were alone together.

Karla led her into an in-the-home office, closing the door behind them. "Please sit down, Dina."

She complied, sinking down to a sand-colored suede love seat. "What do you want to talk about?" Dina asked Karla when she took a matching chair a few feet away.

"Sybil's private parties."

"What about them?"

"When you say work—exactly what type of work will you be doing?"

Dina stared at Karla, wondering how much she should divulge about her upcoming gig as an exotic dancer for a ballplayer's birthday party. There was no doubt she and Sybil were good friends—why else would Sybil hire someone without a social security card or prior work experience? Besides, she trusted Karla implicitly because how else would she have gotten her name changed legally without a court appearance?

"I'm going to become an exotic dancer." Lowering her voice conspiratorially, even though there was no one in the room to overhear them, Dina told Karla about her training and commitment to perform for Sybil's clients.

Karla felt a rush of excitement as she listened to Dina tell what she had to go through with a professional dance instructor to get her body in shape to perform for rich men living out their sexual fantasies by watching women prance around in next to nothing. She knew firsthand about entertaining men, finding it a power trip. Karla was as good at what she did because she made certain every man in attendance thought she'd become his private dancer. She was smiling when Dina revealed the costume that had been created expressly for her.

Dina's eyes were sparkling with excitement. "I can't explain how I felt when I tried it on for the first time. And the moment I put on the mask I truly felt as if I was Sparkle, the green fairy."

Karla nodded, smiling. "Make them pay, Dina. The men you're going to dance for aren't the guys who hang out at the tits-and-ass bar on the weekend because they have nothing else to do except watch sports channels.

And I know Sybil well enough to know that she's going to charge them through the nose, so in addition to what she's going to pay you, you should match it in tips."

Eyes wide, Dina stared at Karla as if hearing a language she didn't understand. Was the lawyer saying that she could possibly make a thousand or more in tips? "How much do you think I can make in tips?"

"If you don't come away with at least a grand, then it's not a good night. Most of these men will blow that much banging Vegas hookers with fake breasts that make her look as if she's wearing basketballs. You're young, pretty and everything about you is natural. Even within the realm of fantasy, men want reality.

"You'll learn to convey that without opening your mouth when they tuck a bill into your G-string that the bidding starts with fifties. If someone gives you a twenty, then give it back until he ups the ante. If you think top-shelf, then you'll be top shelf."

"How do you know so much about this?" Dina asked Karla, thinking perhaps that at one time she'd had a client who was an exotic dancer.

A faraway look filled Karla's dark eyes. "I used to dance." She ignored Dina's slight gasp. "I needed money to supplement my partial scholarships."

Dina nodded. Like herself, Karla did what she had to do to survive. "Were you good, Karla?"

A secret smile softened the lawyer's lips. "Yes, Dina. I was very good." Her eyebrows lifted. "I suppose you should get back to your friend before he comes looking for you."

Dina stood up. "He probably doesn't realize that I'm missing."

Karla wanted to tell Dina that she was wrong about

Lance Haynes. Although he hadn't hovered over her, he'd been aware of where she was at all times. "Even if he doesn't, I don't want him to think that I'm monopolizing his woman."

Smiling, Dina averted her gaze. It felt good to be referred to as Lance's woman. She wanted to belong to him in every way possible. It'd been more than four weeks since her procedure and she was ready to sleep with Lancelot Haynes.

"It was nice talking to you, Karla. And thank you for the tip about tipping."

"Anytime you want to talk to me—about anything—then call me, Dina. I was where you are now, and if it hadn't been for one of my professors, I certainly wouldn't be who I am today. We all need mentors and I'm personally appointing myself your mentor."

There was a moment of silence as Dina bit down on her lower lip. "Thank you."

Karla waved a hand. "Now go and get your man before some of these sex-starved heifers try to seduce him."

"But—but—they're married," Dina sputtered.

"When does marriage stop a man or woman from straying? Those so-called nice folks lounging around my backyard all have closets filled with rattling skeletons, yours truly included in the mix. So don't fool yourself into believing they're above reproach. What you'll eventually discover is that beyond the mansions and manicured lawns lies a moneyed world filled with sex, power, seduction and an occasional scandal. But we do what we do best—we bury our shit before it starts to stink.

"Lance Haynes is a part of that world, even though he's low-key. When you invited him to come with you, you had no inkling that my husband and Sybil's would know him. It's a very small world in which you're going to become a major player."

"How do you know this?" Dina was certain Karla could hear her heart beating inside her chest.

"You're going to marry Lance, and the moment you do your life will never be the same. You've changed your name but not your face. Now what I'm going to say to you is free advice."

"What's that?"

"You can run from your past, but you can't hide it. When you become Mrs. Lance Haynes, I suggest you keep a low profile. No unnecessary photographs. What may save you is that Lance is quiet and unassuming. Try to live your life away from the spotlight and you'll have your happily ever after."

"Do you think I'll jeopardize my future with Lance if I go through with my commitment as a private dancer?"

Karla shook her head. "No. Right now you're not married to him, and as a single woman you have a right to do anything you want. Even when you marry, you should always maintain a measure of independence and autonomy. The man's your partner, not your jailor or keeper." She waved her hand again. "Go, Dina."

Waiting until the door closed behind the younger woman, Karla walked over to the window and stared out at the beginnings of a Japanese garden. Talking with Dina had sparked memories of her eye-popping, jaw-dropping routine as Chocolate Ice.

She'd loved the money, but craved the attention she got from the men who'd come to see her perform. She'd cautioned Dina about independence and autonomy. In her marriage with Ronald they claimed both. The problem was she was getting bored with their open marriage because there wasn't anyone in their Open Door circle she wanted to sleep with. Sex with her husband was not only satisfying but fulfilling.

The rules for the Open Door mandated couples only, so Ronald wouldn't be able to attend without her or vice versa. Maybe if she told him that he could get another member to sleep with him off-site, then he would be amenable to her opting out.

The urge to return to dancing was something she thought about occasionally. She'd challenged herself when she pushed her body to extremes executing splits and contortions; she'd also loved the attention from the men who were enthralled by her physical prowess and she'd loved counting her tips at the end of the night. The high she'd derived from dancing was something that couldn't be duplicated—not even when she had sex with her husband.

Chapter 50

"**A**re you ready to leave, baby girl?"

Dina opened her eyes to find Lance hovering above her. The sun had set, taking with it the heat. The sky had darkened, and stars littered the nighttime sky like precious stones scattered on dark blue velvet. She couldn't believe she'd fallen asleep on the chaise.

Sitting up, she ran her hand over her forehead and hair. "How long have I been asleep?"

"Not long."

"How long is not long?" she asked, embarrassed that she'd fallen asleep when she should've been interacting with Karla and Ronald's other guests.

She remembered after talking to Karla about becoming Sparkle, she'd returned to the pool area to relax and wait for her food to digest before taking off her shoes to dangle her legs and feet in the heated pool. Although the invitation had indicated that she should bring a swimsuit, she hadn't because she wanted to wait before exposing herself to the chemicals in the water that might react adversely with her surgically altered vaginal area. Dr. Lowe had reassured her that she'd healed completely, but she was still apprehensive.

Dina also recalled drinking a glass of champagne with

the others while enjoying a slice of the most delicious strawberry shortcake she'd ever tasted. She'd discovered the contrast of the premium wine on her palate and the tartness of the fresh strawberries tantalizing; she'd downed two glasses of champagne before crawling up on the chaise and closing her eyes.

Lance cupped her elbow and pulled her gently to her feet. She swayed slightly before he righted her. "Don't worry about it, Dina," he whispered near her ear. "You weren't the only one sleeping."

She glanced around to find others on recliners and chaises, sound asleep. Dozens of lighted votives surrounded the perimeter of the pool and were set out on the tables. The flickering flames competed with light from strategically placed floodlights that reflected off the columns of the towering white Colonial-style mansion.

Leaning against Lance to maintain her balance, Dina slipped her feet into her espadrilles. "You still shouldn't have let me sleep," she chastised softly.

Lance wanted to tell Dina not to agonize over something that wasn't that socially inept, but held his tongue. He didn't want to argue with her. When he'd accepted the invitation to accompany her to Oldwick, he never could've imagined meeting two other African-American men who were also into computer engineering. After viewing a classic Bruce Willis action movie, he, Ronald and Cory had huddled together to discuss the merits of a new program recently introduced by a company challenging several computer giants.

One hour became two, then three, and before long they were deeply engrossed in the pros and cons of testing configurations of software compatibility and other embedded software. While some of the other men discussed sports, they'd discussed high-tech electronics. He'd taken furtive glances at Dina on one of the lounge chairs near the pool, but hadn't suspected she'd fallen asleep.

"Let's make our goodbyes before leaving."

They found Karla with Sybil. The two women were laughing and talking softly with each other. Karla noticed them first.

"I take it you're leaving."

Dina nodded as she swallowed back a yawn. "Yes, we are. Thank you for everything."

Karla smiled. "I want to thank you for coming." Her gaze shifted to Lance. "Ronald and I thank you for the champagne. I'm afraid our very thirsty guests drank more than half the case. Luckily I told Ronald to keep out three bottles for us." Lance Haynes had brought twelve bottles of a much-sought-after imported champagne.

Lance pulled Dina closer to his side. "I'd like to thank you for your generous hospitality. Dina and I would like to reciprocate. Whenever you and Ronald have a free weekend, we'd like you to come up to West New York for some R & R. I've already extended an invitation to Cory and Sybil to join us."

"I'm going to speak for Ronald when I say we'd love to come. Dina, please call me once you select a date."

Dina nodded numbly. She realized Lance had said *we*—not *I*—when he'd invited the Kings and the Cumberlands to his home and wondered if Karla had picked up on the reference that they were a couple. The reality was that she and Lance weren't a couple. It'd been weeks since she'd spent the night in his guest room, and after the one encounter when he hadn't been able to contact her Lance hadn't stayed over at her apartment.

They went out to dinner, took in a movie. He picked

her up after work on weekends, and no matter how late the hour he always saw her to her door. Dina had insisted he take her home to convalesce without bringing his attention to her procedure; she also found that she liked being alone because it gave her time to discover exactly who she was. Sure, she was supposedly the new and improved Dina Gordon, but she was also cognizant that Adina Jenkins lurked just below the surface of her newly created persona.

Whenever alone in her apartment, she spent the time reading books and magazines about those who vacationed in exotic places and hosted spectacular parties that were usually connected to their favorite charities. She'd found out that the privileged lived ho-hum lives but were constantly looking for ways to fill up the empty hours that came from not having a regular nine-to-five.

There had been a time when she'd existed like what she mentally referred to as the PP—or the pretty people—because it seemed as if they wasted countless hours perfecting their appearances. Even the men, who professed to be metrosexuals, were engaging in procedures that kept them physically at the top of their game.

Like the PPs, she'd partied till all hours of the night, then slept during the day. Her only concern was how she looked and how others perceived her. It was important to be seen and even more important with whom she was seen.

She'd changed her identity, yet she felt she was living in a parallel world because the difference between the PP at the Kings' and those in Brooklyn was where they lived and the source of their income. The New Jersey PPs were deemed legitimate because they paid taxes on their earnings while the mantra of the Brooklyn PPs she'd run with was *All I have to do is stay black and die*.

"Lance and I will try to pick a date that is convenient for everyone."

Lance and I. The instant the three words left her tongue Dina knew she'd validated the supposition that she and Lance were a couple. But they weren't a couple. They were friends who had a platonic relationship.

She felt the heat of Lance's gaze on her face as his fingers tightened on her waist. Had he given Karla the impression that they were a couple because that's what he actually wanted? Or was he testing Dina Gordon? And if he was, had she passed or failed the test?

Raising her head, she smiled up at him. "Darling, I'm ready to leave whenever you are." The endearment slipped out as if she'd called him that countless times before. The hand at her waist tightened against her flesh before relaxing.

This was one time Dina hadn't lied to Lance. She was ready to leave. She'd overindulged on food and drink.

"I want to thank you," Lance said as he started up the car.

Dina glanced at his profile. "For what?"

"For asking me to come with you today. I spend so much time entertaining clients that I've forgotten how to socialize without inking a deal."

She smiled. "You're welcome. But weren't you, Cory and Ronald talking business?"

"No. We were talking about computers. That's very different from engaging a client whom you want to sign on with your company."

"So you had a good time."

"I had a great time."

"So did I," she agreed. "I can't believe I had two glasses of champagne."

Lance slowed down as he came to a sign that indicated he was entering a deer crossing area. "I doubt if you drank one glass because—remember—the flute was only half-filled."

Pressing the back of her head to the headrest, she closed her eyes. "I still drank it."

"Don't agonize over it, baby. You're not going to turn into an alcoholic with one or even two glasses of champagne." He pressed a button on the steering wheel, and within seconds the car was filled with soft-playing jazz. "Do you want me to change the station?"

Dina didn't open her eyes. "No. It's nice." And it was. The soothing music was smooth and relaxing. Lance had driven more than ten miles when she said, "I'd like to stop at my place to pick up a change of clothes." She wasn't scheduled to go to work until Saturday night, when she would give her first performance as Sparkle. Lance had surprised her when he'd revealed he'd taken off the rest of the week to spend time with her.

Lance's fingers tightened on the steering wheel. Had he heard Dina correctly or was it wishful thinking because he'd wanted her to stay over with him? He'd told her that he was taking time off from work to take her on a drive up to New England.

"Okay."

The single word failed to convey the feeling of euphoria racing through Lance. He'd waited a long time for Dina to come to him on her own accord. It was the first time in his life he believed the adage that patience was truly a virtue.

Chapter 51

Dina used Lance's guest bedroom to cleanse her face of makeup, brush her teeth then take a leisurely shower. She knew when she'd taken her bag from him and walked into the bedroom, closing the door behind her, he'd been disappointed. His crestfallen expression spoke volumes. What he didn't know was that she planned to sleep with Lance—in his bedroom and in his bed.

After moisturizing her body with a lightly scented body cream, she slipped into a delicate cotton nightgown that ended at her knees. The white garment with narrow straps holding up the lace-trimmed bodice made her look delicate and virginal.

Staring at her reflection in a full-length mirror, she undid her braid, brushed it vigorously. She stood motionless trying to decide whether to braid it or leave it to hang down her back. Every man Adina had slept with had wanted her to take her hair down. What she had to remember was that Adina was gone and Dina had taken her place. Pulling her hair over her shoulder, she braided it without securing the ends.

Slowly and cautiously she walked out of her bedroom and down the hall to Lance's. Peering into the room, she realized he was still in the shower when the sound of running water came through the open door of the adjoining bathroom. She walked in and got into bed, pulling the sheet up and over her body. The subtle scent of aftershave wafted in her nose. A soft sigh escaped her as she closed her eyes and waited for Lance to come to bed.

Lance touched a switch on the wall between the bathroom and the bedroom, illuminating the space between the two rooms. He didn't notice the small mound on the far side of the California king bed until he sat down to get in. A rush of heat swept through the lower part of his body as blood hardened his sex.

Dina had finally come to him. Mixed emotions of elation and cautiousness made it impossible to move, to get into bed. He was also faced with the responsibility of introducing her to sex—an act so natural and elemental for life.

If Dina Gordon had been any other virgin, he would've run in the opposite direction. But she wasn't, and because he'd fallen in love with her he wanted to run to, and not away from, her. Forcing his legs to move, he eased back the sheet and slipped into bed next to her.

Without warning, Dina turned to face Lance, her chest touching his. "I almost fell asleep waiting for you."

Her smoky-voiced invitation was almost Lance's undoing as he reached for her, but he stopped himself in time. He didn't know why he had to keep reminding himself that this was to become her first time and he wanted to make the occasion special—for her and for himself.

Resting his arm over her hips, he splayed his hand over her hip. "Are you sure you're ready?"

Dina pressed her face between his neck and shoulder. "No, LL, I'm not sure. But I know that I want you to make me feel like a woman."

His hand moved up to her head. "But you are a woman, Dina."

"I'm only half a woman," she admitted. "Help me. Please help me."

Dina needed Lance's touch, his total possession, to exorcise the number of men who'd used her body for their own selfish motives. It'd begun with the man who'd taken her virginity because he saw her when she'd mistakenly walked into the bedroom to find her mother on her knees with his penis in her mouth. She would've run if not for the sucking sounds coming from Bernice. It was the same sound kids made when they licked an ice pop. She'd turned to leave, but she wasn't quick enough. The man had smiled at her, then licked his lips. He came back to the apartment two days later, opening the door and walking in to find her alone. It took less than five minutes, but when he walked out, she was left bleeding, in pain and clutching a ten-dollar bill for the loss of her innocence. It took years before she realized girls who were sexually abused oftentimes grew up to become promiscuous women.

Working for Payne had become somewhat of a blessing for her because if she hadn't had to concentrate on a particular man to seduce, there was no doubt she would've slept with many more men.

Sensing Lance's indecision and apprehension, she pressed her breasts to his chest. "Don't make me embarrass myself by begging you, Big Daddy."

Lance heard Dina's impassioned plea. Didn't she know how much he wanted her, wanted to make love to her? He wanted nothing more than to be inside her, but he knew he couldn't take her as he had other women.

He kissed her hair. "Do you trust me, baby girl?"

"Yes."

"Then I want you to trust me to try to make it special for you. What I can't promise is that I won't hurt you, but I'll try to make it go easy for you."

"Why is it that I just noticed something about you that I hadn't before?"

"What is it?"

"You talk too much."

Lance laughed softly. "Are you telling me to shut up?"

"No," Dina countered, "I'm hoping you'll stop talking."

Lance knew she was frightened because he could feel her shaking, her heart fluttering in her chest like a frightened bird.

Me. Why? he thought. Why did he have to be the one to take her virginity?

Why not you? the silent voice continued, taunting Lance. Was he not worthy to become the first man in the life of the woman he loved? Wasn't it better that she would be introduced to sex by someone who loved her rather than someone who saw her as another conquest?

"Done, baby girl."

Dina sucked in her breath when Lance moved over her and lifted her nightgown and eased it up her body and over her head. The heat from his body and the intermittent brush of his erection against her thigh fired her nerve endings, and she clenched her teeth. When she'd seen Lancelot Haynes for the first time she'd known instinctually there was something special about him, something she could trust. And now that he'd touched her, she realized her instincts had been right. He hadn't ripped her nightgown, as so many others had done in their quest to show her that they were the *man* and that she was only there for their pleasure and domination.

All of the lies, subterfuge, schemes and scams vanished within seconds when Lance stared down at her naked body. There was enough light coming from the alcove for Dina to make out his expression of awe. Pinpoints of hot tears pricked the backs of her eyelids when she whispered a silent vow that she would never intentionally hurt Lancelot Londell Haynes.

Lance placed a hand over one breast. She arched off the mattress with his light touch. She closed her eyes, giving in to her senses as his fingers traced the outline of one breast, then the other, before they trailed down her rib cage to her belly. A soft gasp escaped her parted lips when his hand covered her mound.

"You are so beautiful," Lance whispered in a hoarse tone. He hadn't lied. Dina Gordon's tiny, compact body was even more spectacular naked; her clothes had artfully concealed a pair of full breasts with succulent nipples.

Dina nodded but didn't open her eyes. "That's because you make me feel beautiful, LL."

"No, baby girl, you were beautiful before we met."

Lowering himself while supporting his weight on his arms, Lance cradled her face between his hands and brushed a light kiss over her mouth. He applied the slightest pressure, deepening the kiss until her lips parted, giving him the access he needed to take full possession of her mouth. If possible, he wanted to devour Dina, put her inside him where they were never apart. His mouth tasted the sweetest of her minty breath, their tongues curling around each other in a dance of desire that didn't have to be rehearsed.

Dina curved her arms under Lance's shoulders, feeling the unleashed power in his back, shoulders and triceps. He felt good and smelled clean, the combination a heady aphrodisiac. Her hands slipped away as he moved lower, placing light kisses over her breasts, belly and thighs.

She lay transfixed and unable to believe the ripples of awareness making the area between her legs wet. She screamed once, then bit down on her lower lip to prevent subsequent sounds from escaping when the tip of her lover's tongue moved lightly over her clitoris, resulting in a rush of wetness that for a moment had her believing she'd urinated on herself.

Lance felt as if he were drowning in the feminine scent, the feel of the silky down hiding Dina's femininity and the scrumptious taste of her. His thumbs parted her folds and he buried his face between her thighs. After a while everything ceased to exist as he lost himself in the moment and the woman writhing under him. Only years of experience prevented him from ejaculating. He wanted to bring Dina to climax before taking his own. He was relentless, alternating suckling with a tender nipping of her sensitized flesh.

Dina gasped over and over as delicious sensations gripped her at the apex of her thighs, holding her prisoner for several seconds before releasing her, only to seize her again. The increasing intense pleasure made her feel as if she were going crazy. She wanted to escape the foreign sensations frightening her but couldn't.

"Lance! Please stop."

Dina was pleading with Lance when it was the last thing she wanted him to do, because even though he wasn't the first man to go down on her, he was the first to bring her close to an orgasm. Now she knew what the women were talking about when they said a man had hit their G-spot. The man with his face between her legs had hit G, H, I and all the way to O when the walls of her vagina convulsed, leaving her gasping for her next breath. It happened again, over and over, until Dina dissolved in a paroxysm of ecstasy that left her shaking uncontrollably in its aftermath.

Lance moved up Dina's trembling limbs, positioning himself at the entrance of her sex. Guiding his erect penis, he attempted to ease himself into her vagina. He managed to get the head in before he met resistance. She was tight, tighter than he could've imagined her to be. The pleasure was so intense he feared he was going spill his seed on the sheets. He planned to use a condom, but only after he'd penetrated her. He wanted Dina to have his baby, but that decision would have to be something they both agreed to.

Moisture beaded his forehead as he counted off the seconds it took to fully sheathe his erection inside Dina's deliciously tight body. "Easy, baby girl," he crooned when her soft gasps overlapped his grunts of spiraling fire that made him light-headed.

Dina fastened her hands in the sheet, gripping them in a death grip when she felt the painful burning sweeping through her much like the pain she'd experienced after the vaginoplasty. There was pain, but there was also a particular sweetness to the pain that revived her passion. Locking her hands around Lance's back, she took deep breaths to slow down her runaway pulse.

"Just do it, Lance," she demanded hoarsely.

He shook his head. "I don't want to hurt you, darling."

Dina gasped again. "Make the pain go away, Big Daddy."

Lance knew he couldn't continue as he was or it would take too long to break through the barrier making them both prisoners of pain and passion. Easing back, he thrust upward. He was inside Dina, their breathing coming in unison.

Burying his face in her hair, he counted slowly to three. "Are you all right, baby girl?"

"Yes-s-s-s," Dina slurred. *It's over.* She was no longer a virgin; she'd experienced her first orgasm. Lance's heavy breathing echoed in her ear.

"I'm going to pull out and put on a condom."

"Okay."

He withdrew, reaching for a condom in the drawer of the bedside table. When Dina welcomed him into her body, it was easier than his first attempt. She still was tight, very, very tight, but it only served to increase his desire for her.

Dina knew she'd opened herself and her heart to Lance when she made certain he derived as much pleasure from her making love to him as he had to her. Her hands caressed his back and buttocks as she urged him to love her.

"Love me, Big Daddy," she chanted over and over until he went completely still, then groaned loudly when he gave in to the turbulence of the desire that'd ensnared him what now seemed so long ago at the Old Bridge Township Raceway.

Collapsing heavily on her smaller frame, Lance waited until his heart rate slowed before he rolled over on his back. He'd waited for Dina to come to him on her terms. Now it was up to him to decide when she would become his wife.

He left the bed long enough to discard the condom before returning to the bed. Dina lay on her side, her hair spread out on his pillow. He climbed into bed and pulled her to his chest; her hips were pressed to his groin when he covered their bodies with the sheet.

There was no need to talk. Their bodies had said everything there was to be said.

Chapter 52

"Ladies, we should arrive in another twenty minutes," came the driver's voice on the other side of the partition in the luxury limousine. It was their cue to get into their costumes. Fortunately no one from outside the vehicle could see into the blackened rear windows.

Dina had told Lance that she had to work an out-of-state party for a group of athletes and wouldn't return to New Jersey until early Sunday morning. What she'd neglected to tell him was that Sparkle the green fairy was making her debut.

He'd dropped her off at SJC earlier that evening, where she worked a party. Afterward, she'd used Sybil's private bath to shower and put on eye makeup. By the time the catering staff had left for the night, she, using a comb attachment to her blow-dryer, had straightened out her wavy hair until it hung stick-straight down to her waist. Her dance instructor's reminder that she had to use her hair, tits and ass to make the most of her performance had stayed with her.

Karla's suggestion that she accept nothing less than fifty dollars was branded into her head. What Karla had hinted at was think small, stay small. And what she owed Payne Jefferson was anything but chump change. She'd fled Brooklyn with twenty-two thousand in cash, and after paying Karla and Dr. Howe, she was left with a little more than eight thousand dollars. She needed to come up with twelve thousand dollars in seven weeks. Right now she didn't have a plan B if she failed to make the Labor Day deadline. If she didn't, then she would contact Payne and give him what she had and owe him the balance. Asking Lance for money was not an option for Dina.

A smile parted her lips as she took off her T-shirt and bra, folding them neatly and placing them on the leather seat, when she thought about how her relationship with Lance had changed since they'd begun sharing a bed.

After he'd taken her *virginity* Lance had waited several days before making love to her again. Each time he penetrated her there was some resistance, but nothing like the first time, and what surprised Dina was that she was able to experience an orgasm each and every time. It was she, not Lance, who made the first overture to make love, and this pleased him immensely. What he didn't know was that she had to make up for all the years when she'd believed herself frigid or incapable of achieving sexual fulfillment.

"The next time you should leave off the bra and put it on only after we perform."

Sybil's voice broke into her musings. She'd noticed that Sybil hadn't bothered to wear a bra because she just would have to take it off to put on her costume. When she saw Sybil's costume for the first time, she couldn't conceal her shock. The black latex cat suit, thigh-high stiletto boots, whip and leather bag filled with a variety of gadgets blatantly shouted that the chef's alter ego was a dominatrix.

"Do you have a stage name?" she asked Sybil.

"It's Delectable."

"Delectable the dominatrix," she said, smiling broadly. "I like that."

"So do the men," Sybil said as she rubbed a small amount of scented oil over her body before she slipped into the latex fabric. "I use the oil under my costume because whenever I perspire it keeps the latex from sticking to my skin," she explained when she saw Dina staring at her.

"How long have you been Delectable?"

"Longer than I care to remember. The aunt of my college roommate tutored us when we told her that we were thinking of getting a part-time job but didn't want to wait tables or apply for work-study at the college. I took to it like a duck to water because it permitted me to let out a lot of repressed rage I had toward my father, who'd abused my mother."

Dina halted slipping into her glittering costume when she met Sybil's gaze across the small space in the back of the limo. "Did he abuse you?"

"No. Somehow my sisters and I were exempt, but it still affected us in the long run. My two sisters refuse to marry, and I married Cory because he's the complete opposite of my father. He'll go out of his way to avoid confrontation."

"Do you have any children?"

"No. Not yet. How are you doing with Lance Haynes?" Sybil asked Dina, directing the topic of conversation away from herself. She didn't like talking about herself because invariably she would have to talk about her traumatic childhood.

An attractive blush darkened Dina's face. "We're good."

"Do you know that you've managed to snag one of the most successful black businessmen in the country?"

"I didn't know what he did when I met him. He told me he played around with computers, but little did I know that playing with computers had made him a wealthy man."

"Does he know about Sparkle?"

Dina shook her head. "No. And I don't intend to tell him."

Sybil emitted a soft chuckle. "How long do you think you'll be able to hide it from him?"

"I only plan to dance for a few months."

"Surely you jest," Sybil said facetiously.

"I'm serious."

Sybil sobered. "So am I, Dina. I'd planned to work as Delectable to make a little spare change, but there's something about having men cower and submit to being punished that gives me a rush."

"But you don't need the money—or do you?" Dina asked Sybil.

"You're right. I don't need the money. But what I need is somewhere to displace my frustrations, and Delectable provides the perfect solution. By the way, Karla's going to join us in two weeks. She would've come along tonight, but Patrice is designing her costume."

"You're not pissed that I told her about your private parties?"

Sybil waved a hand. "No. Karla's the only woman aside from my sisters that I think of as a friend. I help her out because she helps me whenever I have a legal problem."

Dina breathed a sigh of relief. She hadn't thought that Karla would divulge what she'd told her about moonlighting as an exotic dancer; but, then again, she realized the two women had known each other longer than she had known either of them. And, although Sybil didn't relate to her as an employee, she never forgot that Mrs. Cumberland signed her paycheck.

As the limo traveled southward, she listened to Sybil talk about some of her quirkier clients. They were laughing like two schoolgirls when the driver pulled up in front of a set of iron gates to a sprawling property with waterfront views of Chesapeake Bay.

"Put on your mask," Sybil instructed Dina as the electronic gates opened.

"How do we make our entrance?"

"We never come in through the front door, where the guests can see us. It's either a side or rear entrance. The host is responsible for providing the music and lighting. Just to let you know, I'm always paid in advance. I had to learn that the hard way when a client stiffed me when he said he'd pay me after my performance. If they want to be entertained, then it's always up front. I'll give you your fee when we get back to Jersey. And don't forget to remove your makeup and shower before going home," Sybil lectured quietly. "It alleviates having to explain where you've been or what you've been doing."

"I don't have that problem because Lance doesn't clock me."

Sybil lifted an eyebrow at Dina's cocky response. "Neither does Cory, but I'm only saying it as a precaution, Dina. Things done in the dark have a way of coming out in the light."

Dina nodded. "Point taken."

Sybil had to admit that Dina looked ethereal as Sparkle. Patrice had outdone herself when she'd glued

Swarovski crystals onto the high-cut lace bodysuit. Sheer lime-green tights and detachable wings, also covered in crystals and feathers, had transformed her into a life-like fairy. With the orange-red lip color and the iridescent green eye makeup, she was certain to cause more than a stir.

Chapter 53

Dina slipped the clear plastic straps to her wings over her shoulders, adjusting them until they were virtually invisible over the crystal-studded straps of her revealing bodysuit. The lace garment was lined with a fabric matching her skin, making it appear as if she were nude when under the lights. She'd pinned up her hair in a bun with the intent of removing the pins during her routine, much like a stripper, to tease and entice those watching her.

She and Sybil waited in a room down the hall from a ballroom where the ballplayers had gathered to celebrate a popular pitcher's birthday. The noise and music reverberating throughout the first floor added to her anxiety. Dina's only comfort was that no one could see her face.

She paced the floor, her gaze fixed on the toes of the ballet slippers Patrice had dyed green to match the rest of her costume. Turning, she stared at her reflection in a large mirror in a gilt frame. What she saw rendered was mesmerizing. Her eyes looked like a cat's—the green mask picking up pinpoints of the same hue in the hazel orbs.

She took a deep breath and her breasts rose and fell above the revealing décolletage. Even without trying, her tits were definitely on display. What she had to admit was that Carlos's intense workout had improved her upper arms and her legs.

"Nervous?" Sybil asked, watching Dina pace back and forth like a caged cat.

"A little," she admitted.

"You're as stiff as a board. Try shaking out your arms and shoulders."

Dina shook out her shoulders, arms, hands and legs, then rolled her head on her shoulders. Within minutes she felt better, more relaxed. Now she knew why people were into yoga and tai chi. Suddenly she remembered the warm-up exercises and cool-down exercises Carlos put her through before and after each lesson. Within seconds she began stretching and was completely relaxed when a tall, masculine-looking woman in a tuxedo walked into the room. Her hair was completely white, appearing incongruent to her deeply tanned face.

She stared at Sybil, then Dina. "Are you Sparkle?"

Dina took in a deep breath, nodding. "Yes." She resisted the urge to roll her eyes at the woman. With Sybil dressed completely in black, there was no way she could be Sparkle.

"Follow me," she announced in a no-nonsense tone.

Sybil gave her protégée the thumbs-up sign when she followed the taciturn party planner. If Karla had joined them, she would've had her go on first to warm up the partygoers because of her prior experience. Dina would follow, then she would end it with her dominatrix routine.

"Good luck, Dina," she whispered aloud even though she doubted whether Dina Gordon needed luck. After all, she was dating and probably sleeping with a man who could afford to buy her anything she wanted. What she suspected was that Dina had yet to realize her power over the opposite sex.

Women who looked like Dina could pull any man— eight to eighty, blind, crippled or crazy.

Dina walked into the room and the babble of voices came to an abrupt halt. The only sound was that of heavy breathing over the strains of a soft jazz number. Her vermilion-colored lips parted when she felt what could be interpreted as lust radiating off the casually dressed athletes. She'd attended several baseball games but hadn't paid much attention to the players. These men, however, looked different out of uniform. Short-sleeved shirts, tees and casual slacks blatantly displayed the power in their toned, muscular bodies.

Slowing her pace to give them an up-close-and-personal look as she strolled casually toward the portable stage, she blew a kiss at the man wearing a black plastic Stetson with the words *Birthday Boy* stamped on the crown. He rushed up to her, grinning from ear to ear. His young, wholesome looks reminded her of a Midwest farm boy. Standing on the stage gave her a distinct height advantage as she leaned down and kissed his cheek while giving a generous view of her breasts.

"Aren't you a special birthday boy," she crooned, the low register of her voice shocking the pitcher. The others roared when he turned beet-red.

A shorter, stocky black player put up his hand. "I'll take one of those, Miss Sparkle."

"But it's not your birthday," Dina teased. She winked at him.

"It's next week."

"Bullshit, Levon," said a deep voice from the back of the room. "Your birthday ain't until the end of the year."

Levon laughed while ducking an onslaught of napkins, chips and popcorn launched at him by his teammates.

Dina strutted across the stage amid whistles and wolf calls, giving all a good look at her costume. She felt her heart rate kick into gear when the music changed. Hands on hips, she leaned forward, seducing her audience, before turning around to give them a good look at the gossamer wings.

Sybil had told her that the clients always selected the music, so she could either perform to country, hip-hop or R & B. She raised her arms over her head and lip-synched with the lyrics of a popular hip-hop song floating through a powerful sound system. Track lights over the stage flashed a kaleidoscope of color off the crystals, turning them into precious jewels.

Someone extinguished the lights, leaving the room in near darkness with the exception of the overhead track lights, while all gazes were focused on Dina as she used her body to seduce grown men who'd reverted to little boys. She was dancing for the man in whose honor they'd gathered, but in reality she danced for all of them, becoming their fantasy whether real or imaginary.

Turning her back, she executed a full split and bounced her hips off the floor like a dribbling basketball. The noise escalated as hands reached into pockets to emerge with fistfuls of cash.

She rose gracefully to her feet, bent over slowly and grabbed her ankles and shook her ass the way she'd demonstrated for Carlos. Dina gave them ass, turned and then gave them a generous display of cleavage. Bills littered the stage like confetti as she became a nasty girl. Once or twice she saw several clutch their crotches while groaning as if in pain.

"Oh, fuck!" someone moaned, eliciting guffaws from the others.

Dina wanted to tell them not to laugh because he probably wasn't the only one with a hard-on. She slid her palms down her belly, then held her crotch, moaning and licking her lips as she'd seen actresses perfect in pornographic videos. Pandemonium ensued when she removed the pins from her hair, one by one, letting it tumble sensuously down around her face and shoulders. She shook it out, bent her head forward, then flipped it back as a curtain of ebony rained down to her waist.

The pitcher removed his hat and passed it around the room while hooting at the top of his lungs. He returned to the stage and placed it in front of Sybil as she took her final bow. Leaning over, she kissed the top of his head before gracefully plucking the bills off the stage and putting them into the hat. Blowing kisses, she skipped out of the room amid thunderous applause. Her face was flushed with high color when she rejoined Sybil, who couldn't stop the grin crinkling her slanting eyes.

Sybil looked at the hat filled with fifty and one-hundred-dollar bills. "Not bad for less than twenty-eight minutes of work."

Dina sank down to the floor as she tried catching her breath. "Is that all it was?"

Sybil nodded. "I timed it."

"It felt like an hour."

"That's because you're working too hard, Sparkle. You have to learn to pace yourself."

"I think it was the music." They'd favored party music

from artists from the Dirty South along with a montage of hits from dance classics from back in the day.

Sybil reached into her bag filled with devices she used to employ pain and pleasure, handing Dina a canvas bag. "Put your money in that because I'll need the hat." She waited until the small sack bulged with Dina's tips. "I'll be back," she crooned, perching the Stetson at a jaunty angle on her head. Reaching for the whip, she flicked it with a flick of her wrist. The snap of leather echoed in the room like a crack of lightning.

"Oh, shit!" Dina gasped audibly. She smiled. "I'm impressed."

Sybil returned her smile. "Let's see if I'm going to impress or scare the shit out of these manly men."

Strutting in her high-heel boots, Sybil walked out, mentally prepared to punish a few men.

Chapter 54

The week following her debut as Sparkle, Dina felt like Alice in Wonderland. She wasn't sure what was real or make-believe. Sybil had given her two thousand, and her tips had totaled twelve hundred. Thirty-two hundred dollars was very nice money for half an hour of work. All of the cash went into the knapsack hidden in her apartment.

She'd spent several nights a week at Lance's apartment. They alternated cooking for each other as she felt herself growing closer to him. After a passionate session of lovemaking, he'd placed a set of keys to his apartment on her belly, but she'd refused to touch them. He took it personally, saying that if she didn't want the keys, then she didn't want him; he refused to listen to her explanation that she wanted to get used to sleeping with him before they took what they had to another level. What they shared was too new and much too fragile to consider blending their households.

Lance didn't take her rejection well. He'd stopped talking, becoming practically monosyllabic, and that annoyed her. His behavior was proof positive that grown men were still little boys.

Dina knew if she did move in with Lance, there was no way she could hide her after-hours activities from him. How could she explain why a driver brought her home in the wee hours of the morning? Sybil secreted her Delectable paraphernalia in a locked closet in her office at SJC Catering, while Dina washed her fairy outfit by hand and, when dry, stored it in tissue paper in a box on a shelf in her bedroom closet.

"There's no need to pout, LL."

Lance glared at Dina. "Do I look as if I'm pouting, Dina?"

She refused to relent. "What else do you call it when you won't look at or talk to me?"

"What am I doing now if not talking to you?"

"Asking me, 'Do you want a doughnut, Dina?' is hardly talking to me, Lancelot Haynes."

"Let's drop it, Dina."

"I don't want to drop it, LL. You need to understand why I can't move in with you."

"Why are you like a dog with a bone, Dina? Let it go."

Moving off the stool at the cooking island, Dina walked over to Lance. Her bare feet made soft flip-flop sounds on the terra-cotta kitchen floor. Wrapping her arms around his waist, she pressed her face to his back and kissed his shoulder over his white T-shirt.

When she woke up earlier, she'd found herself alone in bed. By the time she'd showered and washed her hair Lance had returned to the apartment with doughnuts and coffee. They'd done something the night before that was a first: they'd gone to bed angry.

Lance shifted slightly and stared down at the petite woman who'd become everything to him. When he woke each morning he looked for her beside him, and whenever he retired for bed each night he wanted her beside him.

Seeing Dina one or two nights a week wasn't enough—he wanted her in his bed every night.

He didn't know how he'd become so incredibly lucky to have found her. Beauty aside, she was more than he could've imagined her to be. He wanted Dina Gordon—in and out of bed.

"I hate fighting with you, Dina."

"And I don't want to fight with you, Big Daddy."

As much as she enjoyed playing house with Lance, Dina didn't want to jeopardize her relationship or future with the man she'd become quite fond of because she hadn't resolved her sordid past.

She'd come to enjoy sex so much that she'd begun fantasizing making love with Lance at the most inopportune times. Desire, passion and orgasms were emotions that were new to Dina, so whenever she recalled the passion in Lance's foreplay and the tenderness of his afterplay, her body betrayed her.

Leaning down, he pressed a kiss to the damp hair that hung down her back like black streamers. "Then don't fight with me, baby."

Tilting her chin, Dina smiled up at Lance. "Okay. And, to answer your question, yes, I would like a doughnut."

One morning she'd stopped at a bakeshop to order coffee but when she'd opened the bag had realized the coffee wasn't coffee but tea. The flustered salesclerk had apologized and included one of their honey-glazed doughnuts as a peace offering. The result was that she'd come to crave the incredibly delicious breakfast treat.

Lance patted her behind over a pair of cutoffs. "Go sit down and I'll serve you."

Dina moved over to the breakfast nook. She watched Lance remove two foam cups of coffee from a bag before opening a waxy bag with her favored honey-glazed doughnuts. A slight smile touched her mouth when he washed his hands in one of the two stainless-steel sinks. Although he denied it, he was a neat freak. He, and everything around him, was always neat and pristine. Even when sporting a pair of jeans and a T-shirt, he still managed to look elegant. He poured the coffee into large mugs and placed the doughnuts on a plate.

"Do you want me to set the table, LL?"

Lance shot Dina an incredulous stare. "I don't think so, baby girl."

She wrinkled her nose. "Just asking, Big Daddy."

He placed a mug in front of her and she picked it up and took a deep swallow, savoring the warmth spreading throughout her chest. Even the coffee tasted good this morning. "That's yummy," she crooned.

Lance sat opposite Dina. "It's definitely not yummier than you are."

A blush darkened her face. "How do you taste, LL?"

It was Lance's turn to blush. He shook his head because he knew what she was thinking. "No, Dina."

A mysterious smile tilted the corners of her lush mouth. "Why no, LL? Why shouldn't I find out how you taste?"

"Forget it." Lance wasn't a prude when it came to lovemaking, but he was usually uncomfortable whenever a woman went down on him. It was akin to losing control, and he always wanted to be in control—at all times.

Pushing back her chair, Dina stood up, rounded the table and straddled Lance. Looping her arms around his neck, she angled her head and trailed kisses along the column of his strong neck.

"I read an article in a magazine yesterday," she said in a low, seductive voice.

"What was it about?"

"Fifty ways to drive your man wild in bed." The article had had her laughing out loud because some of the suggestions were downright ingenious *and* outrageous.

"You don't need a sex manual, baby girl. You drive me wild just being Dina."

She pushed out her lower lip. "You're not going to let me try some of the suggestions?"

"Now who's pouting?"

"Please, Big Daddy."

Lance couldn't believe that the incredibly sexy woman sitting on his lap wanted to use him as a guinea pig in a sexual experiment because she'd read something in a magazine. "What am I to you, a piece of meat?"

Rocking back and forth, Dina achieved the reaction she'd sought when she felt Lance's rising erection. She lifted her eyebrows in a questioning expression. "I think your meat is getting hard."

"Dina!" Lance didn't want to believe the little minx was giving him a lap dance in his kitchen.

She increased her writhing on his lap. "Go to the bedroom and get into bed," she whispered near his ear. "I want you completely naked."

He froze. "You're kidding, aren't you?"

"Do I look as if I'm kidding, Lance?"

His gaze went from her face to her chest. Her nipples were clearly visible through her tank top. Dina was just as aroused as he was, maybe even more so, because her eyes were now a dark forest-green. He found it hard to believe that within a week Dina had gone from innocent virgin to succulent, sexy siren.

He stood up, bringing her up with him. He set her on her feet. "No, baby."

Resting her hands over his chest, Dina kissed Lance. "Go to bed and wait for me."

Chapter 55

Lance lay in bed, smiling. He'd gotten up early to get coffee and the doughnuts Dina raved about. He would do anything she asked because he didn't want her to shut him out of her life.

What he'd come to love about Dina was that she was always full of surprises. Even though he'd taken her innocence, there was still a modicum of childlike innocence that she'd managed to retain.

When she first told him she'd never slept with a man, he actually hadn't believed her. It wasn't just the physical evidence but also her reaction to him whenever he introduced something new to their sexual repertoire. It wasn't what she said but what she didn't say. Somehow he'd become attuned to her every expression and had come to know what Dina was feeling by touching her back.

"Are you naked, Big Daddy?"

"Yeah." Lance lay in bed naked as the day he'd come into the world.

"I'm coming in," Dina announced somewhere outside the bedroom.

"I'm ready, baby."

"Close your eyes. Are they closed?"

Lance closed his eyes. "Yes, they're closed."

Dina walked into the bedroom carrying a jar of honey in one hand and a small dish with a doughnut in the other. She'd also removed her clothes. Smiling, she approached the bed to find Lance on his back, his flaccid sex resting against his thigh. His body was tighter now than when she'd first met him. And when she'd remarked about it, he'd confessed to swimming laps in the building's pool several times a week.

She set the plate with the doughnut at the foot of the bed. "Don't open your eyes until I tell you."

"Are you going to tell me what you're going to do?"

"No, Lance. It's a surprise."

"I don't like surprises, baby."

"I think this is one surprise you're going to like."

Dina opened the top on the bottle of honey. Leaning over Lance, she squeezed the plastic bottle and, starting at his throat, she trailed a stream of honey down his chest, over his belly and to his groin. The sticky substance was the same color as the hair on his pubis.

"Don't move," she cautioned softly as she straddled him. Resting her hands on either side of his head, Dina lowered her head and flicked her tongue over his throat.

He moaned softly. "That feels good."

Dina raised her head to check whether he'd opened his eyes. He hadn't. "You taste good."

She moved slowly downward, her tongue lapping up the sweet substance off his warm flesh. "Sorry, Big Daddy, I neglected to introduce myself."

"Who are you?" Lance asked, playing along with her.

"Honey Dip."

Lance gasped, arching off the mattress when her tongue circled his belly button, then dipped into the indentation to lick the drops of honey pooled there. "Baby, please."

Dina glanced over her shoulder to see Lance's growing erection. Waiting until he was fully erect, she reached for the doughnut and slipped it over the head of his penis. It fit. She'd had to use a little kitchen ingenuity to make the hole in the doughnut larger in order to accommodate the girth of his sex.

Smiling, she checked again to see if Lance had opened his eyes. "Now baby girl is going to have her honey dip."

Sitting back on her heels, she bent over and licked the honey off the hair around Lance's magnificent hard-on. She rested a hand on his belly as he bucked wildly when her mouth closed on his sex, she suckling him as if he were a savory treat.

The pleasure from Dina's mouth sent heat then chills up and down Lance's body as he struggled not to come. He opened his eyes to find Dina nibbling at the doughnut perched around his penis. The sight of her hair falling around her shoulders, her sexy pink tongue darting out to lick the honey on his scrotum, was his undoing. A growl that came from deep within his throat exploded as he ejaculated. Pieces of the doughnut were everywhere: in Dina's hair, on her breasts and on the sheet.

His growl dissolved into moans as Dina grabbed his pulsing flesh, squeezing gently until the spasms slowed, leaving him weak as a newborn. "Sweet baby Jeez-us! Swe-e-e-t baby Jeez-zus!" he chanted over and over, the words becoming a litany. He was so overcome with emotion that he wanted to weep. Dina's selflessness touched a core that he hadn't known he possessed.

Smiling in triumph, Dina picked up pieces of the doughnut and popped them into her mouth. "Hungry,

Big Daddy?" she crooned, dropping a small piece into Lance's mouth.

Somehow Lance managed to push himself into a sitting position, his back supported by several pillows. He reached down and pulled Dina to his side. "Big Daddy should spank Honey Dip for that little stunt."

Pressing her body to his, Dina met his amused gaze. "Don't tell me you didn't like it?"

"The problem is I liked it too much."

"Then why are you complaining, darling?"

Lance sobered quickly. It was the second time Dina had called him darling. The first time was at the Kings' July Fourth gathering. Could he hope that her feelings for him went beyond gratitude for his promise to protect her?

He'd walked to the doughnut shop instead of driving because it had given him time to think, think about Dina and what he wanted from her. What he had to remember was that she'd been raised by her grandmother, who'd passed along her outdated ideas about sex and how men and women related to each other.

Dina had managed to scale one hurdle when she agreed to sleep with him, but she wouldn't relent whenever he offered to give her money or suggested that she have a key to his apartment.

Women like Dina Gordon were a throwback to his grandmother's generation, where girls waited until they were married to give up their virginity. He'd taken her virginity, but what surprised Lance was that she hadn't hinted at marriage. Tightening his hold on her shoulders, he buried his face in her hair.

The expression *There's more than one way to skin a*

cat came to mind. Dina Gordon wouldn't accept the key to his apartment, but he knew of another way to get her to change her mind.

Chapter 56

"Mr. Haynes, this is Jack in the lobby. There's a courier from Kazarjian with a delivery for you."

Swinging his legs over the pale gray leather chaise in his private lounge, Lance reached for the telephone on a black lacquer table. He pressed a button on the console, connecting him directly to the building lobby. "Please send him up."

Lance had made a call earlier that morning that he realized would change his relationship with Dina. Her performance as "Honey Dip" had him confused, elated and wondering what he had released in her when he'd taken her virginity. Her passion matched her beauty—both were shocking and breathtaking.

Reaching for his jacket over the back of a matching leather chair, Lance slipped his arms into the sleeves. A soft buzzing echoed throughout the office at the same time he made his way to the entrance. The screen on the closed-circuit security system showed the face of one of the building's security personnel and that of another man.

Lance unlocked and opened the door. Extending his hand, he smiled at the guard. "Thanks for bringing him up." He'd given explicit instructions that the courier was to be personally escorted to his office.

The guard surreptitiously palmed the bill Mr. Haynes had pressed into his palm. "Please call me when you want me to bring him down."

"I will."

Stepping back, Lance opened the door wider and nodded to the courier. "Please come in, Mr. Kazarjian."

Nicolas Kazarjian, a slightly built, swarthy man with a nervous facial tic, stepped into the office of the man who'd called his nephew earlier that morning with a request usually afforded privileged customers. Once his nephew had identified who'd made the call, he'd decided to meet Mr. Haynes personally.

Switching a leather case to his left hand, he extended his right one. "It's a pleasure to meet you, Mr. Haynes."

Lance shook the small, moist hand, smiling. "I want to thank you for coming on such short notice."

"Time is nothing when it comes to love."

"You're right," Lance confirmed. "Would you like something to eat or drink?"

"No, no, no. I'm good."

Lance extended an arm. "If that's the case, then we'll get down to business. Please follow me."

He led the jewelry designer into the room where he'd lain awaiting his arrival. It was a smaller antechamber with a private bath and a Zen bar. Once he closed the door it became the perfect place to unwind. Whenever he buzzed Della to tell her he was "out" she knew not to put through any calls. The only exception was when Dina called. He'd instructed his executive assistant she was to connect him with Dina Gordon anytime or anyplace.

The lightly scented candles on a low table provided a calming backdrop to the semilighted space. When he touched a switch on the wall, recessed lights softly illuminated the room with walls covered in a fabric that resembled oyster-white raw silk.

"Are you certain I can't get you something to drink?" Lance asked again.

Mr. Kazarjian lifted his shoulders under a rumpled pale blue jacket. He angled his head. "Perhaps I'll take a little cognac. I'm not driving," he added quickly.

"Please make yourself comfortable, Mr. Kazarjian."

Lance walked over to a cabinet stocked with bottles of spirits, wines and liquors and poured two fingers of French cognac into a leaded-crystal tumbler. When he returned with Nicolas's drink, he saw that the man had placed an assortment of diamond engagement rings on a small black velvet tray.

He nodded when Lance handed him the glass. "Do you see anything you like, Mr. Haynes?"

"I like them all."

"Then take them all."

Lance stared at the jewelry designer as if he'd taken leave of his senses. The man had brought him eight diamonds rings, no doubt appraising for millions. He only needed one ring, not eight.

Taking a seat next to the jeweler, Lance stared at the rings, wondering which design Dina would prefer. He knew he was taking a risk in buying a ring before discussing marriage with her, but if he hadn't been a risk taker, then he never would've gone and set up his own company.

Everything was a risk and there were no guarantees—and that included life. At forty-nine, he didn't want to second-guess everything he did or every decision he made. He'd fallen in love with Dina Gordon and he wanted to marry her.

Nicolas took a sip of the cognac and smiled. It was excellent. He placed the glass on a matching coaster. "Well, Mr. Haynes, what do you think your lady would like?"

"I'm not sure."

"Does she wear jewelry?"

"I've only seen her with earrings."

"What kind of earrings?"

"I know she has a pair of gold hoops." He didn't tell him about the small diamond heart-shaped earrings he'd given her.

"Are the hoops small or large?"

"They're not too big." Lance remembered Dina telling him that she didn't wear earrings to work because she didn't have a pair that weren't hoops. All earrings had to be studs.

"How does she dress? Is she fancy or conservative?"

"She's definitely not fancy," Lance said. "Her clothes are more along the classic lines." That was what he liked about Dina. She wasn't one to show a lot of skin, yet her style of dress flattered her body.

He pointed to an emerald-cut diamond ring with a cushion bezel and trapezoid side stones set in platinum. "I like this one."

A sly grin parted Nicolas's lips. "You have wonderful taste, Mr. Haynes." He'd selected one of the most expensive rings in the collection.

Lance picked it up. The ring was magnificent. "What's the total carat weight?"

"The center stone is two and one-quarter carats, and the other stones total one and a quarter. The entire ring is three and one-half carats."

He slipped the ring on his little finger. It wouldn't go past his fingernail. "What size is it?"

"They are all fives. You told my nephew that she is a small woman."

"Yes, she's petite."

"If you need to have it sized, we'll send someone to measure her finger, then we'll return it to you the same day."

"Let's hope it fits, because when I put it on her finger I don't want to have to take it off."

"So you want that one, Mr. Haynes?"

Lance glanced at the other rings, some with fancy yellow and pink diamonds and others cut into heart, pear and round shapes. The ring perched on the tip of his left pinky "spoke" to him, and he considered that a good sign.

"Yes, I do. How much is it?"

Nicolas took a deep breath and quoted a price for the ring, watching and waiting for Mr. Haynes's reaction. "Of course, we will give you a written appraisal for the ring."

"Thank you." He pushed to his feet. "I'll be back with your check."

Nicolas waited until Lance left the room before picking up his glass and draining it. He'd never heard of Lancelot Haynes until his nephew told him that he'd Googled the name. What did he know about searching someone's name on the internet? His only concern was whether a customer was pleased with his designs and *if* they could afford to pay the price for flawless and near-flawless diamonds.

He smiled for the first time, exhibiting stained teeth that were the result of smoking too many strong Turkish cigarettes. Mr. Haynes returned with his check. Removing a polishing cloth from his jacket pocket, he rubbed it over the stones. Reaching into his other pocket, he took out a white leather ring box and placed the ring gently into the groove.

"I know your lady will be very surprised, Mr. Haynes," he said, placing the box on the table.

Lance smiled. "You're right. She will be very surprised."

Dina had just gotten into bed when her cell phone rang. She picked it up, smiling when she saw Lance's name. "Hi, Big Daddy."

"Hey, baby girl. Do you mind if I stop by for a few minutes?"

"I'm in bed, Lance." She didn't want him to stay over because she'd told Mr. and Mrs. Foster that she didn't entertain men in her apartment. The exception had been when Mrs. Foster let him in.

"What I have to show you will only take a few minutes."

"Where are you?"

"I'm in my car outside your place."

"Come on up."

Reaching for a cover-up that matched her revealing nightgown, she made her way out of the bedroom and down the hallway to the door. She opened it as Lance stepped off the last stair. She'd barely closed the door when he swept her up in his arms and carried her into the bedroom, placing her on the bed, his body following hers down. He reached over and turned on the lamp on the nightstand.

Dina searched his face. There was a slight puffiness under his eyes, but other than that he looked the same. "What's wrong, Lance?"

"Nothing's wrong, darling."

She lifted a questioning eyebrow. "Why are you here? I thought we agreed that we wouldn't see each other again until Sunday."

Cradling her face between his hands, he brushed a kiss over her parted lips. "I couldn't wait until Sunday to give you something."

"What on earth are you talking about?"

He shifted slightly, reached into the pocket of his slacks and took out the ring box.

"I want to give you this."

Dina's eyes grew large as she stared at the box on the broad palm. She knew it held a piece of jewelry. Lance had given her diamond earrings, but she suspected it was more than a pair of earrings in this box.

"Take it, baby girl."

He moved off her and she pushed herself into a sitting position. She took the box and opened it. Light from the lamp fired the precious diamond winking seductively at her. She covered her mouth with a trembling hand. "Oh, no!"

Lance closed his eyes when the tears flowed down Dina's face. He had no way of knowing whether she would accept or reject his offer of marriage. He opened his eyes. "Will you marry me, Dina Gordon?" There. He'd said the words he'd never spoken to another woman.

Dina couldn't stop crying and she couldn't stop shaking. Everything she'd ever wanted and prayed for had come from a man named Lancelot Londell Haynes. He'd become lover and protector. She wasn't in love with him because she didn't know how to love, but what she did feel for Lance was something so new and pure that she suspected it was love.

His gentleness, his generosity and his lovemaking

made her feel special, like the princesses in the fairy tales she'd read as a little girl. She was his baby girl and he was her Big Daddy.

"Yes," she whispered, smiling through her tears. "Yes, Lancelot Londell Haynes, I will marry you."

Lance took the ring out of the box and slipped it onto Dina's finger. It was a perfect fit. The knuckle-to-knuckle ring would've overpowered her tiny hand if her fingers were shorter. "It's almost as beautiful as you are."

Smiling through her tears, Dina rested her head on his shoulder. "You have no idea how happy you've made me."

"Come home with me tonight, baby."

She sniffled. "We can't do anything because I have my period."

"We don't have to do anything. I just want to go to sleep with you next to me and wake up with you next to me."

"Same here." She pulled out of his loose embrace. "Let me up so I can get dressed."

Lance waited in the living room while she went into the bathroom to wash her face and brush her hair. It took less than ten minutes to pull on a pair of jeans and a T-shirt and slip her feet into a pair of running shoes. She didn't need to take her personal toiletries because since she'd begun sleeping with Lance she'd purchased similar items to leave in his guest bedroom.

Mr. and Mrs. Foster were sitting on matching rocking chairs on the porch when she and Lance came out of the side entrance. She touched Lance's arm. "I'll be with you in a few minutes." Walking up the steps to the porch, she smiled at the couple who'd been married longer than she'd been alive.

"Mr. and Mrs. Foster, I want you to be the first to

know that I'm going to get married." Extending her left hand, she showed them her engagement ring.

Mr. Foster held her hand while his wife gasped aloud. "It's beautiful," he crooned.

"Bless you, child," Mrs. Foster added. "You and your young man."

"When are you getting married?" Mr. Foster asked.

"We haven't set a date." And they wouldn't, Dina thought, until after she settled up with Payne. She eased her hand from her landlord's gentle grip. "We're going out to celebrate." What she didn't tell the Christian couple was that she was going to her fiancé's house to share his bed.

Turning, she skipped down the stairs and crossed the street to where Lance leaned against the bumper of his car, waiting for her. "Honey Dip loves her Big Daddy." Dina didn't know what love actually felt like, but whatever it was she was feeling, she prayed it was love and would last forever.

Resting a hand on her behind, Lance squeezed it gently. "There'll be no more honey dips until after we're married."

"But I thought you liked it."

He opened the door for Dina, waiting for her to sit, then came around to sit behind the wheel. "I did," Lance admitted.

A slight frown furrowed Dina's smooth forehead. "So why do we have to wait?"

"I'd like to save it for our wedding night. That way we'll have something to remember for the rest of our lives."

What Lance didn't tell Dina was that he'd thought he was having a heart attack during her fellatio session. The next day he'd called his doctor for a complete physical. He was still waiting for the results, but if or when anything happened to him, he wanted to make certain Dina would be provided for. Now that she'd accepted his proposal, he would have to contact his lawyer to draw up a will naming Dina Gordon Haynes as his heir.

"It will become a night to remember," Dina crooned.

His hand touched her hair. "How long are you going to make me wait before you become my wife?"

"Not long, LL."

He stared at her delicate profile. "How long is not long?"

"I'd like an autumn wedding."

Angling his head, Lance pressed his mouth to hers. "You will have your autumn wedding. Don't make any plans for us for Sunday because I'd like to go house hunting. Where would you like to live?"

Dina sat, confused and shaken. Everything was happening too quickly. She'd agreed to marry Lance, and now he was talking about looking for houses. She would've thought that they would live in his West New York apartment.

"I like Upper Saddle Brook." She'd fallen in love with the town when she'd gone there for her procedure.

Lance started the car and maneuvered away from the curb. His fiancée had selected an upscale community in northern New Jersey in which to live. It was an ideal place to live and raise a family.

Chapter 57

Sybil sorted through her sock drawer for a pair in black. "Dammit!" she whispered. She'd run out. Then she remembered she hadn't put up a load of wash in over a week.

This was when she wished she had a housekeeper, someone who would take care of the chores that kept a household running smoothly. She enjoyed doing her own housework because it provided her an outlet to work off tension, but lately she hadn't been as tense because Delectable was busy servicing E. Paul Redding every other night now that his wife had extended her European vacation a month.

She shut the drawer in the triple dresser, making her way to the armoire where Cory stored his underwear. Opening the ornately carved doors, she opened one drawer, then another. Cory always insisted on putting away his laundry, so she had to open and close several before finding the right drawer.

She found his sock drawer, then leaned closer to find a pair in black. They were arranged in neat rows in corresponding colors of brown, gray, blue and black. Sybil selected one in cotton. She preferred the natural fiber because it permitted her feet to breathe.

"What the hell…?" Her words trailed off when she discovered, bound neatly with rubber bands, a stack of betting slips. Upon closer examination, she found another wad of lottery tickets.

"The son of a bitch has been gambling behind my back!" she screamed. Not only was he gambling, but judging by the number of slips, he'd also been losing—heavily. "How much have you lost—or won—my darling husband?" she mumbled, continuing her monologue. If Cory Eliot Cumberland had been there, Sybil wasn't certain what she would do or say to him.

What saved Cory and their marriage was that Sybil had to go to work and later on that night she would morph into Delectable. Not only was he lucky but also blessed.

Sybil sat up, her back cradled against a mound of pillows, waiting for Cory to return from the bathroom. She didn't have long to wait. It took him exactly twenty minutes to shave and shower.

He walked into the bedroom completely naked. Her gaze caressed his lean, athletic body. She hadn't wanted to believe what she'd uncovered the day before. She'd ruminated about the excuses he'd come up with for throwing away his money until she felt like screaming. Her frustration escalated, and E. Paul Redding had become the willing recipient.

Cory smiled at his wife. "I thought you'd still be asleep."

Sybil combed her fingers through her hair, pushing it off her forehead. "I wanted to talk to you."

"What about?" he asked, stepping into a pair of boxer briefs.

"Your gambling problem, Cory."

Reaching for an undershirt on the bench at the foot of the bed, Cory pulled it over his head. "I don't have a gambling problem, Sybil."

"You don't? I found a wad of gambling slips thick enough to choke a fuckin' hippo, and you tell me you don't have a gambling problem?"

Cory pointed a finger at his wife. "Talk *to* me, not *at* me, and don't you dare curse at me, Sybil." He'd spoken through his teeth.

This was a Cory Cumberland that Sybil wasn't familiar with. She'd learned early on when dating that he abhorred confrontation and she'd always tried to appease him. "What do you expect me to say? *Cory, darling, it appears as if you've been playing the ponies. Is there something you need to tell me?*"

He glared at her. "Don't be facetious, Sybil, it's not becoming."

"Losing our money isn't becoming."

"It was my money."

Sybil swept back the sheet, swinging her legs over the side of the mattress. "Your money, Cory? Since when is it just your money? I thought we were partners in this marriage. We share everything equally."

Cory continued dressing, slipping into a pair of trousers. "That's easy for you to say, my dear wife, because you bring home three times what I make."

"But you knew that before we married. I've never hidden what I earn from you."

An angry scowl distorted his pleasant features. "Why should you, Sybil? You remind me every chance you get that you're the breadwinner in this family."

"No, I don't."

"Yes, you do, Sybil." He waved his arms. "Take this

house. We bought it with *your* money. Every stick of furniture in it was purchased with *your* money. Everything we have was—"

"Stop it! Just stop it, Cory." A rush of blood turned Sybil's face a dangerous shade of rose-pink. "Please stop it."

Cory closed the distance between them, pulling her gently to his chest. "Syb, baby, I don't want to fight with you."

Sybil's arms went around his waist. "And I don't want to fight with you. All I want to know is why are you gambling?"

"I'm trying to win enough to start up my own business. I love what I do, but I want to work for myself. You know I've never been good at taking direction from someone else."

Easing back, Sybil stared up into her husband's tortured gaze. "Why didn't you tell me this before? We have enough money saved for start-up capital."

He shook his head. "I can't take your money."

Pressing her palms to his back, she closed her eyes. "Yes, you can and you will. Besides, it's not my money but ours."

Cory pushed her back. "I'm not going to argue with you."

"Nor I with you. Either you take the money or…"

"Or what, Sybil?"

Sybil swallowed the threat on the tip of her tongue. "Nothing, Cory. Nothing," she repeated as she walked out of the bedroom and into the adjoining bath. She had to get away from her husband or she would say something that was sure to end their marriage.

There was no way she was going to have a child with

a man with a gambling problem. She'd grown up with an addicted father who drank until passing out. She'd had enough of addicted men to last several lifetimes.

Chapter 58

Dina found herself at a loss for words. She clutched Lance's hand like a frightened child as they followed the real-estate agent in and out of rooms in an estate home designed in classical French Renaissance architecture.

She liked one of the two properties they'd been shown earlier, but Lance's claim they were too small prompted the experienced agent to show them the updated chateau. What, she thought, did two people need with a house with nine bedrooms, eleven baths and a formal drawing room and dining room flanked by a butler's pantry? The master suite had a stateroom and his-and-her private spa baths. There was an upstairs laundry with access to a twenty-eight-foot lavish walk-in closet.

However, she was impressed with the openness of the house that claimed high ceilings, curved wall arches, columns and expanses of glass that made the formal areas grand yet comfortable. If she was a fairy-tale princess and Lance her prince, then the estate home was their castle.

The elegantly attired middle-aged woman turned and smiled at Lance. When first meeting him, she'd blushed, then gushed over him as if he were a celebrity. The encounter made Dina aware of the clout of the man she'd promised to marry and cognizant of Karla's reminder that she would do well to stay out of the spotlight as Mrs. Lancelot Haynes.

"Mr. Haynes, I know you're going to really love this area of the house. Here we have the grand salon with a giant fireplace and media area connecting it to the morning breakfast room and open kitchen. Beyond the kitchen is the conservatory and library, which are connected by the gallery."

Lance exchanged a glance with Dina when they stood in the middle of the library. "What do you think, baby?"

"Do you think it's a bit much for two people?" she whispered.

"How long do you think we're going to remain two people? I want at least two little Hayneses," he added when she gave him a puzzled look.

A shiver snaked its way up Dina's spine. Lance was talking about getting her pregnant, unaware that she'd undergone a sterilization procedure. "What if I can't get pregnant?"

"Don't worry, darling. We have options."

"What kind of options?"

"Insemination or adoption."

She forced a smile. "We'll talk about babies later." If it'd been up to her, they'd never talk about children. Dina hadn't wanted another child because she thought herself incapable of being a good mother.

They left the library and stood on the balcony overlooking the grand salon. "You're going to buy it." Her query was a statement.

"Only if you like it."

What did he expect her to say? *Yes, I like it because you like it?* Or *no, I don't like it because, although beautiful, it's just too big.* Dina took a breath. This wasn't about her—it was about the two of them. The moment she agreed to marry Lance she'd stopped thinking only of Dina. He'd done everything possible to make her happy, and now it was her turn to reciprocate.

"Make her an offer, darling."

Lance placed a hand on Dina's shoulder and slowly turned her to face him. His fingers trailed across her forehead, down her cheek.

Suddenly everything came to a wild stop inside Dina. Lance Haynes loved her! Curving her arms under his shoulders, she buried her face against his chest. They held each other until the agent returned.

"How much, Mrs. Beatty?" Lance asked, meeting the woman's gaze over Dina's head.

"Five."

He shook his head. "Too high."

"It *is* negotiable, Mr. Haynes."

"How negotiable?"

"The owner's willing to go as low as four-eight-ninety."

"I'll give him four-three-ninety—cash. That's my final offer."

"I need to make a call." Edythe Beatty reached into her handbag for her cell phone. She walked a short distance while talking quietly with her client. The owner had set a price of five million dollars for the house and the surrounding four acres of prime real estate, but she knew he would take the four million three-hundred-ninety thousand because a bad investment had left him strapped for cash. The call lasted less than a minute. "My client has decided to accept your offer."

Lance gave the agent his business card. "I'd like to take possession before the end of the month."

Mrs. Beatty nodded. "I'll make certain to expedite the closing."

"We haven't set a wedding date, and you want to move in next month?" Dina asked Lance once they were back in his car.

Shifting on his seat, Lance turned to stare at her. "We probably won't move in before the end of the year. You're going to have to select furniture, then wait for it to be delivered. And that can take months. Once we're married, you'll move in with me."

"What about my lease?"

"Don't worry, baby girl. I'll pay off your debts."

Dina wondered how Lance would react if she told him she needed eighty-four hundred dollars to add to the eleven thousand six hundred she'd put away to pay off an ex-con threatening to hurt her supposedly deceased grandmother.

She wouldn't panic, at least not yet. Sparkle had an encore performance Friday night, this time at a bachelor party.

Chapter 59

Dina plucked the Post-it off her locker. The message was short and to the point. See me—Sybil.

She refused to entertain the notion that Sybil was canceling the bachelor party the following evening. Each time she became Sparkle it brought her closer to her goal.

Dina found Sybil in her office, but she wasn't alone. Karla King sat on a chair, flipping the pages of a magazine while Sybil spoke softly into the telephone. Sybil glanced up, ended the call and beckoned to her.

"Come in, Dina, and have a seat."

Karla put aside the magazine and smiled at Dina. "How's it going?"

"It's all good."

Leaning back in her chair, Sybil stared at the ring on Dina's left hand. "Congratulations."

Dina blinked once. "Say what?"

"Isn't that an engagement ring?"

Dina raised her left hand. She'd forgotten to take the ring off. She thought it best not to wear it when working. "Yes, it is."

"Let me see," Karla said, coming to her feet and grasping Dina's hand. "Damn! It's big enough to choke a horse."

"Lance Haynes?" Sybil asked.

Dina nodded. "Yes."

"Are you and Lance still friends?" Karla teased.

"Yes. But now we're very, very good friends."

Karla let go of Dina's hand and hugged her. "Congratulations. Your ring is incredibly beautiful." She caught Sybil's gaze and mouthed, "Engagement party." Sybil nodded. "Have you set a date?"

Dina pulled away from Karla. "Not yet."

"Do you plan to have a long engagement?" Sybil questioned.

"No. Lance and I were thinking about an October wedding."

Sybil motioned for Dina to sit. "That's practically around the corner. If you're looking to have a small wedding, then you're welcome to have it here."

"It's going to be very small. I don't have any relatives—at least none that are close—and Lance is an only child. Aside from his mother, who lives in South Carolina, he only has his business associates."

Sybil clapped her hands. "That does it. You *will* have it here. I'll set up everything in one of the first-floor rooms." Picking up a marker, she jotted down a note to herself on a Post-it.

"Don't worry about a thing, Dina. Sybil and I will pull it together for you," Karla volunteered. "By the way, where are you going live after you're married?"

The night of their engagement Lance had given Dina a key to his apartment, and although she'd accepted it, she still planned to spend most of her time in Irvington. "I'm going to move in with Lance."

"Where does he live?" Sybil asked.

"He has an apartment in West New York. I'm not certain how long we'll live there because Lance is buying a house in Upper Saddle Brook."

Sybil's eyes brightened with excitement. "Did you buy a new house?"

"It's fairly new. The original owner had it custom-built but never took possession because some of his investments fell through. So he put it on the market before the bank foreclosed on it."

Karla leaned forward. "How many rooms does it have?"

Shaking her head, Dina closed her eyes for several seconds. "Too many," she said when she opened them.

"Maybe I should rephrase my question. How many bedrooms do you have?" Karla asked.

"There're five in the main house and four in the guest wing."

"Damn!" Sybil and Karla chorused.

"If you need help decorating, then Sybil's your girl," Karla said with a hint of pride in her voice. "She helped me design my outdoor kitchen and select the accessories for my guest bedrooms."

Dina expelled a sigh of relief. "I'd thought about retaining the services of an interior decorator, but I don't want the rooms to have that look-but-don't-touch appearance."

"I hear you," Sybil drawled. "I'm sorry, but I have to change the topic. It's about tomorrow night." Within seconds she'd garnered both Dina's and Karla's attention. "I've arranged for a car service to pick us up at eight. We'll be dropped off at a Fort Lee hotel. We'll get dressed in a room adjoining the suite where the bachelor party will be held. We do our thing, then leave. Each of us will have half an hour of stage time."

"Who's the client?" Karla asked.

"He's the son of man who purportedly has the largest black-owned car dealership in the state. The prospective groom has earned the reputation of being a ladies' man. I heard on the down-low that his daddy had to pay out a lot of money to get him out of a *sit-chi-a-shun* after an ex-girlfriend accused him of rape."

Karla grunted. "Maybe Delectable needs to teach the boy a lesson."

Leaning over her desk, Sybil gave Karla a high five. "What Delectable is going to do is tear him a new asshole," Sybil drawled, enunciating each word.

"I hear you," Karla drawled.

Dina sat, listening to the interchange between the two. They were better educated than most women she knew, resided in affluent communities and were married to professional black men, but underneath the fancy trappings they still were sister-girls who lapsed into dialect and laughed at themselves.

Sybil turned to Dina. "I want Sparkle to put something on the son of a bitch that he'll never forget. I want it to be you, not his bride, that he'll fantasize 'bout fuckin' on his wedding night."

Dina turned away, blushing. This was too much for her. This is the type of conversation she would have with LaKeisha Robinson, not her attorney and her employer. What made her their equal was her initiation into the clandestine world of exotic dancing. What separated Sparkle from Delectable and Chocolate Ice was that Sparkle did it for money, while Karla did it for male attention and Sybil for allegedly a release of frustration.

Did her dancing for money make it more acceptable?

No.

Was she exempt from being labeled unfaithful because she was single?

No.

Chapter 60

"Sit down, Sparkle. You're making me nervous with your pacing."

Dina stopped and shot Karla a blank stare through her mask, then continued pacing the length of the room. She'd applied her eye makeup, gotten into her costume and tied the ribbons to her ballet slippers around her ankles. She'd retied them twice because she'd forgotten that the bow went in the back, not the front of the leg. She stopped, shaking out her arms and legs.

I'm never going to get used to this.

And she didn't want to get used to shaking her ass for sloppy-drunk, horny men. She wanted to marry Lance, decorate her new house and host dinner parties, like Karla and Sybil. And like the Mary J. Blige song, her anthem had become "No More Drama." She stopped pacing and sat on the edge of a folding chair. The noise and music coming from the adjoining suite could be heard through the walls.

"I don't think I'll have to warm up this bunch," Karla murmured.

She was stunning in a brown sheer lace jumpsuit. Thousands of rhinestones covered the garment from the stand-up collar to the hem. The brown was an exact match for her skin tone, and upon closer look it was apparent that Karla was completely nude under the sheer fabric. Although a shimmering mask concealed most of her face it failed to disguise the eyes that glowed with a savage inner fire.

Dina glanced over at Sybil, who sat spread-eagle with her whip dangling between her legs. Dressed entirely in black with thigh-high leather boots and flicking the whip, she looked sexy and dangerous.

"We're ready over here!" shouted a strong masculine voice followed by a knock on the door.

Karla strolled over to the door and stepped onto a stage in the adjoining suite. Sybil moved quickly to hold on to the doorknob to prevent it from closing. "Come, Dina, and look," she whispered.

Dina rushed over to the crack in the door, her mouth dropping when she watched Karla pull herself up and swing around a pole to Ludacris's "What's Your Fantasy." All the men were up on their feet when Karla's tongue flicked out like a lizard's along with the lyrics.

She found herself as mesmerized as the men in the room when she stared at Karla. She simulated making love as she spread her legs, clutched her crotch with both hands while throwing back her head in supplication. Chocolate Ice teased, taunted and seduced, utilizing the pole as if it were an extension of her body. Karla King, aka Chocolate Ice, was good—very, very good.

Karla felt as if she'd been injected with a powerful stimulant. It'd been years since she'd danced for men, but the moves, the splits, came back as if it'd been yesterday. She couldn't see the faces of the men staring at her because the spotlight was focused on her, but she felt their rapt gazes and felt the lust in the room that shimmered like waves of heat.

They were no different from the men she'd danced for twenty years ago. Whenever she performed, it was to complete silence. If it hadn't been for the music, she would've been able to hear their accelerated heartbeats. There was something about her routine that required the utmost concentration or else they'd miss something.

She beckoned to the prospective groom, smiling as he came closer. Then, without warning, she slid down to the floor of the stage and wrapped her legs around his neck. Thrusting upward, she pushed her crotch against his face. He stumbled backward as if jolted by volts of electricity. The entire room erupted in laughter. Recovering quickly, he buried his face between Chocolate's outspread legs, inhaling deeply. The scent of raw sex wafted in his nostrils. He reached for Chocolate, but came away empty. She'd scooted to the other edge of the stage, bowing. Her routine ended as bills rained down around her feet.

Karla picked up the money, waving to the men who whistled, stomped and shouted for more. She slipped through the opening in the door, her heart pounding painfully in her chest. A wide grin split her face under the brown lace mask. Chocolate Ice was back!

Sparkle took the stage to a chorus of gasps from the assembled. She knew Chocolate was a hard act to follow, but whoever had selected the music for her opening act had picked the perfect song—Marques Houston's "Naked." She stared at the groom, gesturing to him. He moved toward her as if in a trance. The crooner's melodious voice reverberated throughout the room.

Sparkle saw something in the guest of honor's eyes

she hadn't expected to see—indecision. She didn't know if he was afraid of Sparkle or if he'd had second thoughts about marrying his fiancée. The green fairy managed a full split, her hands anchored on the floor between her legs. She leaned forward, giving everyone close enough a view of her breasts spilling over the revealing décolletage.

She held his head, whispering the chorus in his ear. He hollered, grabbing himself between the legs. Sparkle's hot breath and the sound of her sultry voice in his ear made him come!

One by one Sparkle seduced every man in the room, a few faring no better than the prospective groom. One man approached the stage, credit card in hand. He waved it above his head, shouting, "I need to make a withdrawal so I can pay the beautiful fairy."

Sparkle turned her back to him and squatted. Raising her hips slightly, she gave him an unobstructed view of her bare bottom through the sheer green tights. Smiling at him over her shoulder, she drawled, "Hey, Boo, the ATM is open 24/7." The man ran the edge of the card down the crystal-studded G-string before reaching into his pocket and littering the stage with one-hundred-dollar bills.

Sparkle rewarded him with a kiss to the forehead. She bumped, she grinded, dropped her ass, then popped up like a jack-in-the-box. She put all she had into the performance because she literally was dancing for her grandmother's life, ending her routine with pulling the pins from her hair, shaking it out and tossing the raven mane over her shoulders and down her back. Bowing gracefully, she threw kisses at the men standing on chairs and pounding tables. She scooped up her tips and slipped off the stage.

Dina met Karla's and Sybil's gazes. They were look-ing at her as if she were a stranger. "What's the matter?"

Sybil shook her head. "You were awesome."

Karla, sans mask, hadn't changed because she'd wanted to watch Dina's performance. "You are better than Chocolate Ice ever was in her heyday."

Instead of feeling elated, Dina felt like weeping. She forced a smile. "Thanks."

Sybil and Karla didn't know—they couldn't know that this wasn't what she wanted to do. They may want to perform for the company of men, but she did it because she didn't have a choice. For the ten years Adina Jenkins went on stage each night to perform in a role, she'd had to seduce a man—for money. Adina had retired, but it was now Dina Gordon who'd reprised the role to use her body to again seduce men—for money.

Chocolate Ice and Delectable saw dancing as fun—a way to spice up their rather ordinary lives. While it was a job—drudgery—for Sparkle, who wanted to live a very ordinary life for the first time in twenty-seven years. A roar went up in the other room, and she peered through the opening in the door with Karla to see Delectable strutting onto the stage.

Delectable uncoiled the whip and popped it, the deaf-ening sound getting everyone's attention. Swaggering on the four-inch heels, she pointed the handle of the whip at the prospective groom, who'd changed into a pair of jeans.

He mounted the stage as Delectable asked someone for a chair. She motioned for him to sit, and he appeared vis-ibly shaken when she placed her booted foot on his groin.

"Relax, baby boy. Delectable is not going to hurt you."

Moving backward, she trailed the length of leather on the floor, measuring the distance it would take for the tip of the whip to reach her target. There was no music, no sound except for the whisper of breathing.

Delectable swung the whip over her head, then snapped her wrist. It came over the chest of the man sitting stiffly in the chair. He screamed and peered down at his white shirt, looking for blood where the leather had cut into his flesh. There was none. The only thing missing was a button. The whip came down again and again, leaving the shirt in tatters but not a mark on the trembling body.

There was no applause or shouting when Delectable ended her awesome skill with the whip. One by one the men filed up to the stage and gently placed money on the stage. A knowing smile touched Sybil's mouth when she bent over to retrieve her tips. Physically the men were superior, but it was Delectable who'd established that she was totally in control.

Chapter 61

Karla glanced at the telephone display when a call came through on her private line. Smiling, she picked up the receiver. "Good morning, darling."

"Good morning to you, too. I forgot to tell you that we have a meeting tonight."

"I don't want to go, Ronald."

There came a pause. "This is the second time you've canceled on me, Karla. What's up?"

"Nothing's up. I just don't feel like going anymore."

Karla didn't know when it'd happened, but she'd tired of the swinging scene, tired of having to decide who she was going to sleep with. Once she and Ronald returned home, she compared him to the man with whom she'd had sex. And that's all it was—sex. Swinging had become even less stimulating now that she'd resurrected Chocolate Ice. Whenever she performed, she felt empowered, in control.

"Why didn't you say something before I renewed our membership?" Ronald asked. He hadn't bothered to disguise his annoyance.

Karla picked up a pen and began doodling on a pad. "I don't know. It's only recently that I've begun to feel differently about sleeping with other men."

"Don't tell me you got a dose of morality all of a sudden."

"It has nothing to do with morality, Ronald. Why can't it be that I enjoying sleeping with my husband?"

"As I enjoy sleeping with you, Karla. But that doesn't mean I don't want to sample something else every once in a while."

"Don't let me stop you, Ronald, if that's what you want to do."

"Are you giving me permission to cheat?"

"It wouldn't be cheating. After all, we do have an open marriage."

There came a pause. "You're right, Karla. We'll stay home tonight and I'll think of something fun to do."

Her expression brightened. "Okay." Whenever Ronald came up with an idea for a fun thing, it always meant a new game or sex toy. "I'll see you tonight."

Karla stared at the object cradled between layers of tissue paper. Her gaze came up and fused with Ronald's. "What do I need with that when I have you?"

"It's not for you," he said mysteriously.

"Who's it for?"

Dimples winked in his cheeks when he winked at her. "It's for me."

Her eyelids fluttered. "You want me to strap on a dildo and *do* you?"

Crawling onto the bed, Ronald lay down next to his wife. Although his mouth was smiling, his eyes were serious—very serious. "Yes."

Reaching out, Karla ran her fingers over the length of rubber that looked amazingly like an actual penis. It was large but not as large as Ronald's impressive member.

A slow smile parted her lips. "You know that you're a freak, Ronald King."

He nodded. "Yes."

She picked up the contraption attached to an adjustable belt and fastened it around her waist. "Look at me," she teased. "I have a dick."

Ronald scooped her off the bed. "Let's try in the shower just in case I have an accident."

Wrapping her arms around his neck, Karla kissed his cheek. "Are you a virgin, Ronald?"

He frowned. "What are you talking about?"

"Am I the first woman to sample your bum hole?"

Ronald nodded. "Yes, you are."

If Karla had asked him if she was the first to have anal intercourse with him, he would've said no. However, she would be the first woman.

Chapter 62

"Can I refresh your drink?" Lance asked Ronald King.

Ronald waved his hand. "No. I'm good here."

Cory Cumberland held up a hand. "I've already passed my limit," he said before his host could ask him whether he wanted another beer. He crossed his sock-covered feet resting on a suede ottoman. "I've got to give it to you, LL. You're really doing the damn thing."

Ronald lifted his glass of brandy. "Ditto. You have a nice apartment, a beautiful fiancée who can cook and a thriving, very profitable business."

Lance smiled. "Life has been good," he said modestly.

"Shit," Ronald drawled. "You're doing more than all right. Karla said that Dina told her that the two of you will move to Upper Saddle Brook later on in the year. Every time they get together they go on and on about buying a funny-sounding table or chair. What the hell is the difference between a Chippendale and one of those kinky-ass French kings?"

Chuckling softly, Lance shook his head. "I told Dina what goes on inside the house is her domain and what goes on outside is mine. That translates into I bring home the bacon, and how she prepares it is her business as long as I can recognize it as bacon."

Ronald took another sip of his after-dinner liqueur. Lancelot Haynes and his fiancée had invited the Kings and the Cumberlands to Sunday dinner. What surprised him was that Dina Gordon's cooking skills were exceptional.

He'd thought her nothing more than eye candy who'd managed to pimp an older man into taking care of her. But when he saw Lance and Dina interact he saw genuine affection between them.

Cory, his gaze fixed on the muted television screen, nodded. "Money—it can make a marriage or break it." He'd stopped gambling, but he still refused to accept Sybil's offer to give him what he needed to start up his own company.

"That's not going to be a problem with Dina and myself," Lance said confidently. "All she has to do is call me Big Daddy and my wallet opens automatically."

"Damn, LL," Ronald said. "You don't have to let everyone know you've been pussy-whipped."

Cory shifted his gaze, glaring at Ronald. "Mind your neck, King. It could be the man likes being pussy-whipped."

"Yeah, King, mind your neck," Lance intoned.

Ronald's silky black eyebrows lifted. "Oh, I take that to mean her shit is *that* good?"

Lance felt a wave of heat creep up the back of his neck. In the past he'd never been hesitant to engage in sex talk with his male buddies, yet it was different now. Dina was different. She was the woman he would marry in another two months, and hopefully become the mother of his children.

"I'm not one to kiss and tell, but I have no complaints."

"How about the lady?" Ronald asked. "Does she have

any complaints?" He'd found Dina intriguing because he wanted nothing more than to sleep with her. He knew Karla would never agree to the arrangement, but that hadn't stopped him from fantasizing about her.

Lance didn't like the direction the conversation had taken. "Perhaps I should ask Karla if she has any complaints."

"I can speak for my wife and say unequivocally no."

"Then the answer would be the same for Dina."

Cory, cognizant of the rising tension between his friend and their host, came to his feet. "Lance, I think I'll take that brandy now." He handed Lance the beer bottle. Waiting until he was alone with Ronald, he rounded on him. "What's wrong with you, insulting the man in his own home?"

"I just asked him about his woman."

"No, you didn't. You wanted to know how she was in bed."

Ronald drained his glass, set it on a table in the library, then stood up. "You need a vacation, Cumberland. You're wound tighter than a guitar string. Karla and I plan to head up to our place near Bear Mountain for the Labor Day weekend. You and Sybil are welcome to join us."

"I…I'll let you know."

"Are you okay, man?"

Cory massaged his forehead with his fingers. "I will be. I will be," he repeated.

Lance returned to the library with two tumblers filled with the golden amber liquid, handing one to Cory. He touched glasses. "Cheers."

Cory stared at Lance for several seconds before putting the glass to his mouth. "Cheers," he whispered, taking a deep swallow. The heat spreading throughout his chest seemed to fill him with courage. "LL, whenever you have some time, I'd like to talk to you about something that's business-related."

Lance smiled. "You have my card. Call me early tomorrow morning."

"How early?"

"Better yet, why don't I call you? Perhaps we can meet for lunch or dinner."

Cory felt as if a stone had been lifted off his chest. "I'd like that. Thanks, LL."

"Excuse me, Big—LL?"

The three men turned at the sound of the dulcet feminine voice. Dina Gordon stood in the doorway to the library. She was the epitome of sophistication in a pair of tailored white slacks, a black silk blouse, strappy sandals and her hair pinned on the nape of her neck in an elaborate chignon.

Lance smiled. "Yes, baby girl?"

"May I see you for a moment?"

He nodded to Ronald, then Cory. "Please excuse me."

They watched as he walked over to Dina and placed a protective arm around her waist as he leaned down to hear what she had to tell him.

Yes, both mused, Lance Haynes was really doing the damn thing.

Chapter 63

Dina knew she was taking a risk when she'd accepted the offer, but it was one she had to take. A man who'd seen her perform had slipped her a hundred dollars and his business card with a notation that he would pay her fifteen hundred dollars for a private performance. She never would've considered it if she'd had the twenty thousand Payne had demanded.

She'd sat on her bed and counted every single dollar she'd saved from her tips working at SJC Catering and her tenure as Sparkle. It added up to eighteen thousand seven hundred fifty-three dollars. Even if she closed out her savings account, she still wouldn't have all the money.

The date on the calendar screamed silently at her. It was August thirty-first. Labor Day was four days away. Timing couldn't be better, because Lance had gone to India for two weeks on business, Sybil had closed the catering hall to give the employees time off to spend the week and the holiday with their families and Karla and Ronald had invited the Cumberlands up to the New York mountain hideaway.

Reaching for her cell phone, she dialed a number, listening for a break in the connection. "This is Sparkle," she said softly when hearing a man answer. "I will meet you at the hotel tomorrow. No money, no Sparkle." Without waiting for a response, she ended the call.

Her client had suggested she come to his house, but she'd flipped the script, saying that she would make the arrangements. She planned to arrive at the hotel an hour before she was scheduled to perform, get into costume and makeup, then wait for someone to contact her as to payment. Then and only then would she fulfill her end of the agreement.

Sparkle sat on the edge of the bed, tapping her feet. She sprang to her feet when she heard a knock on the door. "Who is it?"

"It's the front desk, Ms. Gordon. I have a package for you."

A bathrobe concealed her skimpy costume and a pair of oversize dark glasses the garish eye makeup as she made her way to the door. She opened it to find a young man dressed in hotel livery holding an envelope with her name and room number on it. She handed the man a tip while at the same time reaching for the envelope.

Dina closed the door and tore open the envelope, counting the money. It was all there. She hadn't realized her hands were trembling until she attempted to return the bills to the envelope.

She'd done it!

She'd saved enough money to pay off Payne Jefferson.

At exactly eight o'clock she walked out of her room, knocked on the door several doors down the hall and came face-to-face with the man with a sallow complexion who'd given her his business card. She hadn't remembered what he looked like because she never paid much attention to the men who came to Sybil's private parties.

"You look different, Sparkle," he said with a pronounced lisp.

Sparkle stared at him from behind her mask. "So do you."

"How?"

A slight smile parted her rouged lips. "You're more handsome than I remembered."

He gave her a silly grin. "I like you, Sparkle."

"And I like you, too, Mr. Wells. Did you bring the music?"

He nodded, pointing to a boom box in the corner. "It's over there."

Sparkle patted his cheek. "Let the music begin."

His dark eyes were fixed on her chest. "Can you wait a few minutes?"

Sparkle lifted a bare shoulder. "It's your dime, Mr. Wells. I can give you thirty minutes, and right now you're on the clock."

The door to the bathroom opened and two young girls with profusions of braided extensions fell over each other to get out. They couldn't have been more than fifteen or sixteen.

"What the hell is going on here?" Dina shouted.

"Wait, wait!" Mr. Wells sputtered, waving his hands. "These are my daughters. They told me they want to be dancers, so I told them I hired you so they can see your work."

Dina stared at the girls, then their supposed father. "I'm sorry, I don't entertain minors."

"But, Daddy," wailed the feminine version of her father.

Mr. Wells looked as if he were going to cry. "Why didn't you tell me that?"

"Why didn't you tell me about your daughters?" Dina countered. "Good night, Mr. Wells. Contact me again when they're over eighteen—no, make that twenty-one. Don't worry about your money. I'll return it to you, less expenses."

"What expenses?"

"The cost of the room and the driver to bring me here and back. I'll send you a money order in a couple of weeks. She gave him a long, lingering look. "I'm sorry this didn't work out."

She walked away from the eccentric family and into her own suite. Slowly, methodically, she took off the mask, shoes, bodysuit and tights. Dina took off the eye makeup, staring at her reflection in the mirror. Emotion nearly overwhelmed her when she realized Sparkle had just made her last appearance.

Chapter 64

Grand Central Station was teeming with people arriving and departing and those waiting to meet others. Dina Gordon was one of those waiting. She'd called Payne Jefferson and told him to meet her in the waiting room at exactly two o'clock. She'd gotten there at one, hoping Payne would arriver earlier than the appointed time.

She went completely still when she saw him weaving his way through the throng. He reminded her of a teenage boy with his baggy jeans, too-large white T-shirt and top-of-the-line running shoes. A strap of a backpack was slung over one shoulder. Her eyebrows lifted when she noticed a fading bruise over his left eye.

Reaching into her handbag, she took out a manila envelope. "It's all there." He took it, unzipped the backpack and slipped it in. "We're done, Payne. Over. And if I hear that you've gone anywhere near my grandmother or my daughter, I'll make you sorry you ever drew breath."

Payne reached for her left hand and stared at her ring. "It looks as if you've done well for yourself, Adina."

She snatched her hand back. "Better than you think." Her eyes narrowed. "Have a nice life, PJ." Turning on her heels, she walked away and was swallowed up by the crowd.

Payne hadn't thought she would come up with the money. And if she hadn't, he still wouldn't have done anything to her grandmother. He'd busted up Mrs. Jenkins's place because Adina had ignored his pages. If she'd said she wanted out, then he would've let her out. Besides, he had several new recruits he'd been training to replace Adina. Not only was she getting old, but she'd become a risk. It was only a matter of time before she would be arrested and then the police would come looking for him. Bitches didn't know when to keep their mouths shut.

What she didn't know was that it was Payne Jefferson who'd put out the contract on Adina Jenkins. It was the only way he could get rid of her without having it traced back to him. She'd saved her own life when she'd fled Brooklyn.

He knew it would be a long time—if ever—before she would come back.

Chapter 65

It was a warm October Sunday morning when Dina Gordon exchanged vows with Lancelot Londell Haynes on the patio of the house belonging to Ronald and Karla King, with Judge Rhys Weichert presiding over the ceremony. Karla stood in as her matron of honor, and Lance had asked Cory to stand in as his best man.

The two men had begun a business relationship because Cory was in the process of starting up his own quality-assurance firm.

Adele Haynes's doctor wouldn't permit her to fly given her advancing crippling arthritis, so Layne had informed his mother he was bringing his bride to Charleston, South Carolina, so she could meet her.

Pulling her to his chest, Lance kissed his wife, lifting her off her feet. "I love you, Mrs. Haynes."

Dina tightened her arms around her husband's neck and deepened the kiss. "And I love you, Mr. Haynes."

A smattering of applause reminded them they weren't alone. Turning, they accepted the good wishes from their friends.

Lance, resplendent in a navy-blue pin-striped suit, a platinum tie, a white shirt with French cuffs and black leather slip-ons, smiled down at his wife. She looked like a delicate doll with a simple silk platinum slip dress ending at the knee. She'd fashioned her hair in a twist on the nape of her neck, festooned with a large, fragrant orchid. Her small feet were encased in a pair of gray silk embroidered pumps. Her bouquet was a profusion of orchids, gardenias and baby roses.

The Kings had opened their home for the ceremony and Sybil had prepared the food for the small, intimate reception. Smiling, Lance accepted handshakes and pats on the back and Dina hugs and kisses.

Dina looped her hand over the sleeve of Lance's jacket and smiled up at him. A photographer captured the moment for posterity. "I just remembered something," she whispered.

"What is it?"

"I should've told Sybil to make a few honey-glazed doughnuts. You promised me I could let Honey Dip out of the closet on our wedding night."

Shaking his head, Lance struggled not to laugh. "Do you know you almost killed me with that stunt?"

"No, I didn't."

"Yes, you did, baby girl." He escorted her to a long table set up under a white tent decorated with white flowers and ribbons. "You've got to be careful with the old man."

Dina rested her head on his shoulder. "You're not old, Big Daddy. You're going to be around for a long time, long enough to see our children married."

She knew she'd changed when she considered motherhood. Dr. Howe had given her the name of a fertility doctor who would harvest her eggs for an in-vitro-fertilization procedure.

She'd contemplated telling Lance everything about her

past but decided to wait. She had time—they had time. In fact, they had the rest of their lives to learn not only to love but also to trust the other.

Chapter 66

Ronald King clicked the button to download the email attachment addressed to him. The subject line read: Do they look familiar?

He usually didn't check his personal email for days, but because he was waiting for Karla to come home, he'd decided it was as good a time as any. A slight frown creased his forehead when the photographs popped up on the screen. Leaning closer, he clicked on the thumbnail and the photograph filled the screen.

A wave of heat, then chills, swept over him and Ronald thought he was having a heart attack. He clicked the next one, then the next, as bile rose in his throat and threatened to choke him. He couldn't believe it! He didn't want to believe it!

Twin emotions of rage and pain warred within him as he stared at the damning photographs. However, rage won out. He hit the forward icon, then scrolled through the directory for two other email addresses. Gripping the mouse tightly, he pressed the button, forwarding the photographs. Then he leaned back in his chair to wait for his wife.

Karla walked into the house, confused. The house was dark. She'd had automatic timers that turned the lights on and off at different intervals. She knew Ronald was home because his truck was parked in the garage.

"Baby," she called out as she flicked on lamps. She made her way into the home office. The light from the computer monitor shone eerily in the dark.

"Don't turn on the light."

"What's wrong, Ronald? Why are you sitting in the dark?"

Rising from his chair, he touched the mouse and the screen was filled with images that almost brought Karla to her knees. "Where did you get those?"

Someone had taken pictures of Chocolate Ice, Sparkle and Delectable in all of their physical glory. In one, Karla was smiling as she executed a back bend that contorted her upper body. In another, Sparkle executed her famous—or infamous—booty clap at the same time she smiled directly at the camera. And Delectable was caught in the act of planting her high-heel boot into the groin of a man writhing in ecstasy.

Stalking to her, Ronald closed the distance between them. "From my boyfriend."

Karla felt as if the top of her head had exploded. "Your boyfriend!"

"Don't tell me you're going to have a bitch fit because I didn't get your permission to sleep with him." His hands fisted. "If you were a man, I'd beat the shit outta you, Karla. But I did the next best thing."

Karla closed her eyes and took a deep breath. "What did you do?" Her voice was barely a whisper.

Grabbing her arm, he forcibly pulled her over to the monitor. He hit a button. "Look at the email address, baby. I forwarded those pictures to Cory and LL. I'm certain they'd like to know how their wives are spending their after hours."

Karla felt a spasm squeeze her heart. She knew she'd be able to handle Ronald, but she wasn't so certain about Sybil and Cory and Dina and Lance.

Dina and Lance hadn't been married two weeks. The news would devastate him.

"You're a real bitch, Ronald."

He gave her a sly smile. "It takes one to know one."

They stared at each other until Karla turned on her heels and walked out. She'd come home early to celebrate her husband's birthday. Now she would sit and wait for the fallout from her friends' husbands.

Chapter 67

Sybil stared at the back of Cory's head as he sat at the computer workstation. He'd been working steadily on a project for the past two days. She knocked softly on the open door. "I'm going to bed, baby."

Cory swiveled on his chair at his workstation to find his wife standing in the doorway. He was grateful for her interruption because his eyes were burning from spending hours in front of the monitor testing a new software program. His eyebrows lifted slightly. Sybil wore a short black silk nightgown with narrow straps and plunging neckline barely covering her full, lush breasts. It'd been a long time since she'd revealed so much flesh when retiring for bed.

He smiled. "You look nice."

Sybil returned his smile. "When are you coming to bed?"

"I just have to check my email, then I'll be in."

"Don't make me wait too long."

"I won't," he promised.

Cory shut down the program and logged onto his personal email account. A slight frown furrowed his forehead when he saw the subject line: Do they look familiar? with a download attachment icon. Recognizing Ronald

King's address, he downloaded the message, realizing that Ronald had also sent Lance Haynes a copy.

"What the hell..." he whispered to himself when he stared at the photos filling the monitor. There was something vaguely familiar about the petite masked woman in green, but he couldn't remember where he'd seen her before.

Although the pictures weren't pornographic, they were definitely a turn-on. Noting the time on the email, he reached for the telephone and dialed Ronald's cell.

"What's up with the email attachment?" he asked when hearing Ronald's query.

"Don't you recognize your wife?"

Cory leaned closer to the monitor. "What are you talking about, King?"

"Look closely at the woman in black with the whip. Even though she's masked, don't you think she looks like Sybil?"

"No! How did you come up with that?"

"Because Karla is the one in brown."

"You're kidding me?"

"Man, I wish I was. Karla used to be a pole dancer back in the day."

"You're kidding?" Cory asked again.

"You don't know how much I wish I was kidding."

Leaning back in his chair, Cory studied the photograph of a masked Karla King executing an incredible back bend. Karla had an incredible body, but of course he wasn't about to say that to Ronald. His gaze shifted to the dominatrix with her high-heel, booted foot pressed to the groin of a man who appeared to be enjoying his punishment.

"Did Karla say the other two are Sybil and Dina?"

"No."

"Then why are you starting shit, King? Just because you can't control your wife that doesn't mean that mine or Lance's are out there swinging around poles. Besides, Sybil wouldn't have anything to do with violence or pain because she grew up with her father beating and raping her mother."

"It's not about control."

"Then what is it?"

"It's about trust. Karla promised me that she'd never go back to dancing."

"Have you asked her why she's doing it again?" Cory asked.

There was a pause before Ronald's voice came through the earpiece again. "No. If I get into it with her, then I'm going to risk losing her. I don't know if you know, but we have an open marriage."

"If that's the case, then what are you bitchin' about? She does her thing, while you do yours. You *are* doing your thing, aren't you?"

There came another beat of silence. "Yeah."

"Let it go, friend. Maybe she'll stop now that you know."

"That's what I'm hoping," Ronald said.

"I think you made a mistake forwarding this crap to Lance. What are you trying to do? Mess up a marriage even before it gets started?"

"I'll let him know I forwarded it in error."

"You do that. Look, I have to go. I hope everything works out between you and Karla."

"Thanks."

Cory ended the call, logged off and made his way into the bedroom. Sybil was in bed, reading. He sat down on her side of the bed. "Ronald King downloaded some pictures of three women who apparently were entertaining men. He thought one looked like you and the other Dina Haynes. He knows for certain that one is Karla."

Sybil's impassive expression didn't change with Cory's announcement. "How does he know one was Karla?"

"She used to be a pole dancer, and when he confronted her she didn't deny it."

Sybil's jaw dropped as she feigned shock. "No way!" Cory nodded. "I can assure you I've never been a pole dancer."

"What about a dominatrix?"

A hint of a smile parted her lips. "Sybil Cumberland, a dominatrix. I don't think so. I can't even kill a bug. Why would I hurt another human being? I saw pain every day of my life, and I swore when I grew up that violence would not become a part of my life."

Cory leaned over and brushed a kiss on her mouth. "That's what I told Ronald. He's going to email Lance and let him know he sent the document in error."

"Ronald must be going through an early midlife crisis. He should seek professional help."

"You're probably right."

Sybil rested her hand on Cory's cheek. "Take your shower and come to bed. I think it's time we start adding to our family."

Cory fastened his mouth to the side of her neck. "That's what I've been waiting to hear." He pushed off the bed and walked into the adjoining bathroom.

Sybil stared at the space where Cory had been. *Damn!* Someone must have used a cell phone camera to photograph their act. It was time to retire Delectable and go underground. She would continue to service E. Paul Redding, but only when his wife was on vacation.

She was happy that Cory trusted her completely. It was one of the reasons why she'd married him. Cory Cumberland was kind, gentle *and* trusting.

Sybil closed her book, placing it on the bedside table. She thought about Dina. The younger woman had kept her promise, and after Labor Day Sparkle the Green Fairy no longer existed. No amount of urging or the promise of higher fees could get her to change her mind.

Dina Haynes, nee Gordon, had done well for herself. She and Lance planned to move to Upper Saddle River before the end of the year. The invitation to a New Year's Eve celebration in their new home had arrived in yesterday's mail. The gathering would be the perfect end for an incredible year.

Throwing back a lightweight blanket, she went to retrieve her cell phone. She punched in a programmed number. The call lasted less than twenty seconds. She had to warn Dina about the email. Dina's "I'll take care of it" was enough to ease Sybil's conscience. If she hadn't recruited her to become Sparkle, then Dina wouldn't be faced with having to explain her alter ego to her husband.

She returned to bed, feeling more confident. A silent voice told her that Dina Haynes was more than capable of taking care of her husband.

Chapter 68

Lance glanced at the clock on his desk. He'd told Dina that he was coming to bed, but that was more than an hour ago. He'd showered and brushed his teeth, but what he was looking for hadn't come. He was waiting for an email confirmation from a client who wanted to get together for a breakfast meeting. Several messages popped up on his screen, but they weren't what he was looking for.

He noticed there were two from Ronald King, the first one with an attachment. Lance clicked on the newest first.

LL: Please delete the one with the attachment. It contains private information intended for someone else.
—Ronald

Lance clicked on Reply.

Ronald—I reported it as Spam, then deleted it. Let's get together for drinks next week. I'll contact Cory to see if he's available. Let me know when you have some free time.
—LL

Shifting the mouse, he deleted the email with the attachment.

Seconds later, the one he'd been waiting for appeared on the screen. He read it quickly, then typed a reply, pressed a button for Standby mode and left his office. He walked into the bedroom to find Dina in bed, weeping. His knees buckled slightly before he was able to regain his balance. The sound tore through him as he slowly approached the bed. What, he wondered, had upset her enough to make her cry? He'd tried to make her happy. Whatever she asked for he gave her.

He got into bed with her, pulling her to his chest. "What's wrong, baby girl?"

Dina touched her fingertips to her eyes to blot her tears. "Nothing."

Lance kissed her mussed hair. "I know you well enough to know that you don't cry for nothing."

She sniffled delicately. "I supposed I'm just PMSing." She sniffled again. "I'm all right now that you're with me. I don't ever want you to leave me, Big Daddy. Not for anything or anyone."

A slight frown marred Lance's smooth forehead. "Why would I leave you, Dina?"

She lifted a bare shoulder. "I don't know. Maybe one of these days I'll do something naughty and..." Her voice trailed off when she realized there was no need to confess before she heard the charges.

A chuckle rumbled in Lance's chest. "Are you talking about reprising Miss Honey Dip?" He never knew what to expect from his wife. It was as if she searched out different ways to take their lovemaking to another level, a level where he feared dying in the saddle. His doctor told him that he was healthy enough to engage in stenuous sex, but there were times when he doubted the man's advice.

Dina nodded. "Miss Honey Dip is only the warm-up act for what I'd like to do to you."

This time he laughed. "If you think I'm going to leave you because you like being naughty in bed, then think again, baby. You're a sexy little thing in and out of bed, and I'm very aware of the way men look at you. They can look all they want as long as they don't touch."

"You like showing me off, don't you?"

There came a swollen pause before Lance said, "Yes."

There was another beat of silence before Dina asked the burning question that had reduced her to tears, real tears. "Did you finally get your email?"

"Yes. I'm sorry we can't breakfast together because I have an early meeting. Speaking of emails, I got a couple from Ronald King. He asked me to delete one because it contained confidential information that was supposed to go to someone else."

Dina bit down on her lower lip to stop its trembling. "You didn't open it?"

Lance shook his head. "No. It all comes down to ethics. Perhaps there was something in that email I didn't need to see, so rather than be tempted I honored his request and deleted it."

Dina sprang up with the agility of a cat and straddled his thighs. "How did I get so lucky?"

"What are you talking about?"

She pressed her breasts to his chest. "You're the most honorable man I've ever known."

"That's because I'm the only man you've ever known. That is, in the biblical sense."

"You're right about that."

Looping her arms under his shoulders, Dina buried her face against the side of his neck. Sybil had called to warn her about the photos, but it was apparent Ronald King had had a change of heart. For that she was eternally grateful.

Sparkle, like Adina Jenkins, was her past. She'd been given a second chance at life and she intended to take full advantage of it. She knew Lance wanted a baby, and with the advances in modern medicine she would make certain it would become a reality.

She hadn't been ready to become a mother at fourteen, and she still wasn't certain whether she was at twenty-seven. But she'd grown quite fond of Lancelot Haynes, and there wasn't anything she wouldn't do to make him as happy as he'd made her.

"I have to tell you something," she whispered.

Lance closed his eyes. "What is it, baby girl?"

"I love you, Big Daddy." She'd mouthed the words before because she knew it was what Lance wanted to hear. But this time the admission had come from her heart.

"I know," he said, "because I feel it."

"I want to feel you inside me."

Not needing any further urging, Lance reversed their positions and told his wife without words how much he wanted, needed and loved her. It was later, after their respiration slowed, that they lay together, their chests rising and falling in an even syncopated rhythm.

A long fringe of lashes touched Dina's cheekbones when she closed her eyes. She'd changed so much since fleeing Brooklyn that she didn't recognize the woman who she'd been. The day before she'd married Lance she called her grandmother to tell her everything about her relationship with Payne Jefferson, who her baby's daddy was and that she was now Dina Gordon and soon-to-be Dina Haynes.

She'd also told Dora Jenkins that she could never return to Brooklyn, but would continue to send her money to put away for Jameeka's education. Before ending the call she'd made Dora promise to tell her if or when she was ready to leave the housing projects, because she could make it happen for her. After all, she was marrying a very wealthy man.

Don't forget you're a descendant of survivors. At that moment Karla's reminder filled her thoughts. That she was. She'd survived a traumatic childhood where she'd been confronted with alcohol, drugs, prostitution and still she survived.

Reaching for the button on the lamp, she clicked it off, plunging the room into darkness. Shifting slightly, Dina pressed her back to her husband's chest. His arm moved over her waist, holding her close.

"Do you know what I want?" she asked cryptically.

"What?" Lance's voice was still heavy with a lingering passion.

"I want your baby, Lancelot Londell Haynes."

All vestiges of sleep fled when Lance sat up and pulled Dina up with him. "Really?"

Dina didn't know why, but he sounded like a little child. "Yes, really."

Lance discovered that his wife was an ever-changing mystery. She'd told him that she wanted to wait a year before starting a family, but it was apparent she'd changed her mind. "When do you want to start?"

"As soon as possible. We may have to see a fertility specialist."

"It doesn't matter, baby girl. I'll agree to anything as long as you have our babies."

"And I will," Dina said confidently.

* * * * *

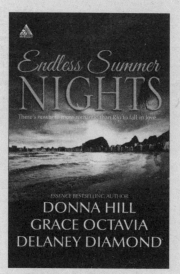

REQUEST YOUR FREE BOOKS!

2 FREE NOVELS
PLUS 2 FREE GIFTS!

KIMANI™
ROMANCE

Love's ultimate destination!

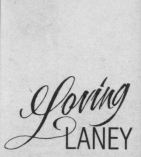
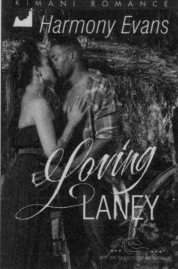